TONIGHT
THEY COME BACK
FROM CONFRONTATION TO CATASTROPHE

NARU K. WILLIAMS II

MILTON & HUGO L.L.C.
4407 Park Ave., Suite 5
Union City, NJ 07087, USA

Website: *www. miltonandhugo.com*
Hotline: *1- 888-778-0033*
Email: *info@miltonandhugo.com*

Ordering Information:
Quantity sales. Special discounts are granted to corporations, associations, and other organizations. For more information on these discounts, please reach out to the publisher using the contact information provided above.

Library of Congress Control Number: 2025906017
ISBN-13:   979-8-89285-508-2   [Paperback Edition]
                  979-8-89285-507-5   [Digital Edition]

Rev. date: 03/25/2025

SHE CAME BACK

S o, Kate," Dr. Malcolm Logan said to the anxious young woman sitting on the couch in front of him in his office, "how do you feel today?"

"Not so fast, Doc," the woman said, fidgeting in her seat. Rubbing her hands in nervous anticipation, she glanced out of a nearby window, her eyes on the skies above Milestone City. After a pensive few seconds, she looked back to Dr. Logan. "It's Martha Johnson now."

"Only out there," Malcolm said, gesturing to the city outside his office. "In here, you're Kate Barrow, former police officer of the Gateway City Police Department." He glanced at the notepad in his lap, then back at his patient, his sharp brown eyes taking her in.

"Emphasis on 'former,'" the young woman scoffed, folding her arms protectively across her chest. She was dressed in black cargo pants, an oversized AC/DC T-shirt, and black boots that made her feet look bigger than they really were. Her dirty blond hair was pulled back in a ponytail, her young face without a hint of makeup.

"Answer the question, Kate," Malcolm said, moistening his lips. He was dressed in a blue button-down shirt, with a darker blue vest over that. His ensemble contrasted sharply with his light khaki pants. Normally, the middle-aged man wore a T-shirt and jeans, but when he was working as a therapist for at-risk youth, he wore the vest and khakis. He found that they gave him a fatherly look and put his patients at ease.

Such a look was integral in getting his patients to trust him.

But it had yet to work on a troubled young woman who had proven to be his most unique patient for the past six months.

"I'm fine, Doc," Kate answered after letting out a long, calming breath. "I'm fine."

1

Seems as though she's trying to tell herself more than me. Malcolm regarded one of his most tragic patients with sympathetic eyes. "Are you sure? Because I can smell the alcohol on your breath."

Kate's brow arched in offended annoyance. "It a law in this town *not* to drink?"

"Milestone City's not a dry town, if that's what you mean," Malcolm answered, determined not to let her words rile him. Kate always brought the stinging barbs when she felt threatened, which was all the time since what happened to her in Gateway City. "Though it is a fishing town." *Despite most people nowadays not eating fish.*

"I know that," Kate said, giving him an irritated look. "I knew that before Witness Protection put me here."

"Do you not like living here?"

"I'm not a fan of living in a town right next door to my old home, where—"

"Where Stan and Francine Solomon live," Malcolm finished in a calm voice. His muscles tensed as he braced himself in case Kate let out another outburst.

Which always happened whenever they broached the subject of the Solomons.

"That too." Kate's shoulders sagged, as if hearing the name of the infamous couple had drained all of her strength.

Perhaps that's why you drink, Malcom thought. "Are you sober right now?"

Kate leaned forward in her seat, giving him a defensive glare. "I got here, didn't I?"

"Do I have to remind you of the conditions of your arrangement with Witness Protection?"

"No." Kate sat back in her seat, looking as though she'd been chastised by a disapproving parent. "No, you don't."

"You *have* to be sober for our sessions," Malcolm continued in a knowing voice. *I sound like I'm reading from a script. No wonder Kate's throwing up barriers.* "That's the only way you can be cleared."

"Cleared for what? Active duty?" Kate laughed, looking at him with cynical eyes. "I can't go back to the GCPD. Not after what the

Solomons did to me." She shivered after saying their name. "Not after …
what happened to me."

"I know," Malcolm agreed in a tender voice. "But there are other
things you can do. You can still have a life, Kate."

"Oh, so I'm being 'cleared' for life?" Kate snapped in a flippant voice.
"That's a thing?"

"It can be." Malcolm kept his voice calm, masking his growing
irritation. "If you *want* it to be."

"You know who won't be 'cleared' for life?" Kate asked in a forsaken
voice. "Brian Solomon."

"I know," Malcolm said, feeling a chill move through him at the
mere mention of the son of Stan and Francine Solomon. "I know, Kate."

"Because I killed him."

"I know that too," Malcolm added, keeping his tone respectful.
Everyone knows that. From coast to coast.

"I … I shot him," Kate stammered, her eyes downcast, looking to
be on the verge of tears. "I didn't mean to, but I did. And I'll never be
cleared of that."

Not until you've cleared yourself, Malcolm thought, looking at Kate
with growing concern. Something that was easier said than done, given
her mental state. "You seem particularly cagey today, Kate. Do you want
to tell me what's going on?"

"I …" Kate paused, her eyes flicking from him to the floor then back
to him. "I don't think so."

"Okay, then," Malcolm said, raising a defensive hand. "You don't
have to tell me anything you don't want to."

"I know, it's just …" Kate's voice trailed off as her eyes went back to
the floor, guilt radiating off her in waves.

"Do you feel you have to?"

"I …" Kate winced as if she'd been hit by a cramp. "Yes."

Malcolm looked to his notepad, seeing what few notes he had
written down. Kate Barrow. Twenty-six years old. Clear symptoms of
PTSD. Anxiety. Paranoia. And trauma. "If I may …?"

Kate rolled her eyes in annoyance. "You may, Dad."

Just going to push past that *comment.* "I took the liberty of checking my calendar," Malcolm said, cocking his head at a calendar on a wall to his right. "Particularly when it comes to your case."

"And?" Kate asked, her voice touched with irritation.

"It's not the anniversary of your abduction," Malcolm said, flipping through the pages of his notepad. "That's not for a few months. Nor is it the anniversary of you being put in Witness Protection. Or the trial regarding Brian Solomon's shooting."

"Kinda weird that you know that," Kate declared, giving him an unpleasant look.

"It's public knowledge, Kate."

"I try not to think about that stuff."

"I have to," Malcolm stated. "It's part of my job. Now, enough deflecting. What's got you so triggered today?"

Kate let out a haggard sigh. "Brian … would've been sixteen, today."

Wow. Malcolm's lips parted slightly, the only telltale sign of shock on his face. "I didn't know you were … keeping track of that."

"Surprised that a heartless child killer would remember a child's birthday?"

And here come those barbs. "That's not what I meant, Kate. You know that."

"That's not what the papers say," Kate said in a somber voice. "And it sure as hell not what everyone back home says."

"You've been back to Gateway City?" Malcolm asked, surprised she still worried about her hometown so soon after her abduction.

"No," she answered defensively, "but I watch the news. I know how people feel about me."

"And how do they feel about you, Kate?"

"They burn me in effigy, Doc!" Kate thundered, her head popping up to flash him an evil glare. "It's been six months since what happened, and the people of Gateway City still burn me in effigy! They had parties when I was taken and rioted when I came back! They hate me!"

—⟋⟍—

Kate heaved a crate onto her shoulder and made her way down the docks, the caws of seagulls and the blare of boat horns filling her ears. She focused on the weight of the crate, the muscles in her arms and back straining as she carried it to its destination.

It was a welcome distraction from her explosive session with Dr. Logan earlier that day, where the pretentious son of a bitch prodded her with questions she didn't want to answer. *How do I feel the people of Gateway City feel about me? He dares to ask me that?! It's been six fucking months, dammit! I know how the people feel about me!*

Six months since Kate was rescued by the GCPD and relocated to Milestone City, a coastal city on the West Coast of the United States. Just a few freeways south from Gateway City.

Why, oh why, did Witness Protection put her so close to her old home?

Focus, girl. Kate tried not to think about Gateway City …

Her old life …

Or the Solomons …

And yet the couple had kidnapped her and changed her life forever. Kate couldn't *not* think about them!

As she made her way back to the loading dock for another crate, Kate caught sight of a figure in the distance, standing at the edge of the pier where she worked. The figure was too far away for Kate to get good look …

But she could feel the figure's gaze on her, and it was intense.

Shit! Kate almost dropped her crate, her heart skipping a beat. *Shit! Shit! Shit!*

Was it Stan? Francine? Or something else entirely?

Stop it, stop it. Kate closed her eyes, gripping the edges of her crate so hard she felt the splinters cut into her skin. *Stay calm, Katie. Stay calm.*

Visions of an alien world danced across her eyes, the sound of exotic chanting filling her ears. The faint aroma of something akin to jasmine filled her nostrils, making her tremble. *No, I'm not back. I'm not back. I'm not …*

Kate opened her eyes and saw, to her relief, that she was still at the dock, still holding her crate.

She also got the attention of her fellow dockworkers, the closest approaching her as though she were a rattlesnake ready to pounce.

He was Ponce Chang, the dock manager who had gotten Kate the job she so desperately needed. He was dressed in a dark overcoat, jeans, and a black skullcap; and his face was the picture of concern. "Martha? Are you okay?"

"I'm fine!" Kate answered loudly, making the dock manager jump. "Just fine!" *Easy, girl.*

Chang glanced at the dockworkers around them, waving at them to get back to work. Then he looked back at Kate. "Are you sure? You need to ... take off today?"

I'm not useless! Kate looked over the stocky man's shoulders, past him to the edge of the pier where the dark figure stood.

But he was gone.

The son of a bitch had scared her, made her make a scene, and fled before she could get a good look at him!

It had to be Stan! Or Francine! There was no one else it could be!

"Martha?" Chang asked again, a slight edge to his voice. "Do you need to go home?"

"Uh, no. I'm fine," Kate answered, trying to shake off the bone-tingling terror she had felt not moments before. "Ready to work."

"Martha," Chang said in a strained voice, "you can't keep having these freakouts at work. That's the third time this week. If you keep having these—"

"Don't worry," Kate cut in, refusing to let him finish that sentence. "You can count on me."

"I hope so," Chang said, giving her a curt nod before turning to head back to his office.

Gritting her teeth, Kate loaded her crate onto a boat tied to the dock. She ignored the stares of various workers, refusing to dignify their behavior with a response.

Finish loading the crates, Katie, she thought to herself. Just finish loading the crates, clock out, and go home. Go the hell home!

—◊—

Sighing wearily, Malcolm looked over Kate's file on his desk. He had really hoped he would have gotten her to tell him more of what she saw when Stan and Francine Solomon took her. From what he had heard, the Solomons' vigilante activities in Gateway City were escalating.

People were disappearing.

Some were notorious crime bosses or low-level thugs.

Others were regular people.

Part of the homeless population, in fact.

Were the Solomons initiating a social purge? Could anyone stop them if they were?

Kate was the only person who had been in close contact with them. She had to know something, even if she didn't know she knew. But how was Malcolm going to learn anything if she didn't trust him?

—◊—

"How does this feel?" Kate asked as she ran her fingers along the call girl's cheek.

"Different," the woman answered, flinching under the caress. "Real different."

You have no idea, Kate thought, smiling sadly. She and the call girl, whose name she always forgot, sat on a bed in a room in a brothel on the edge of Milestone City.

Kate found the place right after arriving in town. She didn't mean to, she really didn't. At least she didn't think she did.

But after what she had been through with the Solomons, the brothel's neon red sign looked *so* inviting!

Besides, she wasn't a cop anymore. What standard did she have to uphold?

You're the first nice person I saw in this damn city, Kate thought, looking into the call girl's green eyes. *The first person to bring me comfort.* She smiled wistfully, thinking that back in Gateway City, she'd be in one of the many bars that catered to the GCPD.

Watching the Playoffs …

Or the Super Bowl …

7

Or a hockey game.

Surrounded by her fellow boys in blue, confident that they would have her back no matter what happened. What an absolute *lie* that was!

"Martha?"

The call girl's words shook Kate out of her reverie. "Huh?"

"You always do that," she said, giving Kate a wary look. The call girl was tall, her hair running down her shoulders like a crimson river. Her skin was so pale it was almost white, making the tattoos on her arms and legs stand out like black brands. "You always space out when you're with me."

"I can't believe I'm the first," Kate said, her words portraying a good humor she didn't feel. She gestured to the room around her—a small one-bedroom area on the top floor of the two-story building. "Not in here." *I can practically smell the other people that have been in here.* She looked to the call girl. *And in you.*

"Yeah, but usually that's because of me," the call girl insisted, leaning closer to Kate until she was staring into her eyes. "Not in spite of me."

"Sorry," Kate said, pulling away from her. "I … got a lot on my mind."

"Well," the woman said, reaching out to massage Kate's shoulders, "let me take your troubles off your mind." She cocked a glance at the room around them, which was draped in red fabric. The walls were red, the carpet was red, even the bed they both sat on was red. "You're safe here."

I'll never be safe, Kate thought even as the call girl's nimble fingers started prying apart the tension in her neck and shoulders. *Not as long as the Solomons are out there.*

But only Kate needed to know that.

"Hey." The call girl leaned close to Kate's neck and took a quick sniff. "You smell strange."

Shit. Kate's heart froze in her chest. "I smell strange?"

"Yeah, like …" The call girl paused, her angular face taking on a thoughtful expression, "like … decaying fish drying in the sun."

I thought I'd put on enough perfume to hide that! The perfume Kate put on every day before leaving her house usually hid the odor, but sometimes it got through.

Especially when Kate *really* exerted herself.

Which happened a lot at the brothel.

"Sorry," Kate said, quickly covering herself. "I worked a long shift at the docks. Had to handle some … dicey products."

"Well, if you'd told me, I would've let you wash up in the back," the call girl said, pointing her thumb at a bathroom in the back of the room.

"That part of the brothel package?"

"Only when you're here."

"Are you … the only one that smells it?" Kate asked, afraid of the answer. The smell was a constant reminder of what the Solomons put her through.

And that she would never truly be free of it, or them.

"Yeah," the call girl answered, her fingers getting deep into the knot in Kate's shoulders. "I'm the only one you go to."

Okay, I'm done talking, Kate decided, turning around to face her. "Speaking of 'going' to you …"

The call girl's expression went from flustered to aroused. "Yeah?"

"Take off your top."

The woman whipped off her shirt and flung it across the room, revealing a voluptuous pair of breasts.

Oh my. Kate looked on in awe. "What's your name?"

"Martha, Martha, Martha," the call girl chanted, before throwing her head back and laughing softly. "It's Nina. You ask me that every time you come in here, silly."

"Well, tonight," Kate said, cupping a supple breast in her hand, "you can call me Kate."

—◊—

"You're running out of time, Doctor."

"I can't get anything out of Kate if she doesn't trust me," Malcolm insisted, glaring at his unwelcome visitor.

Topher Madsen, former commissioner of the Gateway City Police Department, sat across from the psychiatrist, tapping his finger on his polished oak desk. "You've *had* six months."

"The mind unravels in its own time, Madsen, not yours," Malcolm said, his eyes going from the former police chief to the clock on the wall behind him. *It's fortunate that I have no other appointments today. Or that you didn't come during my session with Kate.* "I told you this when we started."

"I was told you were good." Madsen had a nervous, jittery energy to him, like an addict that needed a fix.

Or a sinner needing absolution.

"I *am* good," Malcolm declared, keeping his tone calm and even, "when I know all the facts."

"Meaning?" Madsen kept a hawkish glance at the window to the right of Malcolm's desk as they talked, just as Kate did during their session a few hours earlier. He had once been a big, beefy man, but in front of Malcolm, he looked worn down to the nub. He still had the size, practically towering over Malcolm when he barged into his office twenty minutes earlier, but the commanding presence Madsen had wielded when he led the GCPD was gone.

In its place was a gaping hole.

A yawning void nestled inside a wounded, haunted man.

Malcolm saw that void in Madsen's eyes. And yet ambers of quiet desperation flickered in those haunted orbs. Madsen was doing his best to keep it in check, but only just.

"Why are you taking an interest in Kate's welfare now?" Malcolm asked, leaning forward in his chair, hands clasped under his chin. "Where was this concern months ago when Kate was found at the bus station where the Solomons left her? Or before, when she was the pariah of Gateway City?"

The questions made Madsen's bushy red mustache twitch. "I did what I could, Doctor. But I had to think of my department."

"She was *part* of your department."

"I was the one that arranged for her to be put in Witness Protection!"

"And never came to see her," Malcolm continued, noting the man's reaction. "Or check on her welfare."

"I ..." Madsen's jaw dropped in shock. "How do you know that?"

"I have friends in law enforcement," Malcolm answered in a rueful voice. "They told me all sorts of things when I took Kate on as a patient."

He knew that Madsen had good reason to be defensive. He'd been drummed out of the GCPD in disgrace after arranging a disastrous expedition into the Solomons' territory with a news crew.

"We didn't part on good terms," the former police chief answered. "We had words on her last day on the force."

"What kind of words?"

"The *not*-good kind."

—⁊⁊⁊—

Kate sat in the living room of her cheap apartment near the docks, gazing at her laptop. She felt exhilarated from her romp with the call girl earlier and wanted to put her burst of energy to good use.

So she used it to look over an article on her computer chronicling Stan and Francine's ... extracurricular activities in Gateway City.

The article didn't mention Stan and Francine by name, but Kate knew it was talking about them. An oppressive heat moved through her body every time she thought or read about them. And at that moment, her body was sweltering!

They're still Gateway's dark secret, Kate thought, scrolling through the article. *All they've done, and the GCPD still refuses to publicly admit they exist.*

And yet evidence of their work was all over the news.

Criminals disappearing.

Crime families being wiped out.

Low-income neighborhoods, once home to crack dens and bombed-out tenant buildings, transformed into the safest streets in Gateway City.

Hell, crime was even going down.

Article says their activities are random, Kate thought, rubbing her eyes to clear her thoughts. *But I know they're not ~~random~~. Stan and Francine never do anything random. They're planning something. Something big. But what? And for whom?* One thing Kate remembered from when Stan and Francine took her was that they served masters.

11

Masters that had names. Names that Kate couldn't, for the life of her, remember. It was always on the tip of her tongue, at the edge of her thoughts.

But she couldn't see it. Couldn't grasp it. Couldn't say it.

They're in my mind, Kate thought, gently beating her forehead as though it was a TV with bad reception. *Somehow, Stan and Francine's masters are in my head, influencing my thoughts!*

—⁓—

"Kate's record was spotless, you know that?" Madsen declared after nervously licking his lips as he leaned back in his chair. "And her passion for the job was contagious."

Malcolm nodded intently, taking notes. Anything the former police chief said would be good for getting Kate to open up during a later session.

"I took her under my wing," Madsen whispered, his eyes locked on Malcolm's desk. "I had to. Passion like that? Gets burned out if there's no one to nurture it. So that's what I did."

"Is that all you did?"

Madsen's head whipped up as though he had been shot; he looked at the psychiatrist in indignance.

"I have to ask," Malcom clarified in a gentle voice.

"No, dammit!" Madsen thundered after scrunching his lips in disgust. "She's the same age as my son, for God's sake!"

"Had to be sure," Malcolm said, not the least bit cowed by the former police chief's outburst.

"But," Madsen added in a calmer voice, "she *was* the son I always wanted."

Nothing deeper about that, Malcolm thought sarcastically. "How so?"

"Kate *wanted* to be a police officer," Madsen explained, stroking his bushy mustache. "My son doesn't. He wanted to when he was younger, but his time in college fucked him up. Now? He barely talks to me."

Something tells me that's more from your personality than your son's college friends, Malcolm thought. "So Kate was your compensation for having a son that didn't want to follow in your footsteps."

12

"I guess she was," Madsen said, nodding his head. "Huh, didn't see it that way."

"So those harsh words?" Malcolm asked, remembering what Madsen had said earlier. "Between you and Kate, before she went into Witness Protection. What were they about?"

"She was"— Madsen grimaced, as though he was passing a kidney stone just saying the words — "full of guilt after the shooting. She was a ... shadow of her former self."

Seems like you're still having trouble, seeing that, Malcolm realized, adding that detail to his notes. "She *did* kill a child, Madsen."

"She made a mistake," the older man snapped, slamming a heavy fist against Malcolm's desk as though it was a hammer. "And those goddamn 'critics' roasted her for it! I'd like to see any *one* of them do our job!"

"They were doing *their* jobs, Madsen," Malcolm said in a calm voice. "You know that."

"They were complaining! Judging us from their ivory towers," Madsen declared, stabbing a finger at the wall behind him, no doubt in the direction of Gateway City, "while *we're* the ones in the muck doing the real work! How the *hell* can they complain when they're not doing *anything?!*"

Because they didn't volunteer to do it, Malcolm thought grimly. "The fact that you turn the conversation in that direction shows you agree with them, on some level. And that Kate did too."

"She did, damn her," Madsen swore, his lips twisting as though he was chewing on his anger. "She wanted to plead guilty! Can you believe that?!"

"So why didn't you let her?"

"If a crack in our resolve shows, the whole thing crumbles," Madsen answered, looking up from the desk to gaze at Malcolm with self-righteous eyes. "Besides, we'd weathered shit like this before. I was so sure they'd get past it."

"When you mean 'they,' you mean Stan and Francine Solomon?"

"Yeah," answered Madsen, wincing at the names. "But Stan, with his military friends, he wouldn't let the damn thing go."

"Kate. Killed. His. Son," Malcolm said in a stern voice, enunciating every word for dramatic effect.

"And we were willing to make a settlement with him!" Madsen shot back in a frantic, pleading voice. "As much as he and his wife wanted! Just so we could go back to doing our jobs!"

You blind son of a ... Malcolm's hand wavered. He wanted to smack that entitled expression off the former police chief's face, and damn the consequences. As if any amount of money could make up for the Solomons watching their child shot dead before their eyes! *Stay calm, Malcolm.* "And let me guess, Stan and Francine didn't go for it."

"No. Damned fools. I tried to make them see that their bellyaching wasn't helping anyone, but it just made them madder. But we got Kate acquitted." There was a pride in Madsen's voice that made Malcolm want to retch. "They didn't win that, at least."

— ∞ —

After taking a hit of marijuana, Kate sat on the floor of her living room, her legs crossed as she tried to meditate — a practice she had picked up from Dr. Logan. He said it was supposed to steady her anxiety. The weed helped too.

Remember, she said to herself, willing her mind to go back. *You gotta remember, girl. You got to. So just do it.*

And suddenly Kate was back at the night she was taken, seeing Detective Drake, the only cop from the GCPD who came to save her, falling from the sky as the Solomons carried her out of Gateway City. She remembered screaming at them. Cursing them, pleading with them to go back. To save Drake. That it wasn't too late. That they could still save him.

But Stan didn't hear her. He was that far gone. Francine, even farther.

What are they gonna do with me?! Kate had wondered fearfully as the Solomons took her above the clouds. *And where are they taking me?!*

Then she saw her answer, in Earth's lower atmosphere.

A ring of fire, shaped like the symbol on the chest of Stan and Francine's crazy new "superhero" clothes.

The outline of a bird of prey, its wings outstretched.

It hung in the darkness of space, brighter than the stars and getting brighter as they flew toward it. Seeing it made Kate very afraid.

Knowing that if she touched it, she would be damned. Or worse.

So despite being in space, despite falling to her death, or suffocating if she got free, Kate struggled in Francine's iron grip. She kicked and thrashed as Francine drew closer, determined to go through it first. Stan hung back, covering their rear.

He wouldn't even look at her.

The cold shoulder only made Kate kick and thrash harder, like a rabbit stuck in a bear trap. She could feel it in her bones, somehow, that it would be better if she died in space than go through that damn ring of fire.

"Help me," Kate whispered in her living room, the very words she screamed that night. "For God's sake! Help me," she had whimpered, desperately pulling on Francine's arm like a kid afraid of the dark. "I … I don't deserve this!"

But Stan simply looked on while Francine grinned in anticipation.

"I'll do anything," Kate continued, her skin blistering from the ring's heat as they drew closer. "I'm sorry! I'm so sorry! I'll do anything! Anything! But not this! Please, not this!"

But they went through, and Kate felt the ring's heat flay her skin apart with white-hot claws. She screamed as her hair burned away and her eyes popped in their sockets like overripe zits!

—⁂—

"I know you think I'm the bad guy," Madsen said as he sat in Malcolm's office. "And hell, maybe I was back then! But I was trying to protect the people under my command! You at least have to see that!"

I do, Malcolm thought, keeping his poker face, *as much as I hate to admit it*. But he kept silent, refusing to give Madsen the absolution he craved. It was clear he had come, not for Kate's welfare, but his own.

"When the jury gave its verdict," Madsen continued, "Stan shook his head, but Francine? She looked right at me. Not at Kate, not at the jury, not even at her lawyer. *Me.* As if she knew I had done something to influence the jury!"

Malcolm looked at him coolly, his mental alarm on high alert. "And did you?"

"I just … made sure it knew things it should've already known."

Madsen, you idiot. "You *did.*" Malcolm sighed, not bothering to keep the condemnation out of his voice.

"The public needs to believe in us."

"It also needs to know you're accountable."

"That works on paper," Madsen shouted, glaring at Malcolm, "but in real life, our reputation keeps us alive!"

And what of your reputation now? "That's what you and Kate had words about."

"Kate called me a coward for swaying the jury," Madsen seethed, "but I was only trying to help her! Like I help all my people! Like I've always done!"

"I must admit, Madsen," Malcolm declared, giving the former police chief an accusatory look, "it sounds like you were trying to help yourself."

"Maybe it does, but until you've walked in my shoes, you can't judge me."

"But Kate did," Malcolm said, realizing that was why Madsen was so defensive. "That's why you let her go, wasn't it? Because she wasn't grateful."

"No," Madsen insisted, shaking his head, "but after the trial, things got worse."

"I know," Malcolm said, getting another pen pad. He could see why Kate didn't trust this man. Madsen's actions had used her suffering to protect the GCPD's reputation, and shattered her faith. Not just in herself but in the very system she believed in.

"Gateway City turned on us," Madsen continued. "As if it knew too."

"I'm sure Francine had a say in that," Malcolm said. "You'd be surprised how much mileage a military family can get. Especially when *it's* the wronged party."

"People closed doors on us. Even attacked us. And that was just in downtown!"

"Uptown was worse?"

"A lot of those people are military supporters—veterans too—and they were putting Kate through the wringer."

"They took what she did as a personal affront."

"They wouldn't let it die," Madsen complained. "My office was swamped with calls for reform. Internal Affairs was breathing down my neck, and Kate was doing nothing to help."

"She was getting death threats, Madsen," Malcolm declared, giving the former police chief a deadpan look. "Protest groups hounded her on the streets, *especially* during Brian's funeral."

Madsen's brow arched in confusion. "Who?"

"Brian Solomon. The child Kate killed." *How do you not know his name at this point?*

"Oh, well, anyway, I had to let Kate go," Madsen stated, tears streaming down his face. "I didn't want to do it, but I had to! It was either her or the department! I had to let her go! Do you understand?! I had to!" Madsen broke down, his shoulders heaving with the weight of regret.

—∞—

Kate remembered waking to the sounds of marching, and chanting.

She couldn't feel anything. Not the air around her, not her limbs, not even Francine's arms, wrapped around her body like constricting pythons.

Though somehow, Kate could tell that she was ... lighter than before. She had always been a little thing, even with all the working out she did to add muscle. But right then, she felt lighter than air.

Where did her weight go? Why did she feel so small?

Then, with her one working eye, Kate looked down. And screamed! At least she tried to scream, but found she couldn't make a sound!

Kate saw, to her horror, that thanks to the fire at that damn gate, she had been reduced to a charred torso, a head, and a right arm.

Kate should have been dead. At that moment, she *wished* she was dead!

But against all logic, she was alive—and aware.

17

And Kate saw creatures flying around her, Stan, and Francine. Monsters that hurt her good eye to even glance at. And these creatures, they approached Stan and Francine as kin! Spoke to them, *embraced* them as if they were family!

Some of them had three heads. Some had sets of limbs at perpendicular angles. Some were made of different bodies, fused together.

And still others, somehow, looked even more bizarre!

And yet they all wore dark bodysuits similar to the ones worn by the Solomons. How was that possible? Did these creatures make the same deal that Stan and Francine had made?

Or did they agree to something worse?

Kate didn't have time to wonder.

She, Stan, and Francine were approaching the tower.

—⁂—

Malcolm walked from behind his desk and pulled up a seat next to Madsen. He placed a supportive hand on Madsen's shoulder. The former GCPD commissioner had a lot to answer for, but Malcolm knew he couldn't judge him for what he did to Kate, any more than he could judge Kate for what she did to Brian Solomon.

Not until he heard the Solomons' side, and there was no way they were going to sit on his couch!

But one question did plague Malcolm. "Madsen," he asked after moistening his lips in anticipation of the answer, "are the Solomons harassing you too?"

Madsen turned his head to look at the concerned psychiatrist, his eyes wide and desperate as if he were a scared child. "Remember that I mentioned Francine's eyes?"

"I do," Malcom answered, nodding his head.

Madsen looked away from Malcolm, glancing around the dusty office. "I *still* feel them on me."

Malcolm leaned in closer, alarms going off in his head. "When?"

"All the time," Madsen answered, absentmindedly wiping sweat from his brow.

"Where?"

"My home's in a gated community," Madsen answered, seemingly going off topic, given Malcolm's question. "The rent's high, but security's top-notch."

Where is this going? "Yes?"

"I feel them there," Madsen answered in a hushed whisper. "In my home! In all of the rooms! Especially the bathroom!"

"Wait," Malcolm cut in, shaking his head at Madsen's answer. "Why specifically the bathroom?"

"I don't know! I just feel them there, okay?!"

Probably because that's where you feel the most exposed. The bathroom is where we humans are naked, when we're at our most unprotected. "Okay, then let me ask you another question. Why do you feel Francine's eyes on you?"

"Because she stalking me!" Madsen answered, eyeing the window by Malcolm's desk, just as he did earlier in their conversation. "Why else?!"

Good lord! Malcolm's eyes widened, his mouth agape in shock. "Do you have proof of this?"

"No, I don't have proof!" Madsen bellowed, slamming his fists against the armrests of his chair. "But I know it's her! Who else could it be?!"

"There's always Stan," Malcolm stated in a calm voice. "He has as much reason to attack you as Francine does."

"Stan keeps her in check," Madsen stated, reaching out to grip Malcolm's forearm. "But he can't watch her all the time!"

Good lord, Malcolm thought, blinking at the stinging pain from Madsen's grip. *His fingers are like claws!* "Do you feel her watching you right now?"

"No," Madsen answered, his eyes almost bulging out of his head. "Because it's daytime right now! Stan and Francine only come out at nighttime, Doc! Nighttime!"

—∞—

Enough! Kate's eyes shot open, her breathing heavy as though she had run a marathon. *That's enough!* She quickly wrote down what she remembered, the images as much a revelation to her as they would be to Dr. Logan during their next session. *Enough for today!* Kate's hand went to her skull. The right side was throbbing as though she had pulled a muscle. *Fuck, this hurts!*

But at least she had remembered something.

Kate checked her clock and saw that it was 7:00 p.m.

Not staying here, she thought as she got up from sitting cross-legged to head to her bedroom. *Need a change of clothes! Need to get out of the house! Have to be around people!*

Another stipulation of Dr. Logan's treatment: Make friends. Stick to a daily routine. *Especially* when she didn't want to. And she knew exactly where to go.

A hole-in-the-wall dive called, believe it or not, *Kate's Cove.*

—⚡—

"Well, Madsen," Malcolm said finally as he looked over his notes. "You've given me quite a lot to work with here."

Madsen fixed him with an incredulous gaze, rooted to his chair in front of Malcolm's desk. "That's all you have to say?!"

"What do you want me to say?"

"What do you think?!" Madsen demanded, shooting Malcom a desperate look. "I need to know what's in Kate's head!"

"Why?" Malcolm asked, feeling a touch alarmed that Madsen's first instinct was to go after Kate, again. "You just said Francine was after you, not Kate."

"If Francine's after me, she's after Kate too!"

"So you're here for Kate's welfare?"

"Of course I am," Madsen answered, though the shifty way he looked at Malcolm's desk implied that wasn't the case. At all.

Is he thinking about looking through my files? Malcolm wondered, following Madsen's gaze. "Madsen ...?"

"Yes! I'm here for Kate!"

"Why don't you just *talk* to Kate?" Malcolm asked, giving him a wary look. "Like an adult?"

"Like an adult?" Madsen's lips twisted in anger. "Like an adult?! After what I just told you, you're hitting me with sarcasm?! What kind of a psychiatrist are you?!"

What kind of a police chief were you? Malcolm wondered, refusing to feel any guilt for this man. "One, you're not my patient. Two, you bullied your way into my office and are trying to bully me into doing what you want me to do. And, three, I believe that you play a bigger part in Kate's suffering than you're letting on. Oh, and four, I can't tell you anything about Kate or what's in her head. Doctor-patient confidentiality."

"That's bullshit!"

"It's the law," Malcolm said in a firm voice. "Remember what that is?"

"With the Solomons around," Madsen informed him in a sarcastic voice, "the law means less and less these days."

And whose fault is that? "But not in Milestone City, and not in *this* office," Malcolm declared, looking the man in the eye. "You want answers, you'll have to get them yourself."

"Did you not hear me?!" Madsen shouted in Malcom's face. "I'm being *hunted*! I *don't* have time to get them myself!"

For God's sake, give this man something, Malcolm thought as he pulled a business card from a drawer in his desk. *If anything, just to get him away from this office.* "This is to a private security firm called the Razors. There's a woman who works there named Angie Blackfire. Tell her what you told me, and she'll take your case."

"I heard about those guys," Madsen said, eyeing the card. "I can't afford their rates!"

"Her company's in such high demand that she can do some pro bono work. She also has a deep respect for the police. She'll help you, *especially* if you mention the Solomons."

As Madsen clutched the card as though it was a life preserver in turbulent seas, the light of hope finally shone in his eyes. "Thanks, Doc. I'll call her right away." He then looked at the window, again. "What time is it?"

"About 7:45 p.m.," Malcolm answered after checking his watch.

"She's … not working now, is she?"

"She might be," Malcolm answered, seeing that it was evening outside. "Or maybe not. Like I said, her company's in high demand."

"I can't go home, Doc," Madsen shouted, giving Malcolm a frantic look. "Francine will be there!"

"This is Milestone City," Malcolm reminded him. "The Solomons work in Gateway City, remember?"

"I … right," came the shaky but relieved answer. "That's right!"

"If you feel unsafe being on the roads tonight, get a room at a hotel," Malcolm suggested as he escorted Madsen out of his office. "Call me in the morning. I have a session with Kate. I'll use what we talked about to work with her. If I can confront her with this, maybe we can make a breakthrough. Then I'll call you."

"And what if you can't?"

For God's sake, man! Get the hell out of my office! Malcolm clenched his jaw, doing all he could not to let loose with a curse, ready to go, in his throat. "Then we'll try something else."

———※———

Fuck! Kate gasped as she rode her stranger atop a bed in his apartment. *Fuck! Fuck! Fuck!* Their clothes lay in a damp pile in the corner of the bedroom.

It hadn't been Kate's intention to go home with someone she had just met at a bar like *Kate's Cove*, but after the memories she drudged up, she was in desperate need of a huge … reward.

Each thrust was a spark of electricity that sent waves of pleasure and anxiety through her taut, sweaty body. Thoughts raced through Kate's mind; she was questioning why she was alive, what it meant to be normal, and whether Dr. Logan would approve of what she was doing.

Then she realized: It didn't matter whether or not he did.

As for her stranger, Kate knew his name …

Mark?

Ted?

Nathan?

But Kate refused to think about it. It didn't matter who he was—he was just someone giving her temporary relief from the loneliness she felt at home.

"Slow down, woman," the stranger hissed through gritted teeth. "You're gonna break my dick!"

"Fuck!" Kate gasped as she moved faster, feeling the heat of an orgasm building inside her. "I'm almost there, baby! I'm almost there!"

"Slow down," the stranger said again, his voice sounding weaker. "I can't keep up!"

Please, take the pain away! Kate thought, begging God and whoever else was listening. *Please, just for one night! Please! I just want to feel normal!*

She saw the specter of Stan hovering above her somehow, arms folded in disapproval. *Hey you . . .* Her nipples growing rock-hard, Kate fucked faster as her drunken grin widened.

—⟊—

"Kate, this is Dr. Logan. I've learned some things that I believe will help you. I'll tell you more during our session tomorrow morning. See you then."

Malcolm hung up the phone and leaned back in his chair, still thinking over Madsen's desperate words. It took Malcolm calling security for Madsen to leave his office, flanked by two guards.

Malcolm couldn't press charges since Madsen hadn't issued any threats directly against Kate or himself, but he could put in a call to the Milestone City Police Department to keep an eye on the former police chief.

Going from a respected figure of law and order to a lonely pariah, Malcolm thought, shaking his head. *Oh, how the mighty have fallen.* He then face-palmed, thinking over his thought. And how amazingly cliché that was. *Good use of that PhD, Malcolm!*

—⟊—

Ugggh! Kate knelt over the toilet in the stranger's bathroom, vomiting into its bowl as she gripped its edges. She saw the glint of a pistol in the stranger's closet across from his bed and felt the contents of her stomach well up in her throat.

Kate had barely gotten the bathroom door closed before a few spurts of vomit shot out from her trembling lips. She fell to the toilet, grabbed the rim before she face-planted, and unloaded the rest.

I grew up with guns! Kate thought, shaking with impotent anger. *Now I can't even look at one without blowing chunks!*

She wasn't like this before the Solomons took her. Their masters *did* do something to her! They were still playing with her, influencing her actions somehow!

But Brian had been dead for months! Screwing with her wasn't going to bring him back. So why were Stan and Francine's masters messing with her?

Hadn't she suffered enough?

Once the bathroom had stopped spinning, Kate flushed the vomit. *Just get rid of this! No need for anyone to see it!* But she had to look. Had to see what her vomit looked like.

And God help her, she did!

What in the? Kate recoiled from the toilet in fearful shock. *My vomit's black!* Not pink or red, as she expected, but straight black, like crude oil! *Good lord, this came out of me?*

Strange colors danced across the surface of her vomit, and a rotten smell wafted into her nose, making Kate unsteady on her feet. *I've seen these colors before. But where?* The answer came to her a second later. *The place where Stan and Francine took me!* The answer was on the tip of her tongue, again. But this time, Kate grabbed it, like a port in a storm. *The Other Side! Stan and Francine, took me to another world, another dimension called the Other Side!*

And it looked as though she had brought part of it back with her to the human world!

Kate clamped a hand over her mouth to cover a scream and used the other hand to flush her vomit down. Once that was done, she went to the nearby mirror to check her breath for any telltale smells.

And her face, for any other surprises.

Okay, Kate thought, giving her beleaguered reflection a relieved, tired grin. *Nothing here. Let's get back out there.* She opened the door and stepped out of the bathroom. "Hope you're ready for round 3, babe. Cuz I'm gonna ride that dick like I'm ..."

Kate's words trailed off at the sight of her stranger — curled in a fetal position, shaking like a palsy victim going through a seizure. *Oh shit!* Kate ran to his bedside and felt for a pulse. *Shit!* She reached for her phone and called 911.

—∿—

Malcolm's cell phone rang in the darkness of his bedroom, waking him with a start. He banged his head against the headboard, momentarily seeing stars. *Dammit!*

Blinking away the pain, Malcolm snatched the cell phone from its charging station near his bed. Growling in annoyance at the constant ringing, he took a look at the caller ID. *I don't know this number. Who is this?*

There was only one way to find out.

Malcolm took the call. "Hello? Who is this?" *Please don't be something—or someone—horrible.*

"Dr. Logan!' a panicked voice cried out. "I need your help!"

Kate! Malcolm shot up into a sitting position. "Kate? What's wrong?"

"I've done something terrible!" came the frantic answer. "Please! I'm not sure what to do!"

Hearing those words wiped away any lingering grogginess in Malcolm's head, shocking him fully into the world with a rough hand. "What happened?"

"I was with this guy ... he's not waking up," Kate babbled frantically. "I think I did something to him! I need you here, right now! The orderlies won't let me go ...!"

"Until they see me," Malcolm finished as he leaped out of his bed and went to his closet to get his clothes. "Don't answer any questions that might implicate you." *Why am I talking like a lawyer?* "Where are you?"

"I told you! A hospital!"

"I mean *what* hospital?" Malcolm clarified. "What's the name?"

"Nixon General," Kate answered after taking a moment to calm herself. "I'm at Nixon General."

That's not far from here. "I'll be there as soon as I can," Malcolm declared, putting on his shirt and pants. "Now put me in touch with the orderlies. I need to tell them a few things."

—⁂—

Kate waited in the hospital waiting room, eyes downcast. A nurse handed her a cup of coffee, but she didn't drink it.

The air was heavy with the smell of stale coffee and antiseptic. She tried to avoid Dr. Logan's gaze as he approached her from down the hall. Shame burned in her cheeks. The thought that she had almost killed someone—even if it was someone she had met only a few hours ago—kept playing in her mind.

"Are you all right, Kate?" Dr. Logan asked, taking a seat in the chair next to her.

"I'm okay," she answered, still not making eye contact with him. "Just … not great."

"Do you want to tell me what happened? You sounded really scared on the phone."

Oh, did I? Kate wondered sarcastically. "I'm not sure. It's …"

"You can tell me, Kate," he assured her. "Remember, I'm here to help."

Heh, Topher said the same thing once, before all of this, Kate thought, her blood boiling at the mere thought of her despicable former police chief. *But you're not him. And I do need your help.* "I did something awful, Doc. I … I thought that man was going to die."

"That's interesting," Dr. Logan declared, "because according to the nurses I spoke to, your … partner?"

Kate nodded, feeling more ashamed than ever.

"Your partner suffered an allergic reaction. That's all."

To what? To me? "I didn't even ask his name," Kate said, her lips quivering with guilt. "I almost killed him, and I don't even know his name."

"Kate," Dr. Logan said in a calm, soothing voice as he put a hand on her shoulder, "imagine if you *hadn't* called an ambulance. *That* would've been almost killing him."

"If you say so."

Dr. Logan pulled his chair around until he was sitting right in front of Kate. "I have to ask. How long has this been going on?"

"What?" Kate asked, looking up at him. *As if I don't know …*

"Have you done this before?" Dr. Logan asked in a tender voice. "Gone home with men you don't know?"

Dammit, I didn't want you to find out about this. Kate's eyes flickered away from his. She felt a swell of pride despite the crazy situation Dr. Logan had found herself in. "Men *and* women, Doc."

"How many partners have you had?"

"More than I can count," Kate answered, sighing as she leaned back in her chair.

"Kate," Dr. Logan said, sounding as though he was trying to cushion his words carefully. "Have these … partners had the same reaction as this man?"

"Not this bad, but yes."

"I see."

"It's because of the Solomons," Kate whispered, motioning for Dr. Logan to slide his chair closer to her. "They did something to me."

"In what way?"

"I can't get food down. And everything's numb."

"Numb?" Dr. Logan asked, his brow arching in curiosity. "Please elaborate."

"My skin feels like it's wrapped in cling wrap," Kate explained after sucking in a large breath. "I can't feel the heat of a cup of coffee or the chill of a breeze. It's like there's a thick, damp blanket over my body." *God, this sounds weird to me, and I'm the one going through it!* "Nothing smells good. Everything's mushed together. It's like my senses are calibrated wrong."

"How long have you felt this way?" Dr. Logan asked, fidgeting in his seat in front of her.

"Since I got back," Kate answered in a hushed voice.

Dr. Logan blinked in surprise and then cocked his head, letting out a calming breath. "Why didn't you tell me?"

"I thought it was all in my head. PTSD, you know?" Kate let out a weary sigh. *And now he's guilting me. I know he is. This is why I don't tell people things!* "I thought it would go away in time, but it's gotten worse."

"I wonder," Dr. Logan said before pressing his index finger into Kate's shoulder. "Do you feel this?"

She shook her head with a tiny shrug.

"Let's try this." He removed a pen from his pocket and pushed the tip into her shoulder with greater force. "Do you feel that?"

There was no response; Kate's expression was frozen in fear.

Dr. Logan pushed harder, as though trying to break through her skin. "Nothing?"

"Not a damn thing," she replied without batting an eyelash.

Dr. Logan stared intently at the pen. The tip was bent.

"Kate," he whispered, "this may be more than a psychological condition."

———◊———

The next morning in his office, Malcolm sat at his desk, checking his watch. It read 8:00 a.m., thirty minutes before his session with Kate. He had spent the morning researching accounts of mind-body phenomena. Some read like Kate's condition, but they weren't nearly as extreme.

Others were actually worse.

Malcolm was sure Kate's inability to eat well was a psychosomatic reaction to her trauma at the hands of the Solomons. Her skin's toughness? That was a whole other story. On his desk was the pen with the bent tip. After he had talked Kate off the proverbial ledge, he left it in his jacket pocket. He forgot it was there, until he checked his pockets when he arrived in his office.

He had thought a full night's sleep would give him more insight into the phenomena that created the bent pen tip, but his slumber yielded nothing.

Kate was becoming a full-time job.

And he still had to deal with Madsen!

"Sally," Malcolm called out to his secretary as he pressed the speaker button on his phone.

"Yes, Dr. Logan?" she answered from her desk outside his office in a nasal voice.

"Cancel my other appointments," Malcolm answered in a reluctant tone. "Leave messages with our clients to reschedule."

"Yes, sir," Sally said from outside his office.

"When Mrs. Johnson comes in," Malcolm added, "send her straight to my office."

"She becoming a full-time job, boss?"

"You could say that, Sally," Malcolm answered after letting out a weary sigh. *You could definitely say that.*

—⚬—

Topher Madsen sat in a rental car in the parking lot outside of Malcolm's office. He patted the gun in the seat next to him and waited for Kate to arrive.

—⚬—

As Kate drove silently to Dr. Logan's office, she went over the events of last night. She had almost killed a man. By accident, of course, but hadn't Brian's murder been an accident too?

Accidental shooting, Kate corrected herself, keeping her eyes on the road in front of her. *The court ruled it an accidental death. Not murder. You have to plan a murder.*

The specter of Francine Solomon sat in the passenger's seat across from her, shaking her head in disagreement.

"Shut up," Kate hissed before pressing the gas pedal to the floor. "Shut. Up."

—⚬—

29

"Are you wearing a dress?" Malcolm asked as he gazed upon Kate sitting in her usual spot on the couch in front of his therapist chair. "Wait, you are wearing a dress!"

"Is that a crime?" Kate asked, straightening the bottom of her black sundress. It worked with the black tennis shoes, reminding Malcolm of the goth girls he knew in his youth.

"Not at all. It's just a change from your usual clothing."

"I wanted to try a new look," Kate said in a defensive voice. "There's no need to make a big deal about it."

I'd normally agree, Malcolm thought, arching his brow, *if not for what happened last night*. "Kate, are you changing how you dress to appear less threatening to me?"

"C'mon, Doc," Kate groaned, rolling her eyes. "It's not like that."

"You don't have to do that for me. What happened last night has not changed my opinion of you."

"It's sure changed *my* opinion of me," Kate said with grim emphasis. "Speaking of last night, how's my … comatose stranger?"

"Still in critical condition, though he's better than he was."

"Critical condition?" Kate's face fell, her narrow shoulders sagging. "You said he had a nervous reaction!"

"He did," Malcolm stated, "which put him in critical condition. Though according to the nurses I spoke to, he should be okay in a couple of days."

"That's a relief," Kate said, flashing him a grateful smile. "I already have enough deaths on my conscience."

I do not like the sound of that, Malcolm thought, crossing his legs in discomfort. "Kate, I'm not comfortable with you talking like that."

"*I'm* not comfortable talking about me like this, but it's a reality in my life, Dr. Logan. I have to face it."

"We both agree on that," Malcolm stated, glad that Kate was at least taking some responsibility for what had happened with the stranger. "But that doesn't mean you have to beat yourself up about it. I told you, what happened to that man wasn't your fault." *At least not purposefully.*

"Can I see him?"

"You don't have to ask me for permission, Kate. I'm not your legal guardian." *No matter how much I'm starting to feel like I am.*

"I know," Kate said, a distasteful look flashing across her face, "but still, I'd like your opinion."

"If you wish to see him," Malcolm answered after taking a moment to craft a proper, nonjudgmental response, "you can. Though I'd wait a few days."

"That's a good idea, Dr. Logan," Kate said, giving him a respectful nod. "Thank you."

—⚶—

Madsen stepped out of his car, his gun safe and snug in the holster under his jacket. Scowling at the strangely empty parking lot around him, he scanned the area for threats.

When he found none, he patted his gun for comfort, squared his shoulders, and began the lonely walk to Malcolm's office.

—⚶—

"Now that *that*'s taken care of," Kate said, taking a moment to stretch her back and shoulders on the couch, "I'd like to talk about what I saw when Stan and Francine took me."

"You remember?" Malcolm asked, his eyebrow going up in surprise.

"I did some meditating," Kate answered, a pleased expression on her face. "Like you told me to."

"I'm glad my advice helped." Malcolm couldn't believe his luck. *What happened with her lover last night must have inspired her to confront what Stan and Francine had done to her. What a wonderful turn of events, though I am saddened it took a man almost losing his life to kick it off.* "Are you sure you want to do this?"

"After what happened last night and what I told you at the hospital," Kate answered, a determined expression on her face, "I feel like I have to."

"Okay," Malcolm said, noting the firm urgency in her voice. "Whenever you're ready."

"Our sessions are taped, right?" Kate asked, her eyes searching his face for confirmation.

31

"Always." Malcolm pointed to the recorder resting on his desk behind him. "And I'm taking my own notes as well," he added, showing her his notepad.

"A little old school, don't you think? Most people use iPads."

"For some situations, I find the analog approach is best." Satisfied with his answer, Malcolm nodded at Kate. "So once again, whenever you're ready."

"Stan and Francine brought me to a tower," Kate said, getting right to it.

"A tower?" Malcolm asked, noting how she had switched gears in their conversation. *She's showing focus. That's a good sign.* "Where was this tower?"

"In another dimension," Kate answered, closing her eyes as her voice took on a soft edge. "Called the Other Side."

"This dimension has an official name?"

"Yes."

"How did you know that?" Malcolm asked, writing the name down on his notepad. "Did Stan or Francine tell you?"

"No," Kate answered, wrinkles appearing on her forehead as her expression became troubled. "I … I think the dimension itself told me. Or maybe Stan and Francine's friends told me."

What? Malcolm's lips parted slightly in shock. "Friends? What do you mean?"

"We got to the Other Side by passing through a flaming ring in the skies above Earth," Kate said, changing subjects. "It was like a barcode, allowing us passage."

"Like a security gate at an airport," Malcolm reasoned, taking the change in stride.

"Right," Kate said, nodding her head vigorously while keeping her eyes closed. "Once I arrived at the Other Side, every inch of me hurt."

"You were hurt? Do you know why?"

"The heat of the gate, it burned away my skin, Dr. Logan. It burned away most of me, actually.

"How much of you was left?" Malcolm asked, his forehead breaking out in a cold sweat.

"I was … just a torso and an arm," Kate answered, her voice becoming labored. "The rest of me … didn't make it through."

—m—

"Once Stan and Francine got me to the Other Side, they brought me to their masters," Kate said as a sharp pain stabbed the front of her brain, right between her eyes. *Head's never hurt before*, she thought, massaging the pain away. *Means I'm on the right track, sharing all this.*

"Kate?" Malcolm asked, his voice sounding far away despite being in the same room with her. "Do you need a minute?"

"No, I'm …" Kate brought her hand up to her hair as the pain grew worse. "On second thought, yeah." She slowly opened her eyes and saw Dr. Logan. "I might need a minute."

"Why don't we take a break?" Dr. Logan asked, looking from Kate to the door leading to the lobby. "I'll get you some aspirin and a cup of water, give you a few minutes, and we can—"

"No!" Kate blurted out, a claustrophobic sense of panic seizing her as he got up from his seat. "Wait! I haven't told you everything!"

"Kate," Dr. Logan said in a strained voice, "I need you to—"

"Doctor, don't leave!" Kate declared, her panic intensifying. "Not until I've told you everything!"

"And I want to hear everything," Dr. Logan said, his muscles tensing under Kate's fingers. "But in order for me to do that, I need you to *let go of my arm.*"

Let go of your …? It took Kate a few seconds to realize that her hand had fastened around Dr. Logan's wrist like a claw. *When did I grab his arm?* "Wow," she gasped, letting go of the older man. "I am so sorry!"

"It's okay," Dr. Logan said, massaging his wrist. "All part of the job."

"Can you please stay? At least for a little while?"

"If you wish, Kate," Dr. Logan said, sitting back in his chair. "But the second I think you're putting too much stress on yourself, I'm ending the session."

"Agreed," Kate said, taking a moment to stretch. "Now where was I?"

"You were approaching Stan and Francine's masters."

"Right!" Kate shouted, snapping her fingers as her expression brightened. "I met Stan and Francine's masters! All of them!"

"All of them?" Dr. Logan asked, looking spellbound by her words. "How many of these masters do Stan and Francine have?"

"From what I saw," Kate answered, scratching at her forehead, "three. There were three."

"What did they look like?"

"I …" Kate pushed her mind to remember but felt her grip on her memories loosening. "Dammit, I'm losing it!"

"Take it slow, Kate," Dr. Logan cooed in a soft voice. "Let the memories come in their own time."

"They were like fire," Kate gasped, the sharp pain spreading to the rest of her brain, making her blink rapidly. "And they towered over everyone else!"

"Were these masters like giants, Kate?"

"Yes," Kate answered as the aroma of the Other Side wafted into her nostrils. "At least I think so. But that might've been what they wanted me to see. I wasn't altered enough to see their real bodies."

"But you *were* altered."

"Yes," Kate answered, nodding in grim agreement. "Yes, I was."

"Let it out, Kate," Malcolm said, rooted to his seat as Kate described what she saw in a labored, yet clear voice. "Just keep talking."

"Yes," Kate said, becoming swept up in a mania as she continued. "Stan and Francine brought me before their masters. Tossed me in front of them, awaiting their judgment."

Good lord! Malcolm's eyes widened, caught up in Kate's macabre story. "You were put on trial?"

"Yes! For Brian's death!"

"But you were tried in Gateway City. On Earth." *I can't believe I just said that. With a straight face, no less!* Malcolm suddenly realized that his office had become strangely muggy while Kate told her story. *What in the …?* His clothes felt damp, despite having just come out of the dryer in his home last night.

What is this? Malcolm cautiously raised his hand to his face. He dragged his hand across his forehead and came away with a layer of damp sweat on his fingers. *What in the world?!*

"Doctor?" Kate asked, giving him a nervous look. "Are you—?"

"Give me a second." Malcolm got up from his seat and checked the control panel on his room's air-conditioning unit. "Just need to ..." The temperature in his office had risen to an oppressive 70 degrees, with a humidity of 70 percent in the span of a few minutes.

How could that happen? Unless ...

She made the temperature rise. Malcolm turned to face a bewildered Kate Barrow, the hairs on the back of his neck standing on end. *Somehow, Kate raised the temperature of my office just by talking!*

The issues Kate had revealed to Malcolm at Nixon General were strange enough, but at least they were localized to her body.

But altering the environment around her—an environment he lived in—recontextualized her issues in a frighteningly new perspective!

—⁂—

Madsen stepped into the building, into the lobby of Dr. Logan's practice.

The lobby had blue walls, adorned with paintings of serene seascapes. Calming music was pumped through speakers in the ceiling, no doubt to put patients at ease.

Unfortunately, it didn't calm Madsen's nerves. Nothing calmed his nerves, not since Kate Barrow's trial for shooting the Solomon boy.

He marched to the front desk, a lone secretary in his sights.

Two security guards, posted at opposite sides of the desk, watched him approach.

The secretary, a blond woman in a blue dress, blinked in recognition of Madsen, either from his appearances on the news or from his earlier visit with Dr. Logan. "Can I help you, sir?"

"Yes," Madsen said, putting on a charming smile as he leaned against her desk. "I'd like to see Dr. Logan."

The secretary blinked again, this time showing surprise as she checked her computer. "I don't see your name on his schedule. Are you looking to become a client?"

"I'm in the process of becoming one," Madsen answered, eyeing the two guards warily. They, in turn, eyed him with the same wariness. Oh, how Madsen longed for the days when he could walk in to any building, flash his badge, and *not* be seen as a criminal!

"He is in session right now," the secretary informed him. "Can I schedule you for a sit-down later this week?"

"I'd like to talk to him, today, if possible," Madsen answered with forced patience. "Even if it's for only a few minutes."

"Stand by," the secretary said, keeping her eye on her computer screen as she typed on her keyboard. "I will let Dr. Logan know." She cocked her head at a set of chairs in a corner of the lobby. "Please, take a seat."

—⁂—

He's scared, Kate thought, looking at Dr. Logan standing by the AC unit in his office. *I can see it. He's scared, and I scared him.* Dammit, that wasn't what she wanted! *This is why I don't share things!*

But what exactly was he afraid of? What she said or what she had *yet* to say?

"Dr. Logan?"

"Yes, Kate?" he answered, still looking at his AC unit, his brow wrinkled in worry.

"Are you okay?" Kate sat on the edge of the couch. *Please don't freak out on me.* "Do *you* need a minute?"

"Honestly, Kate, I just might." Dr. Logan looked to the door. "I'll be right back. I think I need a glass of water."

Yeah, you go get that water, Kate thought, watching him head for the door. *Just please come back when you're done.* She fiddled with her hands after he left the office. *Please don't drop me as a patient right when I'm on the verge of a breakthrough!*

Kate wouldn't have held it against Dr. Logan if he *did* drop her as a patient, given what she had told him. The idea that she had spent time as a barbecued, desiccated near-corpse, and yet sat in his office looking perfectly fine months later, was enough to scare anyone away!

But she *was* on the verge of a breakthrough, Kate could feel it in her bones. She had clear memories of the Other Side—something she had never had before. Not in the six months since Stan and Francine brought her back to Gateway City, traumatized as hell.

The fact that she remembered the Other Side now, of all times, had to be important. Either to Stan and Francine or their masters.

It sure as hell was important to Kate, and she needed Dr. Logan to help her figure out what it meant!

Kate's gaze remained fixed on the closed door of Dr. Logan's office; she was hoping he would return soon. She missed the sound of his voice, his breathing. But those comforting sounds had left the room with him.

At the moment, it was just Kate, alone with the maelstrom that was her thoughts …

And a growing sense of unease.

At that moment, Kate felt an unexplainable chill seeping into her bones. *What the* … She hugged herself, wishing she had brought a jacket with her as the temperature steadily dropped, as if the room was reacting to her anxiety. *What's happening?*

Was it what caused Dr. Logan to leave the office?

Suddenly, a high-pitched giggle cut through the silence, making her jump.

What the hell?! Kate turned her gaze away from the door and toward the source of the sound. Her heart pounded in her chest as her eyes fell on Dr. Logan's chair.

Sitting there, under the dim light from the window, was the phantom figure of Francine Solomon. She was draped in a dark-blue latex skinsuit, a long cape flowing from her shoulders to her ankles. She sat comfortably, as if the chair belonged to her, her muscular arms folded across her chest in a position of stern judgment. It was a cruel mockery of a scene Kate knew all too well—the trial of Brian Solomon's shooting, where she had been declared not guilty over six months ago.

In Dr. Logan's office, Francine gazed at Kate with green eyes, her shoulder-length red hair billowing in the wind. Even though all the windows in the office were closed.

"What do you want from me?" Kate whispered fearfully, rooted to her spot on the couch, opposite the superhuman phantom.

Francine leered at her, crossing her legs in a mildly amused manner.

"Say something," Kate hissed through gritted teeth, her eyes darting from Francine to the door. "I know you can hear me."

Francine's lips curled into a sinister smile.

"Say. Something," Kate repeated, her voice rising in volume, her every muscle tense and ready to spring.

Francine's smile bloomed into a sadistic grin.

"SAY SOMETHING, DAMMIT!"

—⚊m⚊—

"Madsen?" Malcolm asked as he approached the former police chief, who was sitting in one of the chairs in the lobby. "What are you doing here?"

"I know you're with Kate right now," he answered, getting up from his chair with a grunt. "Your secretary confirmed it."

"Are you staking out my office?" Malcolm asked as he stopped in front of Madsen, seeing the bulge of a gun under his jacket. *Good lord, the man's armed!* He shot an alarmed glance at the security guards flanking his secretary's desk before looking at Madsen. "And you brought a gun here?!"

"For protection, Doc," Madsen said in a hushed tone. He glanced at the guards and saw they were approaching him and Malcolm. "Only for protection. I'm not going to use it here."

"Dammit, man, I see patients here! People in desperate need of psychological counseling! They count on this place feeling safe!"

"And I in no way wanna mess with that," Madsen said, raising his hands defensively. "I simply want to know what Kate said to you."

"I can't reveal that to you, Madsen," Malcolm protested, his heart hammering in his chest. "Doctor-patient confidentiality, as I told you earlier!" *And yet, you're still here!* Malcolm looked behind Madsen to the door leading to the parking lot outside. *Now, please leave! I have to get back to Kate!*

Her ability to affect the temperature of his office, combined with what she had revealed to him about her time on the Other Side, had shaken Malcolm to his core. So much, in fact, that he had left his office to steady himself. The last thing he needed was a belligerent former police chief convinced that a vengeful, grieving parent—altered or not—was on his tail.

But if what Kate had told Malcom during their session was real, didn't that mean that what Madsen had told him was real too?

"C'mon, Doc," Madsen urged, his face twisted in desperation, "I told you things—"

"And I promised I'd tell you things," Malcolm shot back, enraged that Madsen had put him in such a precarious position. "*After* my session with Kate!"

"Francine's eyes," Madsen blurted out, his hands shooting for Malcolm's shoulders. "I felt them last night!"

Oh, for heaven's sake! Malcolm winced, knowing between Madsen's grip and Kate's, he was going to have some bruises when he got home. "They're in your mind, Madsen! It's all in your mind!"

"After what I told you, can you *really* be sure?!"

I don't have time for this, Malcolm thought, shaking his head. He motioned for his security guards to intervene. "I have to get back to my patient, Madsen. We'll talk after—"

"I stay in different hotels around Milestone City," Madsen said, cutting him off. "Some nights in populated areas like downtown, other nights on the edge of the city."

"Why?"

"To keep Francine guessing, you see?!"

"If you believe Francine is tailing you, why would you endanger a civilian population at all?" Malcolm asked, then shook his head, stepping away from Madsen. "Never mind, I'm not entertaining this!"

"But every time, every damn time, she found me," Madsen continued, gripping Malcolm's shoulders so tightly he was definitely leaving welts on his skin. "I feel her, Doc! Right outside my room! On the other side of my windows! In the walls! In my head! I'm telling you, Doc, she's getting closer!"

"There's been no sighting of Francine Solomon at any point in the city," Malcolm hissed, prying Madsen's hands from his shoulders. *I will not be manhandled like a damn slave!* "If there was, she'd be in the news! We'd be at DEFCON 1, for God's sake!"

"She's too smart to be seen! That's why I have my gun!"

If Malcolm knew anything about the Solomons, it was that conventional weapons did nothing to them. But if having a gun gave Madsen comfort, then let him have his gun. He looked back to his office. "I have to get back to my patient, Madsen. When I'm done, I'll call you. But right now, I need you to go. Right now."

"I can't go home!" Madsen shouted, spittle flying out of his mouth. "I can't go back to Gateway City! She'll be waiting for me there! I can't go to any of the hotels in this town. She knows them all!"

"Calm down, Madsen."

"Something slashed my tires last night!" Madsen continued hysterically. "There are claw marks on the doors too! Claw marks!" He hastily pulled some pictures out of his jacket pocket. "I got the proof right here!"

I've been away from Kate too long! Malcolm gave his guards an angry look, wondering why the hell they hadn't escorted Madsen out of the building already. "And I'll look at those pictures *after* I finish my session! Now I have to go—"

A shrill scream erupted from down the hall, snapping Malcolm's attention to his office. "Oh my god! Kate!"

The scream escaped Kate's lips just as Francine leapt onto her like a rabid dog. She found herself on the floor, her eyes inches apart from Francine's maddening gaze.

"Get off! Get off! Get off!" Kate fought as hard as she could, tasting blood as Francine slapped her across the face so hard she cut her lip open. *Please!* Kate shot a frantic glance at the door as she struggled in Francine's grip. *Someone help me!*

At that moment, Dr. Logan dashed in!

—⚏—

Good lord! Malcolm froze at the sight of Kate writhing on the floor of his office, seemingly fighting with ... something. *What the hell is causing this?!*

"Get her off me!" Kate screeched, her eyes pleading with him for help. "For God's sake, get her off me!"

"Who?!"

"Francine, dammit! Can't you see her?!"

"There's no one here, Kate!" Malcolm ran to her side, pulling the delirious young woman up to a sitting position. "There's no one here but you!"

"No," Kate got out, vigorously shaking her head. "She's here! I know she is! She ..." She blinked, coming out of whatever madness she had been lost in. "She's gone!" Kate's eyes searched every corner of Malcolm's office. "She's gone!"

"She was never here," Malcolm said, keeping his voice neutral as his heart hammered in his chest. "It's just *you*, Kate! The only Francine you're seeing is in your mind!"

"No! No! No!" Kate continued shaking her head, hugging Malcolm so tightly that she forced the air from his lungs. "She was here! She was right here!" Kate showed him a cut, bloody lip. "She did this!"

The wound was disconcerting, but it was nothing she couldn't have done herself.

"Wait a minute," Kate said, looking over Malcom's shoulder to the door to his office behind him. "What's *he* doing here?!"

Dammit, Malcolm thought as he turned his head to see Madsen standing in the doorway of his office. *Dammit! Dammit! Dammit!*

"Hello, Kate," the former police chief said good-naturedly, leaning against the doorframe like it was no big deal. Gone was his desperation; it had retreated behind a mask of smug superiority. "Long time no see, eh?"

"Topher," Kate spat, hate dripping off the word as she glared at her former boss. "How *dare* you show up here?!"

Topher? Malcolm's head snapped from Madsen to Kate. "Madsen," he said, not even dignifying his presence with his eye. "For the last damn time, you need to leave. Right now."

"But," the older man whined, his smug mask cracking at the edges, "I have questions—"

"Which can wait until later!"

Madsen tried to force the issue, but Malcolm didn't budge. Seeing he was beaten, Madsen turned to leave. "Good to see you, Kate. Glad you're doing okay."

"You son of a bitch!" Grabbing a nearby vase from the coffee table in front of the couch, Kate lobbed it at Madsen's head as the door closed. "I fucking see you again, I'll kill you!"

"Enough, Kate!" Malcolm bellowed as the vase shattered against the door. *Dammit, that was a family heirloom!* "He's gone, okay? He's gone."

"What the hell was he doing here at all?!"

"He's here to see me," Malcolm answered, closing his eyes to brace for Kate's reaction. Given what he had just seen, he would be surprised if she didn't rip him a new one.

"Freaking what?!" Kate's face was so contorted by surprise that her eyes damn near popped out of her head. "All I told you, and you keep Topher from me?!"

"I figured if I told you," Malcolm answered in a firm voice, "you'd react badly. And guess what? You did, so it's a damn good thing I didn't tell you, isn't it?"

"How long has he been in the city?" Kate asked savagely. "Does he know where I live?! Does Witness Protection know he's here?" Her eyes narrowed, her voice going from ranting to deathly quiet. "Are you spying on me for him?!"

"What?"

"Are. You. Spying. On. Me. For. Topher?!"

"No. Why would you think—" *Wait a minute!* It was then that Malcolm realized she had called Madsen by his first name, again. It implied a level of intimacy that might have explained her reaction to seeing him again. "Did he do that to you in Gateway City? Have people spy on you?"

Kate paused, her lips twisting as though she was chewing on something sour.

"Kate," Malcolm declared, "you just started trusting me. Don't let Madsen win by undoing that."

Kate's expression softened. "Yeah. Yeah, he did."

Damn, Malcolm cursed to himself. "Who, if I may ask?"

"One of his 'special detectives,'" she spat, using air quotes as Malcolm lifted her from the floor and helped her back to the couch, "from Homicide, believe it or not."

"Not the Special Victims Unit?" Malcolm asked, finding Kate's response curious. "They'd be better suited to deal with you, given what you went through."

"Yeah, Topher never had much faith in the SVU. Saw it as more of a PR thing. To make the department look good, and that was it."

"Good lord, and this man was chief of police?!"

"What can I say?" Kate answered, shrugging. "Topher had a lot of pull back in the day. Not so much anymore."

—✶—

The nerve of them! Madsen sat in the lobby; his eyes trained on his hands. He didn't trust himself to look up, afraid of how the security guards would react if he looked even a little upset. *Goddammit!* His leg almost shot out to kick the chair in front of him in growing disgust, but he stopped it in time.

Kate's words bounced through the corridors of Madsen's mind, making him heated. *She has the gall—the absolute gall—to threaten me?! After all I did to keep her safe!*

Glancing at the security guards, who gave him a mean look, Madsen felt his gun under his jacket. He was almost sad he didn't use it on Kate.

—✶—

"So," Kate said after a moment of silence in Dr. Logan's office, "what Topher was saying about Francine, is that true?"

43

"About her hunting him down?" Dr. Logan asked while pouring a cup of coffee for himself at a sink in the far corner of his office, his back to Kate. "I'm afraid it is." He paused, wincing as though he had told a lie. "Or at least he thinks it's true." Once he finished making his cup, he turned to face her. "Do you think it's true?"

Well … Kate paused, looking at the floor as she thought about Dr. Logan's question. "Francine has the power to."

"Good lord …," Dr. Logan whispered anxiously.

"But … I don't think she would."

"What makes you think that?"

"Because Stan wouldn't allow it," Kate answered. *Don't ask me how I know that. Well, no, he's going to ask me, because if I were in his shoes, I'd ask me!*

"Kate," Dr. Logan asked, turning around to lean against his sink as he gazed at her. "How do you know that?"

I knew it! Kate wanted to suck her teeth in disgust. But she figured that Dr. Logan had been through enough for one day.

"Well?"

Don't rush me! "Because when the Solomons kidnapped me, the only reason Francine didn't kill me in my home was because Stan was holding her back," Kate answered, looking up at Dr. Logan. "Keeping her in check. If he can do that when the woman who killed their child was right in front of her, he can do the same when the person that got her off for the crime is a whole city away."

Dr. Logan almost dropped his coffee. "What?"

Damn, Kate winced painfully. *Cat's out of the bag now.* Her eyes widened, a long-overdue thought coming to her. *Wait a minute, why am I defending Topher?! He hung me out to dry!* "You heard me, Doctor. Topher got me off for Brian's death."

"I was under the impression that the jury got you off. By declaring you not guilty."

"And who do you think helped them come to *that* decision?" Kate asked, giving the psychiatrist a sardonic smile.

"Good lord," Dr. Logan whispered, his features twisted in disgust. "I can't believe Madsen went so far as to manipulate a jury just to save you."

"He manipulated a jury to save his *department*," Kate clarified in a sour voice. "He needed me to look clean. To look innocent, untouchable, so that the department would remain untouchable. If I was found guilty, if I even spent one night in jail, he'd lose it all." Kate sat back against the couch. "His influence and all the perks that came with it."

—m—

I heard that the Gateway City Police Department was corrupt, but I never dreamed it went so deep, Malcolm thought, gazing at Kate in disbelief. *At this point, it sounds less like an institution of law and order and more like a gaggle of criminals!* "I'm starting to see why Stan and Francine have been going on their rampage."

"Yeah," Kate admitted in a said voice. "Me too."

"Not that I agree with it," Malcolm added quickly. "There are other ways to change things besides bullying people. Or taking them out of their homes."

"Sometimes, Doctor, it's the most effective way."

Let's try another tact, Malcolm thought, not wanting Kate to go down *that* road. "Kate, why were you struggling with Francine when Madsen and I came in this office?"

Kate's head shot up, her eyes wide with shock. "So you believe I was fighting her?"

"Let me say it another way," Malcolm said, cursing himself for not phrasing his question better. "When did you start seeing this phantom of Francine Solomon?"

"After I was released from intensive care," Kate mumbled, looking away from Malcolm, clearly ashamed. "A month after Stan and Francine brought me back from the Other Side."

Wish I had my notepad, Malcolm thought, glancing at his easy chair. The pad lay on the seat of the chair, a whole five feet away from him. He wanted to walk over and grab it but was afraid any movement in front of Kate might make her lose her train of thought. *I'll have to reconstruct the details of her story from memory later.* "Why do you think you see them?"

"You really want to know?"

45

"I asked, didn't I?" Malcolm braced himself. Kate always asked that question right before letting out some mind-blowing revelation.

As if making sure he could take the shock.

"Yeah," Kate agreed, pulling down the collar of her sundress. "Yeah, you did. So here's the reason."

Oh my word! Malcolm, to his shock, saw a tattoo on her skin. No. Not a tattoo, a brand. Of a bird of prey, wings outstretched, right above the swell of Kate's right breast.

It was the same mark on the walls of the Solomons' home and on their costumes in the files Malcolm received when he took Kate on as a patient. He never imagined he would see it burned into a person's skin. "How long have you had this?"

"Ever since the Solomons brought me back from the Other Side."

"I take it the doctor who examined you after you came back saw this?" Malcolm sat next to Kate on the couch, his eyes glued to the tattoo.

"Actually," Kate answered, watching him with curious, borderline-amused, eyes, "no."

"No?"

"No," Kate answered, her eyes staying on him as though seeing him from a new perspective.

"Why not?"

"Because," she answered, taking a quick glance out a nearby window, "they didn't see it. Hell, I didn't see it. Not until after they let me off with a clean bill of health."

"A diagnosis I have issues with," Malcolm declared, fighting the urge to touch the bird-shaped mark carved into Kate's chest. "More and more every day."

What the hell is taking them so long? Madsen wondered, checking his watch. *Dammit, Dr. Logan, I need to talk to you!* He craned his neck to look at Dr. Logan's office, his face awash in panic. *Hurry the hell up!* Madsen then looked to the door leading to the parking lot of Dr. Logan's practice and the skies above.

The sun was going down.

—ɯ—

Kate squirmed a little under Dr. Logan's gaze, trying to look anywhere else in the office but at him.

Or that damned mark the Solomons gave her.

You wanted me to open up, Kate thought, watching the good doctor's brow jump up and down on his face. *How's this for opening up?*

Kate had tried her damndest to ignore the tattoo the second she was released from the doctors six months ago. Tried to feel grateful that they gave her a clean bill of health.

And then the mark came.

It just showed up on her skin when she was taking a shower. Just seeing that thing on her chest, like a demonic tag, made her scream so loud she damn near woke the neighbors!

The way it moved, the way the skin underneath it got warm freaked Kate out to no end. How was it she couldn't feel any temperature from the world outside but she felt the heat of that mark as clear as the sun's heat?

"I tried covering it up," Kate said, realizing that Dr. Logan hadn't said anything in the last few minutes. "Just wrapped my upper torso in gauze every day before going to work."

"You never told anyone about it?"

"You're the first person I've ever told about this, Doctor."

"Well, in that case," Dr. Logan said, giving her a warm smile, "thank you for the privilege."

"That's what you call this thing?" Kate lightly ran her fingers over the mark, hissing as her skin tingled, as though covered in a nest of spiders. "A privilege?" She blew a strand of blond hair from her face. "I call it a nightmare. A reminder of another one."

"You seem"—Dr. Logan paused, as if searching for the right words—"pretty calm about it, all things considered."

Yeah, I look calm, Kate thought, giving him a mirthless smile. *But I don't feel calm.* "I've had six months to get used to it. Besides, I got other tattoos, Doctor. This one's just one more."

"Have your lovers," Dr. Logan asked after clearing his throat, "and the people you've been with since arriving in Milestone City, seen this mark?"

"I told you, Doc, I keep it covered."

"I know, Kate. But in the throes of passion," he explained, "gauze can slip despite the most vigilant of efforts."

Now that you mention it … Kate thought for a second, then shook her head. "No. I'd know if any of my partners saw it."

"Not to badger you, but how?"

"I'd … feel it."

"You'd feel it?" Dr. Logan's brow arched, a slight tremble growing in his voice. "Does this mark … communicate with you?"

"Heh," Kate chuckled, catching his meaning, "you mean like talk to me?"

"I normally wouldn't ask, but given what you've revealed to me …"

"No, Doctor," Kate answered, shaking her head again. "It doesn't talk to me. Not with words, anyway."

—w—

I need a moment to digest this, Malcolm thought as Kate covered the tattoo again behind the top of her sundress. Was it his imagination, or did the mark throb before his eyes? "I think here is a good place for us to stop for today."

"Getting too out there for you?" Kate asked, the question sounding like a dare. Was there amusement twinkling in her eyes?

"I will admit," Malcolm answered quickly, "it is beyond my experience, but I knew something like this might happen when I took you on as a patient."

"You didn't take me," Kate said in a patient voice. "I was forced on you." She cocked her head at the door leading to the lobby. "I'm guessing by Topher out there."

She's still giving Madsen power, Malcolm realized darkly, *even after seeing the mess he's become.* "Witness Protection sent me your file, and I accepted. You know this, Kate. I told you this during our first session."

"That's true," Kate admitted, shrugging in agreement. "Sorry, Doc. I forget sometimes."

"Madsen had nothing to do with it."

"And yet he knew that I come here for therapy," Kate declared in a grim voice. "Knew where to find me down to this office."

"He's a former police officer, Kate," Malcolm said patiently. *Assure her, old man. Keep her from spiraling.* "I'm sure he used his detective skills to find you."

"How much you want to bet he knows where I live?"

"Are you worried that he'll find you?" Malcolm asked, his concern for Kate's mental state rising. "That he'll do something to you?"

"After how he acted in this office, aren't you?"

Got me there, Malcolm thought, swallowing nervously. "If it really bothers you, I can speak to Witness Protection tomorrow. The marshals can put a restraining order on Madsen to keep him away from you."

"I'd rather they do something more permanent," Kate scoffed, an anxious breath escaping her month with a shaky weight, "but that will do." She got up from her seat, looking around to make sure she didn't leave anything even though she came in with nothing. "Time for me to go, Doc. If you don't mind, I'll take the back exit."

"I'll have one of my guards escort you," Malcolm agreed, walking to his desk to make a much-needed phone call as he glared at the door to the lobby. *Damn you, Madsen, for putting Kate through this.*

—⚏—

"Took you long enough," Madsen muttered, elbowing his way into Dr. Logan's office after a freaking eternity sitting in that damn lobby. He took a quick look around the sparse office, the walls as blue as the lobby's outside. *Man sure loves his primary colors.* He looked at the older African American man. "Let me guess, Kate's gone."

"She left ten minutes ago, escorted by my guards," Dr. Logan snapped as he sat down behind his desk, no doubt where he felt the most powerful. "You're lucky I don't have you escorted off the premises for what you did."

Whatever, dumbass. Madsen plopped down on the couch, then shivered. "Let me guess, Kate sat here."

"Have her smell memorized, do you?"

"Watch it, Doc."

"Or what?" Dr. Logan leaned forward over his desk, his hands clasped under his chin in what his people called "careful introspection." "What will you do? Shoot me?"

"All right," Madsen said, waving off his words. "I get it. Kate told all kinds of shit to make me look like the bad guy. Like some pervert using her for my jollies."

"I'm not at liberty to share anything from our sessions," Malcolm answered in a strained voice. "Though it is interesting that you would take it there."

I got no time for posturing, you pencil-necked jackass, Madsen thought, gritting his teeth so hard in smoldering anger he was sure he cracked a molar. *The sun's going down!* "Doc, can we skip all this bullshit? I'm in trouble here!"

"Because you believe Francine's after you," Dr. Logan said in a voice that stank of sickening superiority. "You made that *abundantly* clear."

"Because I know *Francine's* after me!" Madsen clarified in a frantic voice. *For God's sake, listen to me!*

"You've no proof of this!"

He's treating me like I'm *the nutcase!* Madsen gawked at Dr. Logan in quaking disbelief. *All his "sessions" with Kate, and I'm the nutcase!* He frowned, a sour taste building in his mouth. *What's she doing? Fucking him on the sly?* He gave Dr. Logan a suspicious once-over. *Shit, is she fucking you?* Madsen wouldn't have put it past Kate, given what he had heard about her … extracurricular activities in Milestone City. "I got instincts, honed from decades on the force. Doesn't that mean anything anymore?"

"What do you want me to do?"

"Tell me what Kate told you," Madsen answered desperately. "Together we can use her knowledge to stop Francine! It's the only way to save everyone!"

"You mean to save *you!*" Dr. Logan damn near shouted at him.

"You think she's gonna stop with me?" Madsen shot back. "Do you, really?"

"Are you *really* sure Francine's trying to kill you?"

Why am I the only one that can see it? Madsen gawked at Dr. Logan in bewilderment. *Did the Solomons pull the wool over his eyes too? Or*—he looked over his shoulder at the door to the lobby—*is that Kate's job now?* "I told you, Doc! I heard her right outside my door in all the hotels I've been in!"

"What makes you think Kate can tell you anything?" Dr. Logan asked skeptically. "How do you know she's even still part of the Solomons' craziness?"

"For one thing, because she still sees Francine," Madsen answered in a matter-of-fact voice, "despite not being anywhere near her for months."

"She has PTSD, Madsen," Dr. Logan declared. "Anyone would, given what she's experienced. And given how she was treated by the people in her department."

Is that a shot against me, you freaking jerk?! Wait, that is a shot against me! "Oh yeah, and because Kate wears the Solomons' mark! Above her right breast!"

Dr. Logan arched an eyebrow in surprise. "How do *you* know about that?"

Bingo! "You *have* seen it!"

"Dammit," the beleaguered psychiatrist cursed, running a hand through his graying hair, "so much for doctor-patient confidentiality."

Heh, Madsen chuckled to himself, pleased that he'd gotten the self-righteous prick to slip up a little. *As if* that *matters anymore.* "If it helps, Doc, I won't say anything."

"And that fills me with *so* much confidence, Dr. Logan said in a less-than-amused voice. He let out a resigned sigh. "Well, in for a penny, in for a pound. Now, how did you learn of Kate's mark?"

"She showed it to me," Madsen answered, puffing up his chest with pride.

"When?"

"When I saw her at the hospital, after the Solomons dropped her off."

"Medics let you see her?"

"I told them I was her next of kin."

"Madsen," Dr. Logan hissed in warning.

"What?" Madsen shot him an annoyed look, his brow furrowed in steely resolve. "I was the freaking chief of police, Doc. Bending rules was the name of the game."

"No one was supposed to see her except trained doctors!"

"I got those trained doctors to treat her," Madsen snarled. *You self-righteous son of a bitch!* "I'm not the bad guy here!"

"Did you take advantage of her?"

Did he seriously just ask me that? Madsen recoiled from the doctor, almost falling out of his chair. *By God, he really did just ask me that!* "I helped her!"

"Then why does she hate you?"

"I don't know!"

"Madsen, I have a traumatized woman in my care," Dr. Logan stated, stabbing a finger at the door to the lobby as though Kate was waiting on the other side, "and I'm seeing her former boss harassing her after *six months* of keeping his distance from her!" He pounded the surface of his desk at each word. "Now tell me something!"

"I'm trying to help her!"

"Really? Because it looks like you're trying to help yourself!"

"I'll admit I'm trying to do that too," Madsen admitted, his shoulders sagging with shame. *My word was good as gold once.* He let out an exasperated sigh, his strength failing him. *God! How far I've fallen!* "Look, just tell me what I need to know. I'll only pry enough to get the answers I need. I won't violate your ethics. Or Kate's peace of mind."

Kate sat on her couch in her apartment, gingerly rubbing her cheek where Francine had slapped her. The skin was still tender despite thirty minutes having elapsed since Kate saw her. *Only part of me that feels anything. How's that for a laugh?* She winced at the sting of the mark under her gauze. *Well, not the only thing.* Thunder rolled as rain fell on Milestone City, a light drizzle happening just outside her window.

Seeing it reminded her of the Other Side.

Kate closed her eyes, her mind retreating to that hellish place.

To the coliseum.

And the trial.

Stan and Francine were nowhere to be seen, but she felt their eyes on her as she stood on a stand, a harsh light shining above her. By her side was some hellish creature arguing in her defense. It wore a suit and everything, even glasses, trying to look all smart and official.

The Other Side's surreal version of a lawyer.

There were words spoken in a tongue too garbled to be understood. Kate had tried to say something in her defense, but her body, grown from one of their vats, was still tender.

In her apartment in Milestone City, Kate sweated amber-colored droplets, the sting of the mark intensifying.

—⚉—

I can't believe I'm doing this. Malcolm sat in his office with Madsen, telling the former police chief what he could without violating Kate's trust. As he spoke, he noticed that Madsen kept glancing at a nearby window, as though expecting Francine to break through the glass at any moment.

A manifestation of guilt, perhaps?

Madsen took a deep breath after hearing Malcolm's words. "Thanks for telling this to me, Doctor."

Huh, Malcolm thought, giving him an amused look. *From Doc to Doctor.* "I barely told you anything, Madsen."

"Seeing Kate on the floor wrestling with a Francine only she could see? It filled in the blanks."

Of course it did. "She had a hallucination, Madsen. Conjured by a fevered mind."

"Like mine, right?"

"Yes, Madsen," Malcolm answered, "like yours."

"Walked right into that one," Madsen cursed under his breath.

Yeah, you did. "Listen to me, please. You and Kate both share an all-consuming guilt," Malcolm declared in a knowing voice. "She for killing Brian, and you for getting her off for the crime."

"You're making me sound like I'm some criminal mastermind." Madsen sighed in disgust. "Is that what you think I am?"

"It doesn't matter what I think," Malcolm answered in a nonjudgmental voice. "You know you did something terrible. So terrible, in fact, that your subconscious won't let you rest, conjuring Francine to punish you. Just like Kate's is doing."

"You're assuming she's crazy," Madsen declared, folding his arms across his chest. "The Solomons *took* her, Doctor. All this stemmed from that."

Malcolm had considered that. It would have been stupid of him not to. And yet he refused to go all in on the idea. Not until he had exhausted all logical options.

"You're thinking," Madsen said, giving him a hopeful look. "I can see it."

"I need proof," Malcolm said, rubbing his chin. "If what you're saying is true, there must be proof."

"I showed you pictures of Francine's claw marks on the doors of the hotels I've stayed in," Madsen protested, going from hopeful to angry in a second. "What more do you want?!"

"I'm talking about forensic evidence," Malcolm answered, standing his ground. "Blood, hair, skin samples. And you found none, or you'd be talking to the police instead of me."

Madsen bristled but said nothing.

"Because there is *no* forensic proof, is there?"

"No," Madsen answered after a few seconds of lip-chewing silence.

There he is, Malcolm thought, having finally gotten past Madsen's wall of blue silence. *The scared man within!* "*That's* why you wanted to see Kate. She was your last hope that your theory was correct."

"I want to see Kate because what's happening to me is real!"

Likely story! "You *don't* want her to be mentally ill," Malcolm continued, pressing his advantage, "because if she is, that would mean you are too."

"That's not true!" Madsen shot to his feet, fire in his eyes. "That's not true, damn you!"

I almost got him! "That's what this is," Malcolm continued, convinced he had him on the ropes. "Harassing Kate Barrow. Feeling pursued by Francine Solomon despite there being *no* sightings of her in any part of Milestone City. Symptoms of your guilt." *Time for the big push!* "And you won't have any peace of mind until you move past it."

"Don't you think I want to?" Madsen asked, the question a pitiful squeak.

"You're here, Madsen. You could've gone anywhere else, but you came here," Malcolm said, relieved that his gamble had worked. "I can help you. We can get you past this. But only if you make an appointment."

"That's not why I'm here," Madsen protested with the final rage of a dying spark in his body.

Time for one more push, Malcolm thought, treating his final words as though they were the knockout punches in a cage match. "Isn't it?"

"Fine. Fine." Madsen shook with impotent rage but sat back down in his seat. "We'll play it your way, damn you."

Yes! Malcolm thought, his skin flush with the rush of victory. "Good. Now let's set up an appointment.

Back at her apartment, Kate staggered to the bathroom, her thoughts shrouded in pain. Her back twisted, the sounds coming from her lips shifting between screams and howls.

Those howls combined into one long roar as she thought of Topher.

Coming to *her* therapy!

Judging her!

Just like the Solomons!

They stood before her right then, in her bathroom! Bathed in light. Stan in soothing blue, Francine in angry red.

"What do you want from me?" Kate whispered tersely, falling to her knees before them. "Just tell me! What do you want?!"

Stan frowned while Francine grinned as thunder shook Kate's apartment.

55

—⚏—

Can't believe I caved! Madsen fumed as he walked to his car, having left Dr. Logan's practice a few minutes earlier. *Never would've happened a year ago!* He was so angry at himself for falling for Dr. Logan's trap that he didn't even notice the light drizzle of rain blanketing the empty parking lot around him. *I'm not crazy. I know I'm not.*

He just needed hard evidence.

I'll go to Kate's apartment, Madsen decided as he wrenched open his car door. *I'll get the truth from her! Forcefully if I have to!* He was about to get into his car when he felt something land on the pavement behind him. *No ...*The hair on the back of his neck stood on end as he felt the same moist heat he felt during Kate's trial over six months ago. *Francine's found me!*

Teeth chattering in fear, Madsen whirled around, gun in hand, ready to fire ...

Only to feel something cold and scaly crush it, and his hand, in its grip!

"You're not Francine!" Madsen screamed as he was lifted off the ground, red eyes staring at him with animal contempt. Madsen shook his head, doing his best to deny the horror standing in front of him. *You're not Francine! You're not Francine! You're not Francine!*

"Look at me." His attacker pulled him close, its nose furrowed in rage. "Look! At! Me!"

Realizing karma had caught up to him at last, Madsen looked his attacker full in the face. *Oh God.* He squeaked out his final words. "Why me?"

"Why not?" His attacker plunged his talons deep into Madsen's gut as the light drizzle became a heavy downpour.

—⚏—

Malcolm heard the screams as he was leaving his building right behind Madsen intending to go home for the night. *What in the ...* He saw something monstrous standing near what had to be Madsen's car, his body crumpled at its feet. "Get away from him!"

Madsen's killer swung its massive head to face him, horrifying details revealed in the streetlights that littered the parking lot.

Malcolm's breath froze in his throat.

It was seven feet tall, covered in golden scales that shone like armor. Spines grew from its back, reminding Malcolm of a dinosaur from his nightmares. Iridescent red eyes glared at him. Sharp claws dripped with blood and meat, droplets flying through the air as it whirled about in a macabre victory dance.

Madsen's nightmare creature was real, and it had killed him, on Malcolm's doorstep!

But it *wasn't* Francine Solomon!

It turned its head to the sky as wings poked out of its back. Rain obscured Malcolm's view as it took off into the night, howling in triumph.

—⚡—

Shit! Kate's eyes shot open. She was breathing hard as she picked herself up off the floor of her apartment. *Fuck, that was crazy!*

The amber-colored puddle under her feet made that difficult.

Water. Making her way to the bathroom, Kate licked her bone-dry lips. *Need! Water!*

She grabbed two tablets of aspirin and a glass of water from the cabinet above her sink and downed both. Then she grabbed the edges of her sink, waiting for the bathroom to stop spinning.

—⚡—

It's real. Malcolm left the police station after an hour of giving statements and answering questions regarding Madsen's slaying, still reeling from the sight of Madsen's mutilated corpse. *It's actually real!* The only way the coroner could recognize Madsen under all that flayed, skinned meat was through dental records.

But Madsen's monster was real.

He'd been telling the truth, and Malcolm had done nothing to help him.

57

I swore to do no harm, Malcolm thought as he got in the squad car that would take him home. *And tonight, I've done more harm than ever.*

And Madsen's killer was still out there.

"Kate!" Malcolm whispered fearfully. He tapped the driver on the shoulder. "Sorry, Officer, change of plans! Take me to Fifth and Fifth! Quickly!"

—⚊—

Water! Kate thought as she hobbled to the shower. *Need more water!* As she gingerly stepped under its spray, she winced at the sound of a gavel coming down at the end of her trial on the Other Side.

The Solomons' masters—their peers—had reached their verdict.

And found Kate guilty as sin.

Francine howled with excitement.

Stan nodded in grim agreement.

Under the heat of the overhead lights, on the stand before the Solomons kaiju-sized masters, Kate had tried to hold Stan's gaze. To tell him she was sorry for Brian's death and for the pain she had put him and Francine through.

To Kate's surprise, Stan had looked back, a contemplative expression on his African American features. Was he going to forgive her?

But Francine stepped between them, her gaze exuding scalding hate. Kate looked away, resigned to her fate. She expected their masters to kill her.

What they did was worse.

They dropped her right outside their city's walls.

—⚊—

The squad car came to a stop in front of Kate's apartment.

"Follow me, Officer!" Malcolm said as he dashed out of the back seat and inside Kate's apartment building. "She's on the top floor!" He had never been in her place before and wished his first time was under better circumstances.

But with Madsen's killer at large, he had no time for permission.

Malcolm found the elevator, jumped inside, and headed for the top floor. He hoped the officer was calling for reinforcements. For all he knew, Madsen's killer was already in the building!

Don't think about that, Malcolm thought as he took a stun gun from his jacket pocket. It was easier to get than a handgun, and not nearly as difficult to conceal.

After two minutes that felt like an eternity, the elevator came to a stop at the top floor of Kate's apartment. *Finally!* Malcolm took quick looks at both sides of a curiously dark hall, then sprinted out of the elevator. *Down the hall!* Kate told him her room was at the end of the long hall. It was the most affordable place she could get near the docks.

Malcolm ran as fast as he could, careful to stay quiet in case Madsen's killer was nearby.

Or was already in Kate's home.

Kate's apartment wasn't that far from his practice. On the wing, it would take Madsen's killer mere minutes to get to Kate!

Oh no! Malcolm forgot the monster could fly!

When he arrived at Kate's front door, Malcolm saw, to his mounting horror, that it was ajar.

Maybe Madsen's killer was already inside!

—⁂—

Kate lay in a fetal position on the floor of her shower, shaking as more hellish memories flooded her mind.

Stan and Francine's masters left her to the elements, her only protection being the suit they had forced her into, and the body they grew for her to replace her original one. "Don't leave me," she whispered tearfully in her shower. "Please ..."

"I won't leave you, Kate."

"Ah!" she yelped at the sight of Dr. Logan kneeling over her, a towel in hand to cover her nakedness. *What's he doing in my bathroom?!* "How'd you get in my house?!"

"The door was open," he answered apologetically. "Sorry to barge in like this, but—"

59

Something's happened. Kate bolted to an upright position, every iota of her body on high alert. "What is it?"

"Madsen's dead," Dr. Logan revealed.

The revelation was so out of the blue it took Kate a few seconds to react. "What?"

"Madsen is dead," Dr. Logan repeated. "Killed by something I'd never thought I'd see outside of a horror movie! I was afraid it would come for you next, so I came straight from the police station!"

"You're with the police?" Kate blinked, disbelief flooding her mind. *Topher's dead?*

"They're right behind me," Dr. Logan said, pulling her close as the urgent footsteps of the Milestone City's finest echoed from Kate's living room. "Everything's going to be okay!"

—⚏—

Malcolm sat with Kate in his office the next morning, both of them staring off into space.

The bags under Malcolm's eyes made him look ten years older than he really was as he sat behind his desk. He ran his hands along the top of the desk, the solid wood making him feel safe. Safe in a world that was no longer safe—or normal.

Malcolm scratched at his hair, the strands feeling brittle under his fingers. The black vest and blue jeans he wore felt shabby and slept in despite him showering and dressing at his home before arriving at his office.

The bags under Kate's eyes made her look like a boxer who had gone eight rounds with a heavyweight as she sat on the couch in front of Malcom's desk. She wore a white sundress, the fabric looking so flimsy and thin it might as well have been translucent.

From the look of her bodice, one could see Kate didn't bother to put on a bra, either, because she didn't feel like it or because she didn't think to. Kate didn't look at Malcolm; instead, she concentrated her gaze on her legs, which she crossed and then uncrossed in quick movements.

The police grilled us so hard after Madsen's death, Malcolm thought, giving Kate a worried look. The looks of disgust the officers gave her during her interrogation were hurtful for him to see. *Will she ever get a fair chance?*

Malcolm handed her a cup of coffee from a tray he had prepared a few minutes before Kate arrived at his office for their session. *Will anyone treat her fairly ever again?*

"I'm all right, Doc."

"Hmm?" Malcolm blinked, Kate's voice snapping him out of his thoughts despite the softness of her tone.

"I can tell you're worried about me," Kate declared, giving him an equally worried look. "I'm all right."

"Kate, what's happened to Madsen was *not* all right. How those police officers treated you last night was *not* all right. *None* of this is all right."

"All of this is kinda my fault," Kate stated, slouching in her seat, "so it kinda makes sense."

So quick to blame yourself. "Not all of it," Malcolm said tenderly. *Could be a sign of a martyr complex.* "You were tried for Brian Solomon's shooting and found innocent."

Kate gave him a pointed look. "You know what *really* happened, Doc. You have to after talking to Topher."

I keep forgetting how perceptive she is. "I do, Kate, and I must say you're a strong woman to make it through such an ordeal. The strongest I've seen."

"I …" Kate blinked, her mouth open in shock. "Thank you."

"You're welcome," Malcolm said, giving her a warm smile and a nod.

Before Malcolm could stop her, Kate got up from the couch and walked up to the front of his desk.

What is she doing? Malcolm wondered, before Kate leaned forward on his desk and gave him a quick kiss on the lips.

"Sorry," Kate said, stepping back from Dr. Logan's desk. It had been so long since she had heard such … kind words. "I didn't mean to…" Her hands went to her mouth, as if to try to cover any evidence of the kiss.

"It's okay," Dr. Logan said in a way that was downright saintly. "I understand the need for comfort after what you've been through."

"Thank you."

"But don't do that again."

"Right," Kate said, chuckling nervously. *Move past it, woman!* "So what did the police say?"

"That they'll be on the lookout for Madsen's killer," Dr. Logan answered, also seeming eager to move past that damn kiss. "But I'm not confident they'll find him. If it even is a him."

"It—I mean, he didn't leave any evidence?"

"Not a single hint. Based on the state of Madsen's body, coroners surmised that a bear had killed him. Or a tiger."

"But that's not what you saw."

"Unless tigers can stand on their hind legs," Dr. Logan said, giving her a pointed look, "look human, and are covered in gold scales."

"Look human," Kate whispered, her eyes taking on a faraway cast. *Like the aliens on the Other Side. Good lord, did one of them follow me here? Is that possible?* She winced, realizing how stupid it was to ask if anything was possible, given what she had been through in the past few months.

"What are you thinking?" Dr. Logan asked, his eyes never leaving her face.

Ease up on the staring, Doc, Kate thought, squirming under his gaze. "I saw a *lot* of human-looking aliens on the Other Side."

"Kate," Dr. Logan asked, his voice taking on a tentative tone as he stayed behind his desk, "when I found you in your shower—by the way, sorry for just barging in without asking—did other memories come to you?"

"More and more," Kate answered, realizing he hadn't moved from behind his desk. "Like water from a broken damn."

"Seeing Madsen, confronting him last night, must have taken away your mental blocks!"

Is that what happened? "Please don't sound so enthusiastic about that," Kate cautioned, giving the psychiatrist a pained expression. "Seeing him last night wasn't a good thing."

"I told him the same thing," Dr. Logan said, finally walking out from behind his desk to lean against its front, perhaps to show Kate that he wasn't creeped out by her despite what he had seen. "In fact, I think they were the last words I said to him."

"At least your words were kind words." *Not like mine.*

"Well, it didn't do any good," Dr. Logan said, folding his arms over his chest. "In the end, I didn't even believe him. Which is pretty silly when you think about it, because I believe what you've been telling me."

"And thank you for that," Kate said, placing a hand on Dr. Logan's knee. It was a simple gesture, one she didn't really think about. She just wanted to comfort the man who had been comforting her for so long.

But it was enough to make Dr. Logan clear his throat.

Right, got it. Kate took her hand away, her cheeks burning with embarrassment. *Stupid, Kate! Stupid!* "So, about my new memories?"

"Right," Dr. Logan agreed, snapping his fingers in agreement. "What do you remember?"

"Walking for days in that world, lost and alone."

"Oh my," Dr. Logan whispered, his hand shooting up to his mouth. "If this is too hard for—"

Don't interrupt! Kate shot him a stern look. "There were no trees. No grass. Not even flies."

"I wish this were fantasy," Dr. Logan declared, shaking his head. "I truly, truly do."

"Well, it's not. I got the scars to prove it," Kate said, scratching at the mark under her dress. "I got bit by one of their animals. Turned out they'd been hiding from me."

"What did these animals look like?"

"Part snake, part fly, part … something else," Kate answered after letting out a calming breath. "White, like the sands I walked on."

"Can you draw them?"

Are you serious? Kate looked at Dr. Logan, and saw that he was serious. *He wants to understand. He really wants to understand!* First he took her mark in stride, and now this? It was too much to hope for! "I'll bring some pictures next time."

—⁂—

63

Once Kate had left his office a few minutes later, Malcolm put in a call to Chief McLane of the Milestone City Police Department. Letting out a tired sigh, he raised the receiver to his ear right as she started speaking.

"So how is Kate Barrow?" McLane asked in a gruff voice from the other end of the line.

"She seems stable."

"How's she *acting?*" McLane asked, the sounds of a busy police station ~~slightly~~ muffling her powerful voice.

"Like someone suffering from intense trauma," Malcolm answered, careful to keep his voice respectful. "Your people didn't have to be so rough on her last night."

"My heart bleeds," McLane said, her voice sounding like it was doing anything but. "I've put them on the report."

"I hope that's enough."

"Doc, why *are* you helping her?" McLane asked in a curious, if not irritated, voice. "I get being loyal to a patient, but you're playing with fire here."

"She came to me," Malcom answered, realizing that wasn't exactly true. Kate didn't originally come to his office of her own free will. She had been brought there by US marshals working in Witness Protection. "I opened my door."

"Right," McLane answered, her tone thick with doubt. "Well, since she came to your door, do you have anything to tell me? Anything you feel that I *really* need to know?"

"I can tell you this much," Malcolm answered, then stopped. *I reveal this, it might affect her ability to trust me.* He paused, the receiver shaking in his hand. *Might also affect my integrity. Do I really want to be on her watch list?*

"Doc?" McLane called out from her end. "Getting irritated over here."

In for a penny, in for a pound. "I believe Kate's forming a romantic attachment to me."

McLane chuckled, the sound as grating as nails across a chalkboard. "That 'attachment' must be really good, Doc."

"There's no need to be vulgar, Chief," Malcolm said, catching the double entendre in her words. *Good wordplay, though.*

"Just be careful, Doc. People she forms personal attachments to don't live very long."

—⚌—

I kissed him, Kate thought, her finger brushing over her lips as she drove from Dr. Logan's office. *I can't believe I kissed him.* She pushed the thought to the back of her mind, keeping her eyes on the road in front of her. There was a bigger problem to worry about. Something had followed her from the Other Side and killed Topher on Dr. Logan's doorstep.

How long until it came for her?

Or someone else she knew?

—⚌—

The nerve of that woman! Malcolm hung up the phone, letting out a shaky breath as he sat in his chair behind his desk. He didn't sign up for this craziness, but he shouldn't have been surprised. When it came to the Solomons, nothing went the way one expected things to go.

That extended to anyone touched by them.

And Kate had been "touched" the most.

—⚌—

Malcolm saw it, Kate thought as she brought her car to a stop at a traffic light. *He saw the thing that killed Topher. And he came to check on me.* She gripped the steering wheel, waiting for the traffic light to turn green. Kate was so focused on the light that she didn't realize she was referring to Dr. Logan by his first name. *Might not have been his first thought, but it sure was his sweetest one.*

Sweet and foolhardy.

Topher's killer, whatever it was, would be after Malcolm now.

How'd it follow me? Kate wondered, tapping the steering wheel impatiently. *And what the hell is it?* She absentmindedly scratched at the mark under her bodice, remembering how she wandered for days in the white-hot desert of the Other Side, its alien sun cooking her skin.

How the water bloated her throat.

Kate had lost the ability to talk on the fifth day, her tongue so large she couldn't close her mouth. All she could manage were grunts, groans, and whimpers.

—m—

Madsen's killer came from the Other Side, Malcolm thought, leaning back in his chair. *But how?* Kate had traveled through space to get there, according to what she had told him. *By way of Stan and Francine Solomon, as a matter of fact.*

Did Madsen's killer do the same thing to get to Earth? Did Stan and Francine give it passage? And if so, why? Just to torment Kate one last time?

Something as alien as Madsen's killer doesn't just stay hidden, Malcolm surmised, his hands clasped under his chin. *Yet according to McLane, it has. Despite its strange appearance!*

Only Madsen had seen it, and that was because it had wanted him to see it.

To know it was ending Madsen's life.

Malcolm glanced at the door of his office, then at the window. Was it stalking him too?

—m—

On the fourth day of her time on the Other Side, Kate saw the monsters.

Some were the size of mountains. Some were the size of a horse. And others the size of a dog. All wore the colors of the rainbow on their bodies, claws, and teeth.

And they couldn't wait to use them on her!

The monsters! Once the traffic light turned green, Kate drove to a nearby parking lot. After pulling into the closest parking space she could find, she pulled a sheet of paper from her glove box. *Gotta get them down while I still can!*

Malcolm said he wanted to see them, after all.

———

"These pictures look good," Malcolm commented as he looked through Kate's drawings the next morning, in his office. "I had no idea you were such an artist."

"They're just sketches," came the humble reply.

"Don't sell yourself short," Malcom continued as he looked upon another picture of a monstrous creature rendered in charcoal. "You drew this from memory?"

"I have a very good one," Kate declared, blushing as she gave him a smile. "Now at least."

She sat across from him on the couch. She was wearing yet another sundress, one that showed off her shoulders. Her blond hair had grown out enough to frame her face and draw attention to her neck. Malcolm wondered if she had gotten it done just for him, given her kiss yesterday.

Get over yourself, you ass, Malcolm chided himself. *Just because she's taking the time to look good doesn't mean she has a crush on you!*

"Do any of these sketches look like the thing that killed Topher?"

"A few are close, but the creature that killed Madsen walked on two legs," Malcolm answered, Kate's question breaking his train of thought. "These walk on four."

"Sorry," came the meek reply.

"It's okay, Kate," Malcolm said, giving her a sympathetic smile. "Maybe it was one you didn't see."

"I was trapped on the Other Side for ten years, Malcolm," Kate revealed, giving him a sly grin. "If Topher's killer came from that place, I would've seen it."

"Hold on," Malcolm said, his eyes shooting open in surprise. "Did you say ten years?"

"I did."

"That's impossible! According to your file, you were only gone six months!"

—⚓—

Here we go, Kate thought disdainfully. "Time moves faster there."

"I'll say," Malcolm exclaimed in agreement.

"Took me a few weeks to work out the calculations once I got back." Kate glanced at her hands, in case she had to do it again using her fingers. "For every day that passes here, fifteen pass there. It's the only way to explain what happened to me the longer I stayed."

Malcolm swallowed, apprehension on his face. "Happened to you?"

"To my body," Kate clarified gently. "I was … mutating."

"Mutating?" Malcolm's right eyebrow arched. "How?"

"Maybe from drinking some bacteria in the water. Or breathing in some microbe from the air. Whatever it was, I was becoming like the creatures I saw …" Kate's voice trailed off as a realization hit her. *A human-looking creature, maybe like the one that killed Topher!*

Malcolm didn't flinch. "When did you realize what was happening to you?"

Kate was silent for a full minute, still going over her realization in her head. "When I stopped feeling sick."

—⚓—

Kate was mutated from her time on the Other Side, Malcolm repeated in his head, not bothering to hide his surprise as he gawked at Kate Barrow. *Transformed.*

"It's like the clothing Stan and Francine's master's gave me grew over me," Kate continued in a low voice. "Merged with the synthetic body they put me in."

"I still can't get over that," Malcolm said, shaking his head in disbelief. "According to their report, the medics that examined you found nothing amiss. As far as they were concerned, you're as human as me."

"Yeah, well, the body they gave me was very good," Kate revealed, smirking at the headshrinker. "I can pass. Problem was, it was extremely adaptable."

She's talking about this very casually for someone that's been through something so traumatic. "That's what you call what happened to you on the Other Side? Your body adapting to its new environment?"

"How else would I explain what happened to my legs?"

Oh, good lord, she's going to take me through it. The color drained from Malcolm's face. Quite a feat since he was a black man. "What happened to your legs?"

"They grew longer," Kate answered quietly. "So did my arms. My nails grew into talons."

"You *were* adapting," Malcolm whispered in an awestruck voice.

"Yup," Kate said, shrugging. "Didn't know it at the time, though. Don't even think I cared. All that mattered was that I could eat things and not get sick."

Malcolm tried to imagine the woman sitting before him transformed into a newly minted animal, her humanity forgotten. He had read of such things only in horror novels.

To know that it was real—that it had happened to someone he knew—was a lot for his mind to wrap around!

How did Kate survive?

And how did she come back looking human?

—m—

"Look," Kate said, noticing Malcom's discomfort. "If this is bothering you—"

"No, no," Malcolm answered, shaking his head while raising his hand. "If I have the presence of mind to ask, I have the presence of mind to know."

"Okay, then," Kate said, impressed by his stomach for her story.

"My question is, can you handle telling me this? This is reliving some pretty traumatic memories. I don't want to do any more damage to you than has already been done."

He's worried about me, Kate said to herself, her breath catching in her throat. *Actually worried about me.* It had been so long since she had been treated like a person worth being worried about.

69

It floored her to know there was still genuine human kindness in the world.

From this gentleman before her, no less!

Watch it, Kate thought, catching herself. *He's already on guard from that kiss.* "I didn't have time to think about that. I was too busy fighting for my life."

"Against the monsters," Malcolm stated in an expectant voice.

"Yeah," Kate said grimly. "I got attacked. Every day. It never stopped." She took a moment to swallow. "They never stopped."

"How'd you, in all that, maintain your sanity?" Malcolm asked, looking spellbound by her story. Not disgusted. Not frightened. Just intrigued.

If only Mom and Dad reacted like this, Kate thought, her expression darkening.

"You okay, Kate?"

"I'm just thinking about Topher," she answered, lying to his face. "I'm actually sad he's dead."

"It's called compassion, Kate," Malcolm said in a kind voice. "That's not a bad thing."

"I said such horrible things to him before he was killed."

"Things I'm sure he deserved on some level," Malcolm said, nodding his head. "But yes, he did go out in a horrible way."

"Dismembered by a creature from the Other Side," Kate whispered, lying back on the couch. "No matter how much he hurt me" — she rubbed the mark under her shirt, which hadn't stopped throbbing since she last saw Topher — "no one deserves to go out like that, Malcolm."

—⟨⟨⟨—

She's referring to me on a first-name basis, Malcolm realized as he watched Kate scratch at her mark under the bodice of her sundress. *Going to have to keep an eye on that.* "Did you see the Solomons again while you were on the Other Side?"

"No," Kate answered, sitting up straight in her seat. "I saw their friends, though."

Malcolm tilted his head, needing more information. "Their friends?"

"Their fellow aliens," Kate explained in a sarcastic voice. "They flew over the jungle I lived in all the time."

"Like they were on patrol?"

"Yeah." Kate winced regretfully. "Something like that."

Like lawmen policing a province, Malcolm thought, his eyebrow arching in thought. Kate did say they wore the same uniform as the Solomons.

Was Madsen's killer one of them?

—∞—

Kate headed for the parking lot of Malcolm's practice after he ended their session. Whistling to herself to calm her nerves, she glanced at the sky above.

It was almost noon.

Her boss at her job on the docks had heard about Madsen's death and gave her the day off. To "decompress," he said. *Like he cares.*

Still, Kate had the day off. She decided not to waste it.

—∞—

Kate had been gone from Malcolm's office for five minutes before his cell phone rang. *Let's see who this is,* he thought, pulling it out of his pocket to check the caller ID. Seeing it was McLane, he felt his stomach drop. "Hello, Chief," he said, putting the receiver to his ear. "How can I help you?" *Funny how you got to me right after my session with Kate ended. Almost as if you'd planned it.*

"I need you to come to the station," McLane said in an urgent voice. "Right now."

Oh no. Malcolm's mood darkened. "Did you make a break in the case?"

"You … need to see it yourself."

Not liking the hesitation in that answer. Malcolm grabbed his coat and headed for his car. "I'm on my way."

—∞—

71

Best place to start investigating any murder is at the scene of the crime, Kate thought as she approached the spot in Malcolm's parking lot where Topher had been murdered. *And lucky for me, I'm right near this one.*

Right where Topher had parked his car before barging into her session with Malcolm.

Freaking bastard, Kate cursed as she knelt at the bloodstain at the far edge of the parking lot, a full fifty feet from the entrance to Malcolm's practice. *Kicked out of the GCPD, and he still thought he could just barge in on my pain and take what he wanted from me.*

The bloodstain was faint, the CSI's having done their work. There wasn't even any crime-scene tape around the area, which struck Kate as strange. *No crime-scene team moves this fast,* she thought, leaning close to examine the pavement that had caught Topher's blood from his dismemberment. *It's not even been a day, and the scene's already been released?*

It normally took police one to forty hours to process and release a crime scene to the public, but that was only when it came to normal murders.

Topher had been killed by an inhuman creature from the stars. That, at the very least, warranted longer than a couple of hours!

So why had the MCPD released the scene so quickly?

Whoa! Kate's ears perked up at the sound of a door being opened. Looking over her shoulder, she saw the door to Malcolm's practice opening from the inside. *Who's that?* She sniffed the air, not sure where the idea for such a thing had come from, and took in Malcolm's scent. *He's leaving for the day? He doesn't normally leave until 5:00 p.m.* Kate checked her cell phone, seeing it was just after noon. *Why are you leaving so early?*

Kate ran to her car and ducked behind it just as Malcolm stepped out of his building. It wouldn't do for him to see her poking around the crime scene where Topher had just been killed the night before.

Taking a quick peek over the hood of her car, Kate saw him sprint to his Prius, which was parked right next to his building. *Looks like he's in a hurry.* She ducked back behind her car, waiting for Malcolm to drive out of the parking lot. When she saw his Prius leave, she scurried back to the crime scene. *I'll ask him about that at our next session.*

On one knee, Kate took a quick scan of the pavement, detecting only faint traces of Topher's blood. *CSIs wiped it clean*, she reminded herself, getting to her feet. *Means I only got one place left to go to get any clues.*

The hotel where Topher lived while he was in Milestone City.

—⁓—

Malcolm stood in the morgue of the MCPD, which was filled with bodies on slabs, spread out before him like a macabre tableau. Each body had been mutilated, like Madsen's had been.

His killer had been busy.

"How many?" Malcolm asked in a hoarse voice. He swallowed back a wave of gorge as the aroma of putrefaction wafted into his nose.

"Twenty," Chief McLane answered as she stood by his side. "And these are the ones we *could* find."

McLane was a tall woman, taller than Malcolm, in fact. With a mane of lustrous black hair held in place in a ponytail, she looked like one of the Amazons of legend, complete with broad shoulders and piercing blue eyes.

She wore pants as black as her hair, topped by a white shirt, her badge dangling from a chain around her neck. Her arms were crossed in a jaunty pose, her eyes solemnly taking in the bodies, as if seeing them was a tragedy.

Which, in this case, it was.

"There are so many." Malcolm walked among the bodies, thankful that the black bags covered the grislier details. He stopped at one, looking over his shoulder at McLane. "Can you tell me about them?"

"All of them are mutilated," McLane started after clearing her throat. "Just like Madsen's body had been. Guess we can rule out a tiger or a bear."

"Not that I ever believed that theory, but why?"

"Because a tiger or a bear doesn't have the sense to sneak into someone's home," McLane answered. "To open doors, get past security systems, and bypass cameras. Some of these people were killed while at work, Doc. Working late, based on the time of death."

"How late?" Malcolm asked, staring at the body back on the slab in front of him. *Don't open it, Malcolm. It won't do you any good.*

But the bodies inside these bags had once been people. Living, breathing people with dreams and hopes and futures.

All reduced to meat for being in the path of Madsen's killer.

But why? Malcolm wondered, growing paler the more he thought about it. *Why would the creature that killed Madsen kill these people too? Why them and no one else?*

"All have their heads," McLane added from right behind Malcolm, making him jump, "though they're scarred up in the same way."

"At least its consistent."

"Not too consistent," McLane corrected him. "Pieces are missing too."

Good lord. Malcolm's hand was over his mouth before he had a chance to think. "As in, body parts?"

"Oh yes," the police chief answered. "We believe that Madsen's killer took them, either as trophies or lunch."

Given what I saw that night, Malcolm thought, remembering the creature's supernatural appearance, *I'm thinking lunch.* Then he remembered how the creature had danced over Madsen's corpse. Like it was happy, celebrating the completion of the act. Didn't seem right that anyone that has the sense to do that would eat any part of their kill. But they would take samples, perhaps as a souvenir?

Or proof of the kill to show someone later. But who, or *what*, would the creature be showing them to?

Perhaps, God help him, another creature like itself? One that had journeyed with it from the Other Side?

"How long have you had them?" Malcolm asked once he was sure he could talk without vomiting.

"A few days," McLane answered in a solemn voice. "We're finding them all over the city."

"And yet I'm not seeing this in the news."

"We're keeping it on the hush-hush," McLane revealed, giving Malcolm a conspiratorial look. "We don't want to start a panic. You get me?"

Oh, I get it, Malcolm thought, realizing that he was to keep quiet too. "Keeping this from the public isn't protecting anyone. It's making them targets."

"Speaking of targets, we happen to have a common denominator linking these unfortunate souls together."

That's a terrible segue. "Don't tell me …"

"Uh-huh," McLane answered, nodding her head like a dog after getting a sweet treat. "Kate Barrow."

I think I know how, Malcolm thought, *though I don't want to say it, yet.* "Tell me."

"All these victims were seen with her," McLane answered dryly, "at a bar on the docks called Kate's Cove on the nights of their deaths."

—✹—

Topher had lived in a Motel 6 on the outskirts of Milestone City.

The motel was part of a circle of two-star hotels meant for people visiting Milestone City either for business or for pleasure. It was only a few blocks away from the docks and from Kate's home.

Topher was watching me, Kate realized as she stood outside his hotel room. She had arrived at the hotel ten minutes ago. After finding the manager, she slipped him a hundred-dollar bill to let her into Topher's room, then encouraged him to give her some time alone.

In case she saw something she didn't want anyone else to see.

Standing in the middle of the room, Kate took in all the details. It was a small room, with a polished floor, a bed covered by stained white sheets, and a bathroom, awkwardly crammed next to a sink in the side of the room.

Smells like the Other Side. Kate's nose wrinkled at the sickly sweet smell of the alien dimension. *Topher's killer was here. It was here, in this room, after it killed him! But why?*

—✹—

Kate's Cove, Malcolm thought, rubbing his chin as he stood with Chief McLane, looking at the bodies. *What are the odds that the very bar Kate loves shares her name?* "Then I know where I must go next."

"Doc," McLane said, putting a hand on his shoulder, "let us handle this, for God's sake."

"Oh, believe me, I am." Malcolm patted her hand, so that she would know he appreciated the gesture. "I just want to go to *Kate's Cove* before you guys. To get my own answers."

"You're not a detective, Doc. What 'answers' do you think you'll find there?"

"I don't know, Chief," Malcolm answered grimly, "but I'm mixed up in this. I have to see it to the end. And maybe get some answers."

"We've already talked to everyone there," McLane declared, looking as though she was not happy with Malcolm's plan.

"But as police officers, thanks to the Solomons, everyone's leery of you."

"You got me there," McLane admitted, wincing in agreement.

I know, Malcolm thought, giving the police chief a sympathetic look. *And what an unfortunate turn of events* that *is*. "So as a civilian, I can get more information."

"Which you'll share with us, right?"

Seriously? Malcolm turned to face her, his hands on his hips. "What do you think, Chief?"

"I think," McLane said, knowing when she was beaten, "that I'm gonna have to arrange for some backup."

—⁂—

Red ghostly images materialized before Kate's eyes, leaving her frozen in fright. *What is this?* Her mouth agape, she watched as the apparitions grew more substantial. Then she realized they were of Topher. *What are these? Afterimages?* A sharp pain lanced her brain, making her touch her forehead. *How am I seeing these?*

More memories flooded Kate's brain. Memories of her, fully transformed into a majestic creature of the Other Side, soaring above jagged mountains on leathery wings.

All Kate knew was that world—it's jungles, mountains, hilltops, and rocky crevasses. She was the master of her domain. After years of battles, no one dared challenge her, except the Paladins from the shining city, but she kept her distance from them.

And yet she could sense something else was watching her.

No! Kate leaned against a wall for support, almost falling onto the nearby bed as the pain in her head intensified. Her vision blurred, making her blink repeatedly. *I'm not there anymore! I'm here! I'm right here!*

And yet she was seeing apparitions! Seeing them with sight that wasn't human! How was that possible, unless she never got out of the Other Side?!

God help her, what if she was still there?! Still asleep in her burrow, plotting to hunt for her next meal?

What if the last six months were just a dream? An illusion? The last gasp of a fading humanity?

No! No! No! Kate thought, grabbing her head as the pain traveled down her spine. The mark on her chest burned, as though in resonance with the pain in her brain. The aroma of sizzling skin made her head swim. *I got out! I got out!*

And then, as if her hellish experience couldn't get any worse, Kate saw Topher's killer standing in the middle of the hotel room. It was a phantom, a ghost image, but it took her breath away all the same. Madsen's killer was clothed in gold scales. Human looking, but very tall. It had to stoop to move about in the room, but it did so with stealthy ease. How it had gotten onto the motel's property, let alone in one of its rooms, without anyone seeing it was beyond her.

Smart, Kate thought as beads of sweat ran down her face. *Smart like me.*

Just like he was when they first met on the Other Side.

He had revealed himself to Kate during her third year. She had sensed him way before but had ignored him. He hadn't tried to kill and eat her, so she hadn't tried to kill and eat him. That was what Kate's intellect had been reduced to. Killing and eating. And mating. Not that anything on the Other Side was worth opening her legs for.

Except Madsen's killer.

Such a sweet, succulent specimen!

—⚒—

"Martha Johnson?" a bartender asked, giving Malcom a suspicious eye. "Why do you want to know about her?"

"So she *does* come here," Malcolm answered, recalling that "Martha Johnson" was the name the marshals had given Kate when she joined Witness Protection.

Standing in *Kate's Cove* put Malcolm's mental alarm on high alert, more from the clientele than the bar itself. On the outside, *Kate's Cove* looked like a simple rectangular shack made of wood, more at home in the backwoods of Virginia than on the pier of Milestone City.

On the inside, *Kate's Cove* looked like the hold of an ancient ship. Everything was made of wood, even the bar that Malcolm stood in front of, addressing a bartender who looked as though he had been in way too many fights.

And lost a good portion of them.

A black eyepatch covered the bartender's left eye, and his right eye scanned not just Malcom but the entire bar in frantic jerks, as if working overtime to pick up the slack. His beard was as black as oil, covering his entire chin in a coarse, hairy chain that extended from ear to ear.

A black captain's hat covered a lumpy bald head, implying he had been in charge of a ship.

My, my, you are a big one, Malcolm thought as he looked up at the towering bartender. He shook his head; he needed to focus on his goal. "I'd like to ask you some questions about her."

"We don't snitch on people," the bartender stated, folding his arms as he looked down his nose at the psychiatrist. "Not when it comes to a woman who has seen more suffering than anyone I know."

Why would you ...? Malcolm's brow arched in curiosity. "You know what happened to her?"

"Don't need to," the bartender boasted, his one good eye flicking from Malcolm to the bar behind him. "Hey! Get your ass back here and pay for that!"

What is he looking at? Malcolm looked over his shoulder to see a dockworker tiptoeing to the exit, holding something in his coat.

"Where the hell do you think you're going?"

What is that clicking sound? Malcolm turned back to the bartender, startled to see him, holding a shotgun in his thick fingers. *Good lord! He just has that out in the open?!*

The dockworker froze like a deer in the headlights, and his hands raced. "Easy, Preston. Easy."

"Put back what you stole," the bartender demanded, clicking the hammer on his gun.

With quaking hands, the dockworker placed a few pieces of silverware on a counter next to the exit. "Sorry, Preston. Just needed some money, that's all."

"Get the hell out of here," the bartender growled. "And never come back."

Without another word, the dockworker ran out of the bar like a bat out of hell.

The whole encounter took only a few minutes.

—⚒—

Back at Topher's hotel room, Kate shuddered as a flood of forgotten memories threatened to drown her.

Madsen's killer came upon her in the night, in the cave she called home. Kate stood in defiance of him, her kill cooling behind her. He was almost a head taller than she was, big in all the right areas. The curved horns added to his majesty, sitting atop his head like a crown. The way his chest heaved got her blood going.

Kate circled him like a wary cougar.

Madsen's killer did the same, as if daring her to attack.

As one, they pounced, clawing and slashing at each other in a macabre courtship, their blood mingling. Soon that slashing and clawing turned to thrusting and grinding.

Overcome with the carnal power of those memories and the perfume of the Other Side flooding her nose, Kate fled Topher's room, her pulse racing as though she had snorted a line of cocaine.

She had to put this shot of energy to good use!

—⚭—

Now that we have that *past us,* Malcolm thought, gawking at the gun in the bartender's large hands. "So, about Martha …?"

"First off," the bartender said, putting the gun back behind his counter, "who are you?"

"Dr. Malcolm Logan." *Please tell me you like psychiatrists!*

"Whoa!" The bartender's eyes widened in happy astonishment, a grin breaking out on his craggy face. "So *you're* Malcolm!"

I'm Malcolm? "Martha's told you about me?" Malcolm asked, taking a step back in happy surprise.

"Oh yeah! She mentions you a lot!"

"Hopefully, only the good things." *She talks about me,* Malcolm realized, turning over that new bit of information. *And refers to me by my first name. Seems she's been doing that way before she did it in my office.*

"What brings you here?" the bartender asked, turning around to grab an empty glass. "You want something to drink?"

"Is it on the house?" Malcolm didn't normally drink on the job, but he felt this was a special case. Actually, he wasn't in his office, so did this really count as "on the job"?

"For you? Yeah, it is," the bartender answered, giving me a friendly over-the-shoulder-glance.

"In that case, I'll take a drink," Malcolm answered, nodding his head in return.

"What's your poison?"

"Bartender's choice."

"Ahh!" The bartender gave Malcolm a wink before turning away to make his drink.

Don't lose sight of why you're here. "So, about Martha …"

"Oh yeah," a nearby patron, slumped over the bar to Malcolm's left, cut in. "We've always wanted to meet the man that captured the heart of the bull." He was an elderly man, a long white beard acting as a pillow for his heavy head. He grinned at Malcolm, revealing a disturbing lack of teeth. "Nice to put a face to the name!"

"Dammit, Mort!" the bartender cursed, sliding Malcolm a drink. "What do I gotta tell you about spillin' customer business?!"

But you were doing the same thing, Malcolm thought, taking a sip of his drink. It burned like fire as it went down, making him cough.

"Aye," the bartender said, "it's a strong brew! Martha's favorite!"

Kate drinks this?! Malcolm rapidly blinked away the tears forming in his eyes. "It's certainly … memorable!" *What the hell is even in this?!*

"I'll let Martha know you like it."

"Yeah, she goes through three of those in one sitting," the bearded patron cut in, his voice so loud it threatened to blow out Malcolm's left ear. "Downs 'em like shots!"

"Dammit, Mort!" the bartender cursed again. "We talked about this!"

"What?! I thought he wanted to know about Martha!"

"I do." Malcolm looked from the patron to the bartender, then back, deciding he needed to use this banter to his advantage. "Is she a regular here?" He already knew that Kate came to *Kate's Cove*, but he wanted to know how *long* she had been going there.

"Oh, Martha comes here every night," the bartender answered as he poured Malcolm another glass of Kate's mystery drink.

"In more ways than one," the older bar patron added, getting hearty laughs from all the other patrons at *Kate's Cove*.

—⟶

Rebecca Delcroix was a young woman who had just graduated from college. Like most people her age, she learned that having a degree wasn't a surefire ticket to the job of her dreams. And like most people her age, she tumbled down the rabbit hole of employment, looking for any job that could pay the rent and allow her to save up for the job she wanted.

Given her attractive looks and physical prowess, she found herself performing as a dancer in a strip club called the High Horse. She usually worked from 6:00 p.m. to midnight, the only one she could get given her inexperience.

When she came in for work that night, Rebecca figured it would be like every other night.

Until she caught the eye of the hungry blond lurking in the back room of the club. She wasn't one of the regulars, but she had such a magnetism about her.

She had said her name was Martha Johnson, but Rebecca couldn't hear her.

Not when she had such beautiful eyes ...

—⁊⁊—

Not liking the implication of that *statement*, Malcolm thought, eyeing the other patrons in the bar. *Let's try a different tack.* "Mort, could you tell me what you mean by what you said?"

"Great," the bartender muttered, face-palming in disgust. "Now you gone and done it."

"C'mon, Preston," Mort said, giving him a mirthful look. "Don't you wanna show this fine gentleman here the real side of Martha?"

Preston? Malcolm looked from Mort to the bartender. *You do not look like a Preston!* "Mr. Preston, could you show me what Mort's talking about?"

"Depends," he answered, holding back Malcom's second drink. "What are you gonna do with what I tell you?"

"I'll only use it to help Martha, I promise."

"Help?" Preston and Mort asked in unison, their eyes focusing on Malcolm like laser sights on a gun. "She in trouble?"

What to tell you? Malcolm looked at the two men, biting his lower lip in indecision. *Last time I revealed anything about Kate's therapy, it was to Madsen, and look what happened to him!* "She might be."

"How?" Preston demanded, brandishing his fists. "Who's causing Martha trouble?!"

"Martha's in trouble?" an old man, sitting by a window in the back of the bar, called out.

"What's going on with Martha?!" a pear-shaped man demanded from his seat near the entrance.

"Hold up!" a brutish-looking woman shouted as she played a game of pool with what had to be her date. "Who's hurting Martha?!"

All the voices in the bar blended together in a cacophony of concern.

Looks like Kate's got herself a new family, Malcolm thought, smirking at the fact that Kate had taken his advice to meet people. *One she never mentioned in any of our sessions!*

Looking around the *Kate's Cove*, it suddenly made sense why Kate felt so at home there. The gruff and macho patrons no doubt reminded her of her former comrades at the Gateway City Police Department. Complete with a sense of kinship.

Would these patrons feel that same kinship if they truly knew what Kate had done to arrive at *Kate's Cove*? Or worse, how it had changed her?

"Everybody, calm down!" Preston called out, shouting above the clamor of voices. "I'll handle it!"

"Yeah, you handle it, Preston!" another patron, unseen from Malcolm's perspective, shouted in a slurred voice. "You handle it!"

"Thank you," Malcolm said, shooting him a grateful look. *Seems she's got a replacement for Madsen here too. A better one, from the look of it.*

"Sorry about that. Look, Martha's one of us," Preston declared once everyone in the bar had gone back to their own business. "She's always comin' here after busting her ass on the docks just like the rest of us."

"What does Martha do when she comes here?" Malcolm asked in a confidential tone. "Besides drink, that is."

Preston leaned close to him so that no one else would hear. "Promise you won't tell anyone?"

"By anyone, you mean …," Malcolm asked, just for clarification.

"The cops," Mort answered, giving him a shrewd look.

Technically, I am working with the cops, Malcolm thought. *But you don't need to know that.* "I won't tell anyone, as long as no one under eighteen is being hurt."

"Oh, some folks are gettin' hurt," Preston revealed, stepping out from behind the bar. "But they ain't eighteen."

"What is that supposed to mean?"

"Come on," Preston said, gesturing for Malcolm to follow him to the back of the bar. "I'll show you."

—๛—

"God!" Rebecca got out in heavy gasps as she and Kate grinded against one another on top of a bed in the back room of the strip club. "You're so strong!"

Kate let out a feral hiss, so overcome with animal lust that she couldn't form words.

"Fuck!" Rebecca's breaths became haggard as she struggled to keep up. "Fuck! Fuck! Fuck!"

The touch of Madsen's killer, his taste were etched in Kate's brain as she went down on the young woman, juices rolling down her chin.

"Oh God," Rebecca rasped, feeling the heat building in her body. "You're gonna give me bruises!"

Kate's thoughts were a maelstrom of fury, at the center of which was the savage roar of Madsen's killer.

"You're making me so hot!" Rebecca panted, her tongue hanging out of her mouth. "So … fucking … hot!"

A snakelike whisper in her ear demanded that Kate go until she was spent, as she did with Topher's killer, on the Other Side.

"I'm gonna cum! I'm gonna cum!" Rebecca howled, her every muscle clenching so tightly that veins stood out on her skin. "I'm gonna cuuummmmm!"

—๛—

Malcolm followed Preston into the kitchen in the back of *Kate's Cove.* He had one hand in his jacket pocket, on his cell phone, ready to dial McLane if he felt even a hint of trouble. *He'd better not be intending to cut me up and eat me, away from witnesses.*

It was such a random thought—one that Malcolm wouldn't normally entertain, or take seriously. But given what he had seen over the past few days, it seemed plausible!

Preston opened a door in the floor in the back of the kitchen, revealing a set of stairs that descended to what looked like the bar's basement.

A secret passageway, Malcolm thought, remembering the spy novels he read as a youth. "Intriguing, Preston."

"Thanks," the bartender said, descending the stairs. "Follow me, eh?"

We're going down? Malcolm looked behind him, worry on his dark features. "What about your bar? Are you really going to leave it unguarded?"

"Unguarded? Mort's out there. He'll keep the peace. Besides, I got more employees here than just me."

"Right," Malcolm laughed nervously. "Of course." Giving the bar outside one final look, he descended the stairs. When he finally got to the bottom floor, he let out a silent gasp at what he saw. *What is this?*

A rectangular fighting cage took up most of the floor, its walls made of chain-fencing. The walls extended six feet from the floor. Black matting covered the inside of the cage, as if it was made for fighting matches.

The smell of dried sweat and blood that permeated the room told Malcolm that the cage was being used a lot. "Preston, what is this?"

"What we do in our free time," the bartender answered, a look of pride on his stubble-encrusted face. "Doesn't she look good?"

Not sure how to respond to that. "What happens here?"

"We have battle matches here, Doc. Boxing, extreme fighting. Nothing too crazy. These guys have to get to work the next day, so they can't afford to be injured too badly."

"You hold matches down here?" Malcolm wasn't sure he heard correctly. "Is this why you wanted to know if I'd tell the police earlier?"

"Yeah," Preston answered, nodding. "Can't be too careful."

"Why, though? Nothing I'm seeing here is illegal."

"Those pigs wanna shut down anything that's remotely fun," Preston answered, throwing a disdainful look at the floor above. "If it ain't anything 'intellectual,' it's seen as bad, you know? There was a time when people were allowed to be athletes, you know? Get in touch with their inner animal. But all that's going away with this 'enlightened age.'"

Malcolm nodded, seeing what Preston was trying to say. He wasn't the first person to decry the "softening" of American culture. Especially when it came to physical sports. Sports like boxing, football, even basketball, were being put under the microscope as more scientific data revealed the long-term damage of playing those sports to everyone involved.

As long as scientists placed more limits on those sports to keep its players safe, there'd always be a group of people who played in those sports who longed for the old ways.

It was clear that Preston, and at least some of the patrons of *Kate's Cove*, shared that belief.

But how exactly did the boxing cage figure into Kate's extracurricular activities?

—⟪⟫—

That's better. Kate Barrow slept soundly, her nude body covered in a thin layer of sweat. *So much better!* Whatever energy she had received from Topher's room, she had spent on the woman named Rebecca Delcroix.

Kate pulled her close, smiling as the brunette woman lightly kissed her neck.

—⟪⟫—

"What does this have to do with Martha?" Malcolm asked as he ran his fingers over the bars of the cage. He already had a good idea, but he wanted Preston to confirm it.

"Don't you mean Kate?"

He said her real name! Malcolm's brow arched. "You know, huh?"

"That Martha Johnson is actually Kate Barrow, the cop that killed a kid, creating Stan and Francine Solomon?" Preston slowly nodded, a grim expression on his face. "Yeah, I know."

"She told you?"

"Kate's lips get pretty loose when she's drunk. Which happens all the time around here."

"I've been trying to help her with her guilt in therapy," Malcolm explained, "but it's been slow going." *Until recently, that is.*

"I'm not surprised," Preston said, giving him a sympathetic look. "That woman carries a lot of guilt on her shoulders. I've tried to help her with it as best as I can."

"And I take it the cage here is part of it?"

"Oh yeah," Preston agreed, nodding his head. "Kate drinks to forget, ya see. That doesn't work, she brawls down here."

"She fights in this cage?" Malcolm asked, his voice growing hoarse at the prospect. *Why else do you think Preston showed this to you, man? Think!*

"Oh yeah. Wins 'em all too."

Wish Kate had shared this during our sessions. Malcolm was having trouble reconciling the troubled, neurotic young woman he had been working with for months with the undefeated fighter Preston hinted at. But after everything he had seen, he couldn't ignore the possibility. "What kinds of brawls does Kate take part in?"

"The savage stuff," Preston answered, cocking his head at the cage. "Real MMA shit."

Mixed martial arts? I didn't know Kate had those skills! "How many nights does Kate participate in these fights?" Malcolm asked, though he already knew the answer.

"Every night, when she could get in," Preston answered, giving him an amused chuckle. "Girl's got stamina. I tell ya, there were times Kate didn't even feel the guys beating on her!"

Malcolm's eyes grew as wide as dinner plates. "She was fighting men?"

"Women don't last long against her. Too fragile, I guess. We boys"—Preston beat his chest—"we're the only ones that can handle her!"

Heightened abilities from her time on the Other Side would *give her an edge*, Malcolm reasoned, remembering what Kate told him during their latest session. "I'm afraid to ask, but what was her prize for winning these bouts?"

"Anyone she wanted," Preston answered, rubbing his bushy beard. "Women *and* men. I tell ya, Kate's gotta be one hell of a lay, because they keep coming back, every night, to see her."

How utterly barbaric, Malcolm thought before checking his privilege. *These are adults, Malcolm! Not everyone in the world has to live by your standards!* "They're adults, right?"

87

"Of course, Doc. We're not monsters."

"I'm sorry, Mr. Preston, I had to be sure."

"Hey man, I get it," the bartender said, giving Malcolm a friendly shrug. "And by the way, it's just Preston. I know too much about you for all that official crap."

"Thank you, Preston," Malcolm said, trying the name out. It didn't feel right for him to just call someone by their first name without having earned the right, but if Preston was okay with it, who was Malcolm to argue? "About these people that Kate's sleeping with …"

"Whoa, whoa, whoa!" Preston said, raising his hands defensively. "Hold on, I never said Kate slept with any of 'em!"

"I know, but she's told me that she has been." *I've also seen other evidence*, Malcolm thought, remembering the bodies in the MCPD's morgue. *Wait a minute!* A light bulb went off in his head. *Those people in the morgue. Kate must have met them here. After her fights, she takes them back to her home, or theirs, and sleeps with them. They then have the same allergic reaction to Kate's otherness that her latest lover, who ended up in the hospital, had!*

As for how they ended up in the morgue, that would be because of Madsen's killer.

I never asked if the claw marks matched the marks on Madsen's body. Malcolm swallowed back a rising wave of gorge in his throat. *What's left of Madsen's body.*

But why would Madsen's killer target Kate's partners? It was obvious, at least to Malcolm, why the otherworldly beast targeted Madsen.

The disgraced former police chief had been a subject of ire for Kate.

But her various other partners? They had brought nothing to Kate's life but joy. At least, according to Preston. For a little while, at least.

"Doc," the bartender said, giving Malcolm a worried look. "What aren't you tellin' me?"

"Preston," Malcolm answered, returning his worried look "I believe that you and your establishment may be in terrible danger."

Preston gawked at Malcolm for a second, as if digesting his revelation. "Words like that deserve a drink."

You don't know the half of it, Preston, Malcolm agreed as he followed him up the stairs.

—⁓—

A few moments later, Malcolm and Preston sat at a table in the far corner of *Kate's Cove*. Preston had called one of his employees to take over running the main bar, allowing him to talk to Malcolm undisturbed.

"So what you're saying," he started, leaning close to Malcolm so no one else would hear, "is that there's some creatures out there in the city killing folks?"

"Yes," Malcolm answered, nodding. He held a pint glass of beer in both hands but was too focused on telling his story to take even a sip. *Need to stay sober for this one.*

"And these folks are connected to Kate?"

"Yes, indeed," Malcolm answered, nodding again.

"So what are you doing here, then?" Preston asked after taking a gulp from his goblet of beer. "For all you know, this thing might be chasing you."

"If it was, it would've killed me right after it killed Madsen," Malcolm said, giving the bar around him a quick glance. "And it's had ample of opportunity. But it didn't, so it's safe to assume it's not after me."

"So," Preston asked, "why haven't we heard this on the news?"

"Because the police don't want to cause a panic," Malcolm answered, pursing his lips in embarrassment after saying that. *Which I probably just contributed to by telling you that.*

"Are they serious?!" Preston demanded, throwing a baleful glare at a nearby window, as though the MCPD was outside. "We can't protect ourselves if we don't know what we're protecting ourselves from!"

"I said the same thing," Malcolm agreed, "which is why I need to talk with one of Kate's partners, if you get my meaning? Do any of them frequent this place?"

"Now that you mention it," the bearded bartender answered, cocking his head at the window, which gave him a perfect view of a patio right outside, "right there."

Right where? Malcolm wondered, following Preston's gaze. The patio was full of patrons, making it hard at first to see who he was talking about.

"The far corner," Preston answered. "The lady drinking by herself."

There she is. Malcolm's eyes zeroed in on a redhead woman drinking at a table all by herself. Her back was to the two men, but something about her told Malcolm that she was Kate's kind of girl "I'd like to talk to her, if you don't mind."

"By all means. Just don't try anything funny, eh?"

"I won't," Malcolm assured him, getting up. "I promise."

"Heh, yeah," Preston snorted dismissively. "Famous last words.

Hopefully not, Malcolm thought as he headed for the patio.

"Shit," Kate whispered, her head pounding from something that felt like a hangover even though she hadn't had a drop of alcohol all day. "God, why does my head hurt?"

As careful as a ninja, she slid her body off the damp bed, allowing Rebecca—she was sure that was her name—to get her sleep. Taking one look at her, Kate winced, mentally kicking herself. *Dammit, I did it again.*

What would Malcolm think of her if he saw this?

What would her parents think of her?

What would old me think of what I've become? Kate wondered, sitting on the edge of the bed. She looked over her shoulder at Rebecca resting comfortably. *Least she's quiet. And young.* A horrifying thought came to her. *Too young!* She looked to the foot of the bed, saw her clothes in a pile on the floor. *Please tell me she's at least eighteen!*

Kate knelt over the pile of clothes, sifting through them to find Rebecca's clothes. *Right, she doesn't have clothes!* But a relieved smile spread over her face. *Stripper clothes! She's a stripper! Means she's got to be at least eighteen!*

Because there was no way a seedy gentlemen's club would ever hire someone underage!

—⚒—

"Hello, ma'am," Malcolm started as he approached the redhead sitting at a table in the corner of *Kate's Cove's* patio. "I need to ask you—"

Then she turned around to face him.

"Questions," Malcolm finished, struck dumb by the beauty before him. The woman grinned, revealing a set of pearly white teeth and the most arresting set of green eyes. Her skin was pale—so pale, in fact, that it was almost porcelain white, clashing against her luscious red hair.

"Hey," she said, holding out her hand for him to shake. "Good to meet you at last, Dr. Logan."

"Same here," Malcolm said once he had found his voice. Still staring at the young woman, he shook her hand, seeing that her arm was covered in intricate black tattoos that reminded him of vines on a plant.

The woman smiled, clearly aware of her beauty's effect on him. "First time you've been out of the office, eh?"

"Huh? Uh, no," Malcolm stuttered, looking away from her eyes. *I'm actually tongue-tied around this woman!* He managed an embarrassed smile, hoping he wasn't blushing. *No wonder Kate likes her so much. She's got good taste.* "No, I've been out of the office once or twice."

"Could've fooled me," she said, retracting her hand. There was no judgment in her words—at least not openly. Instead, the words were easy, laid back, much like she was. Just her voicing her opinion.

Get to it, man, Malcolm thought. *We don't have time for these feelings.* Clearing his throat, he got to it. "You know my name."

"Oh, yes," the woman agreed before taking a sip from a glass of water sitting on her table. "Yes, I do."

Once again, no judgment. Just a nice, laid-back answer.

Malcolm could feel a quiet sense of superiority in the woman. Another reason Kate was drawn to her, perhaps. "Then you know why I'm here."

"You want to know about my relationship with Kate."

"You know her real name too?" *Does everyone in this bar know Kate's real name?*

"She told me, Dr. Loga—" The woman gave Malcolm an embarrassed look. "Can I just call you Malcolm?"

"Yes, you may, Mrs. ..."

"Nina Cameroon," the young woman finished, holding out a hand in greeting. "Not that you'll remember later."

"Hello, Nina," Malcolm said, shaking her hand. *Strong grip!* "Why don't you think I'll remember that name?"

"Because Kate never remembers, no matter how many times we're together."

I could recommend the two of you for couple's counseling, Malcolm thought, giving her an odd look. *If you're even a couple.* "Nina, I'd like to ask you questions about things that'll seem like they're none of my business. But in fact, it's for Kate's welfare. And yours."

"Ask away, Malcolm." Nina's inquisitive eyes never left his. "I'm an open book."

"Okay, then." Malcolm wet his lips. *Just get into it.* "How'd you two meet?"

"We met at my job."

"And your job is?"

"I work at the ..." Nina paused, shifting uncomfortably in her chair. "At the bordello on the edge of town."

"I see." Malcolm's mind conjured an image of Nina and Kate meeting every night in some opulent room, far from prying eyes. Kate needing comfort. And Nina taking advantage.

If that was how it happened.

"I can already feel you judging me," Nina said in a defensive voice.

"I don't have the luxury of judging anyone in my line of work," Malcolm declared, hoping to calm her fears. *Or the time.*

"Right, because *you're* the psychiatrist."

"I was going to say because I listen to people," Malcolm corrected politely, "but let's go with me being a psychiatrist." He cleared his throat before continuing. "What made you come back to Kate after your initial meeting?"

"Actually," Nina answered, shifting her weight atop her barstool, "she comes to me."

"And how many times does she do that?"

"Once or twice a week," the redhead answered, counting the numbers off on her hand. "Three times if she's really stressed."

Must cost a pretty penny. "If you're so used to Kate coming to you, what brings you here?" Malcolm asked, gesturing to the bar around them.

"I come here once a week to let off some steam," Nina answered, giving him a wry smile. "I like this place. It's quiet, and Preston keeps the riffraff off me."

Looks like Kate's guardian angel's got more than one person he likes to keep an eye on. Malcolm smiled despite the odd way he and Nina had met. "Do you know of Kate's reputation? Here, that is?"

"I do," Nina answered, nodding her head confidently. "That's the other reason I'm here. I wanted to see if the rumors were true." She pulled a pocket watch out of her shorts pocket. "Kate should be here any minute."

"During your intimate times together, did Kate ever open up to you?" Malcolm asked, wanting to broach the subject carefully. "Tell you about her past?"

"More like she opened *me* up," Nina answered, giving him a mischievous smirk.

Keep it clean, kid. "Did you notice anything strange afterward?"

"Now that you mention it," Nina answered, keeping her eerily calm demeanor. "I don't feel cold anymore."

Just like Kate, Malcolm thought, his mental alarm on high alert. "Just cold?"

"Yeah, just cold. It's the only reason I'm wearing this revealing number," Nina answered, showing off her outfit, which consisted of a T-shirt, jean shorts, and flip-flops. "It's like I got a blanket of heat around me."

The heat of the Other Side, perhaps? Malcolm looked at Nina's hand, so engrossed in their conversation that he had forgotten he had been holding it. *Wait a minute.* "You're not just warm—you're hot." *How did I not notice that?*

"I'd say so too."

Malcolm was too focused on Nina's body temperature to even acknowledge whether she had made a pass at him. "Have you noticed any other side effects?"

"I have to drink water all the time," Nina answered, gesturing to the pint glass sitting on the table in front of them. "If I don't, I dry out pretty quick."

Dehydration, Malcolm thought darkly. *Just like the man Kate sent to the hospital!*

"And there are the dreams," Nina continued in a freaked-out voice. "They haunt me every time I close my eyes."

—⚏—

"Dreams?" Malcolm did not like the sound of that. He shifted uncomfortably in his barstool. "What dreams, Nina?"

"Wet ones," she answered, gripping the handle of her pint glass. "I have them whenever I go to sleep."

"What exactly are these dreams of? What do you see?"

"A jungle," the young woman answered in a nervous, unsure voice. "Of flying aliens in the skies. Creatures the size of mountains. And I know these dreams aren't from me. I don't have the imagination to conjure things like that."

No kidding, Malcolm thought, his breath caught in his throat. *I know who does.*

"But Kate could," Nina continued, a faint trace of alarm in her eyes. "I started having these dreams after we were together. That's the real reason I'm here, hoping to run into Kate."

"You want an explanation," Malcolm declared, looking over his shoulder at the entrance to Kate's Cove. *She's seeing the Other Side. How is that possible? Dreams don't jump from one mind to another!*

Unless a mental link perhaps? Forged when Nina and Kate became intimate?

The man that Kate had sent to the hospital—had she formed a mental link with him too?

Malcolm needed to find the answer, but there was no way he was going to do so at Kate's Cove. "Nina, this is going to sound strange, but I need you to come with me. You're in great danger."

"Huh?" Nina looked at him, her expression becoming more alarmed. "What are you talking about?"

"You're not the only partner Kate has been with."

"I know that."

Why am I not surprised? Malcolm arched an eyebrow in shock. "How do you know that?"

"Someone as hot as her doesn't settle for just one partner," Nina answered, trying to sound casual. "I sure as hell don't."

What is with this generation? "But you are the only one still alive. And conscious."

Nina's eyes grew as wide as dinner plates. "What?"

"All of Kate's lovers are dead, save one," Malcolm continued, leading her away from her table. "Murdered, by a killer that's after you too. I have no idea how it finds them, but it has, and they're all in the morgue. I believe you're next, which is why I must get you in protective custody."

"It?!" Nina asked as she let him lead her away from the patio. "What do you mean *it*?!"

"It's a long story," Malcolm said as he pulled out his phone. "Tell you on the way—"

The change was so quick he didn't catch it.

One second, the front of Kate's Cove was in his sights …

The next, a wall of seething gold was in front of them.

No. Looking up, Malcolm's breath caught in his throat. *I'm too late!*

Madsen's killer had found them at last.

He's here, Kate thought, her eyes snapping open with new awareness. *Madsen's killer, he's here! I can* feel *him.* An oily black film spread across Kate's eyes, throwing her vision into a turbulent infrared as she went from sitting on the edge of the bed to crouching on its edge like a gargoyle.

Rebecca moaned, turning over in her bed just behind Kate.

But she might as well have been a world away, because Madsen's killer was close!

Kate could *feel* him!

Must go to him! Kate closed her eyes tight, her mind having trouble forming the words for some reason. *Have … to …* She shook her head, trying to clear a dense fog that had crept into her mind. *Have ... to ...* Kate fell from the edge of the bed and found herself on the floor. She had landed on all fours, as quick and as quiet as a cat.

Didn't she always walk on all fours?

No ... Kate shook her head again, her intellect fading, drowning in a sea of instincts that were both foreign and familiar. *Not ... me ...* Her head snapped up, her ears zeroing in on the sound of breathing coming from the mattress.

Sleeping. Something was sleeping. On her mattress.

No, her nest!

My ... nest, Kate's mind got out, the effort making her whimper. *My ... mate!* She circled the foot of the mattress, the words making her pulse race. *My ... nest! My ... mate! My ... territory!* The city was her territory. And her mate from the Other Side was in it! Without her permission! Defying her!

My ... mate! My ... first mate! He killed ... Kate gritted her teeth, her head throbbing from the effort. *Mad ... Mad ...! Madsen!* Kate's eyes shot open; she was breathing heavily as though she had run down prey in the jungle. *Mad-sen!*

His killer, her mate—he was in her territory!

Kate circled the foot of the mattress, hissing at the idea of Madsen's killer coming into her territory! Without permission! Without announcing himself!

Must go ... to him ... now! Drooling like a hungry dog, Kate looped to the nearby window. Her shrinking intellect didn't even register the shards of glass in her shoulder as she crashed through it, leaping to the wall of an adjacent building. Her nails lengthened into claws that dug into the brick and mortar of the wall. Thick ripping sounds echoed in her ears as her skin sloughed off, revealing the black scales of the Other Side underneath!

Find him! Kate scaled the building, reaching its roof in what felt like seconds. Turning her head in the direction of Kate's Cove, she raced toward the roof's edge. Find! Him!

She took a swan dive off the roof's edge as batlike wings poked out from her scaly shoulders and lifted her into the dusky sky.

—⚏—

The creature—Madsen's killer—hurt Malcolm's eyes the longer he looked at it.

A set of horns topped its head like a crown, the light from its golden scales causing a strobe effect that bathed the entire patio in its radiance. It looked down on Malcolm and Nina with eyes the color of amber, glowing in the faint light of the setting sun.

A tail whipped behind it, cracking against the floor of the patio like an oversized, thick whip.

My god, Malcolm thought, taking a step back, motioning to Nina to do the same. *Did it get bigger since it killed Madsen? That was only a few days ago!*

The creature stomped toward them, shaking the patio.

Malcolm was the first to snap out of his stupor. "Run!"

"Get down!" Nina shouted, pulling him into the patio as bullets sailed over their heads, heading for Madsen's killer. The second he hit the patio, Malcolm looked to see where the bullets had come from. *Thank you, Preston!*

The bartender had somehow rallied the residents of *Kate's Cove* into a firing line at the bar's entrance. Comprised of determined dockworkers, ready to defend their home away from home, they faced Madsen's killer, guns in hand.

For the first time, Malcolm was thankful for the Second Amendment.

Letting out a roar that sounded like the wails of a thousand damned souls, Madsen's killer launched itself at Preston's firing line, sailing over Malcolm and Nina as they kept their heads down. Malcolm winced as the creature collided with the line in a bone-splitting crash.

Time to move! "Get up," he shouted, yanking Nina to her feet. He pointed at the patio railing a few feet in front of them. "C'mon!"

"That thing!" Nina screeched as she and Malcolm made a break for it. "It's from my dream!"

"I know!" Malcolm pushed her forward, trying to ignore the bloodcurdling screams from behind him as Madsen's killer tore people limb from limb. *Preston! I'm so sorry!* He and Nina vaulted over the patio railing and hit the beach. "Keep going!" Malcolm whipped out his phone. "McLane! Where are you?!"

"We're close," the police chief answered, sounding thousands of miles away. "What's happening?"

"It's at *Kate's Cove*!" Malcolm shouted into his cell phone's receiver. "Madsen's killer! It's here!"

"Shit," McLane cursed loudly. "I got officers on the way! Where are you?!

"On the beach! Can you have someone meet us?!"

"Of course," came the urgent reply. "Just stay alive, Malcolm! We'll find you!"

"We'll try," Malcolm said, ending the call as he and Nina ran, putting distance between them and the carnage at *Kate's Cove*.

—⚊⚊—

He's close … Kate's primitive brain thought as she flew through the skies above Milestone City. *Near … water.*

The docks!

With a screech of anticipation, Kate changed direction and headed for the docks.

—⚊⚊—

"That thing! It was in my dreams!" Nina shrieked as she ran ahead of Malcom, away from Kate's Cove. "Jesus Christ, it's real!"

"I know!" he agreed, sucking in frigid air as he ran behind her. "And it found us!" *But how?! How did it find us?!* He glanced behind them. *How fast can it move?!*

"I don't hear anything," Nina said, slowing to a stop amid the nighttime surf. "Maybe it's not following us." She looked to Malcolm, a hopeful expression on her face. "What do you think?"

"Oh, it's following us," he insisted, taking a moment to catch his breath. Bent over, his hands on his knees, he looked to Milestone City in the distance. *And it's going to keep following us.* His brow furrowed. *Unless someone slows it down.*

"Malcolm?" Nina gave him an unsure look. "What are you thinking?"

With a resolute look on his face, Malcolm pointed to Milestone's cityscape just ahead. "Nina, I want you to run as fast as you can. Head for those buildings. Do not stop. The police will meet you. Don't look back."

Nina looked at him as though she already knew what his plan was. "It'll destroy you."

"But you'll be safe."

"Malcolm ..."

"Go, Nina." Saying it gave his resolve strength. "I'll be all right."

Looking at Malcolm as though she would never see him again, Nina leaned close and kissed him on the cheek. "Thank you."

Then she ran.

Have a good life, Nina. Watching her leave, Malcolm felt a heaviness in his gut. *Really wish I could go with you.* Taking a breath to steady himself, he turned in the direction of *Kate's Cove. Come on, you bastard. Let's finish this.*

—⁂—

The creature that had once been Kate Barrow could feel Madsen's killer nearby. Him and one other.

A man. Not meat. A man.

She soared over a place called ... Kate's Cove? Had Kate gone there before?

No matter, death was there. Kate could smell the blood on the wind despite being hundreds of feet in the air. It meant Madsen's killer had been there. And was still there!

No, wait, he wasn't there anymore!

So where was he?!

That was when Kate caught his scent on the sands.

—⁂—

Madsen's nightmare killer landed a few feet from Malcom, its scales glistening. It wrung gore from its claws, wearing a mark like Kate's—so big it almost took up its entire chest.

Was it serving a sentence like Kate did? Had it served longer?

"Hey!" It croaked in a wet voice, looking right at Malcolm with crimson eyes. "Get away from him!"

The words I said when I saw it kill Madsen, Malcolm realized, taking a step back in shock. *It heard them. My god, it knows me!* Had it come to Kate's Cove looking for him? Had Malcolm gotten all the denizens of the pier-side bar killed by asking about Kate?

The creature's eyes narrowed, nodding its head, as though it had heard Malcom's thoughts.

Oh, screw you, monster! "Well, here I am," Malcolm said when he found his voice. He raised his arms high as if daring the creature to attack him. "Your move."

—❦—

Kate saw Madsen's killer, and one other, below, in a face-off on the beach. She dipped toward them to face the winner.

—❦—

Malcolm knew that if he moved, the creature would cut him down. *What are you waiting for?*

What *was* it waiting for?! A favorable wind?

Malcolm saw scores of wounds on its golden body. Bullet holes that dripped blood on the beach. A chunk of its right shoulder was gone, flayed to the bone. As the creature stood before him, its breathing was labored, pained. *Maybe it's hurt more than I realized.* Malcolm heard the sound of approaching sirens in the distance and let out a sigh of relief. *Thank you, McLane!*

Then he heard the flapping of wings right above him.

Of course, Malcolm thought, his spirits sinking at the realization. *You were waiting for backup.*

—❦—

Here. Kate landed on the other side of the meaty man. *He's here.* Keeping her body close to the sand, she growled at Madsen's killer, towering over him.

The man turned, his eyes wide with fear. From his body language, Kate could see that he knew her.

How? How did he know her?

A demanding click from Madsen's killer snapped Kate's mind back to their standoff.

—⁂—

Kate? Malcolm didn't need a degree to know that the winged creature crouching behind him was her. Sure, she was covered in scales and sporting smaller horns and wings, but the facial structure was identical.

Somehow she had transformed into what she was on the Other Side.

Dammit, McLane, what is taking your people so long?! Malcolm's eyes flicked between Kate and Madsen's killer. "Okay, then. Who's first?" *Such bravado! With nothing to back it up!*

Malcolm then heard a strangled croak from Kate.

"Malcolm. Duck."

—⁂—

With an angry screech, Kate launched herself over Malcolm's head, straight at Madsen's killer. Seeing the scared therapist had brought her back to her senses, like a bolt of lightning.

She was Kate Barrow, dammit! KATE BARROW!

Invigorated by the realization, she slammed into the creature's chest, her claws digging into his flesh. She sank her teeth into his neck, hoping to tear out meaty chunks.

He fought back, throwing elbows on her head, neck, and shoulders. Then he drove her into the ground.

Madsen's killer growled, communicating with Kate in a language only they knew. One he had taught to her on the Other Side. And he demanded answers.

Why was she betraying him? Hadn't he protected her? Shown her how to survive on the Other Side?

Madsen's killer had come to take Kate back to the Other Side where they belonged! Where they could be free!

—⚶—

No! Kate violently shook her head. *This is my home!* She glanced at Malcolm amid the blood and gore flying in front of her face. *With him!*

Malcolm had come to her rescue again. He could have run. Could have turned his back on her, like everyone else. But he didn't! He cared about her too much!

Using that singular thought as a compass for her thoughts, Kate lunged at Madsen's killer again, aching to finish him, once and for all!

—⚶—

I can't believe I'm seeing this! Malcolm stayed perfectly still, lying on the sands of the beach. *I wish I wasn't seeing this!* But he couldn't turn away, mesmerized by Kate and Madsen's killer ripping into each other like oversized lions. Blood and gore flew off their bodies like chips from a woodchipper.

How can anything lose that *much blood and* still *stand?* Malcolm wondered when he saw the growing black pool under their feet.

—⚶—

"*There's* my blood goddess!" Madsen's killer boasted as he dodged Kate's attacks. "Just beneath the surface!"

"Shut up!" she fired back, carving a chunk of meat out of his side. "Shut up, damn you!"

"This world's forgotten you!" the creature declared. "Only I understand you!"

"How did you find me?!"

"I followed the Solomons," he answered, backhanding her across the face, "when they brought you back to this stifling place!"

102

"They ... brought me back?" Kate's eyes blazed with battle lust as she collided with the beach. *I knew that!* Saliva dripped from her chin as she circled Madsen's killer, envisioning sinking her teeth into his throat. "Why?"

"To hide you from me," Madsen's killer answered. "But I *knew* you were alive! I just had to bring you out! And there was only one way!"

Madsen's murder, Kate realized, her reptilian eyes narrowing shrewdly. "You killed Madsen to impress me?"

"Not just him," the creature snorted, "but all of your other lovers!"

Other lovers? It took a second for Kate to realize what the creature meant. *He didn't just kill Madsen! He killed my sex partners too!* Kate's stomach sank in her reptilian gut. "Why?!"

"Because if they want the privilege of bedding you," Madsen's killer snarled, beating his chest with a thick claw, "then they must earn it! They must fight for it, as I did!"

"That's not for you to decide!"

"It's *our* way," Madsen's killer declared, giving her a challenging gaze.

"It's *my* body!"

"But it's *their* blood," the creature said, pointing a curved claw at the space behind Kate.

Their blood? Right then, Kate felt Stan and Francine's presence just behind her.

"They watch you even now," Madsen's killer screeched, his eyes wide with fear. "Don't you see?!"

No ... Kate refused to turn around despite the Solomons' energy warming the air around her. *He can see them too!*

"You think you can hide from them?!" Madsen's killer frantically gestured for her to approach him, curling its index claw toward the palm of its hand. "Come with me, please! We'll go where they'll never find us!"

—m—

Are they talking to each other? Malcolm wondered as he looked from Kate to Madsen's killer, confusion on his face. *Wait a minute, they* are *talking to each other!*

—◈—

Overcome by a feeling of dread, Kate turned around to see the Solomons standing a few feet behind her.

Stan stood to her left. His arms were folded, and his face was stern and cold.

Francine was on her right, grinning in devilish anticipation.

Despite their mouths not moving, Kate could hear their voices in her ears, buzzing like a swarm of angry bees.

—◈—

They're just standing there! Malcolm lay on his side, too afraid to move. *Why?* He couldn't take his eyes off Kate and Madsen's killer, not even reacting to the sound of approaching sirens.

It sounded that Nina had gotten to McLane's people after all.

They're looking at something! Following their eyes, Malcolm slowly, carefully turned his head in the direction Kate and Madsen's killer were looking.

To the space right behind Kate. To the left and right of her, in fact.

What are they looking at? Then Malcolm remembered Kate's tussle with Francine in his office a few days earlier. *Are they sharing a collective hallucination?*

Were they both seeing the Solomons?!

—◈—

Why are you here? Kate trembled before the Solomons like a wet dog, her eyes wide with fear. *Why now?!*

"Don't talk to them!" Madsen's killer hissed, reaching for her. "They lie!"

Did you know? Kate panted heavily, her fearful stare becoming an angry glare. *That he was here? All this time?*

"They're lying to you, even now!"

Is that what you were trying to tell me at Malcolm's office?! Kate's eyes searched Stan and Francine's faces for any hint of their thoughts. *At that man's house?!*

"They cannot be reasoned with!" Madsen's killer bellowed in a voice so strong it created shock waves that kicked up sand everywhere. "None of their kind can!"

Do you want me to kill him? Kate kept her gaze on the Solomons, waiting for an answer. *Will you leave me alone if I do? Will you let me rest?*

Stan's and Francine's eyes narrowed ever so slightly.

So be it, then, Kate thought, squaring her shoulders. *So be it.*

—∞—

Good lord! Malcolm flinched as a strangled cry came from Madsen's killer.

Faster than his eye could track, Kate swiped at its throat. Blood sprayed like a fountain from the wound. A mortal one. Madsen's killer staggered away, flailing as it let loose a howl that hurt Malcolm's ears. A death call that sounded like the screams of a thousand damned souls.

Then it died, collapsing in a bloody heap.

—∞—

It's over! The rage left Kate's body, leaving her giddy with relief. *It's over!*

She looked in the Solomons' direction. *Please! Tell me it's over!*

But they were gone.

Her eyes wide in shock, Kate looked around. *No, it can't! It can't end like this!* She gawked at the spot. "Come back," she whispered, too tired to move. "*Please, come back…*"

She could feel her body cooling. She saw soft skin where hard scales had been.

Kate was covered in his blood. She could taste him in her teeth.

She felt Malcolm nearby.

105

He saw me like this, she realized. *He'll … he'll run from me like all the others!* Tears streaming down her face, Kate punched the sand in frustration. *Dammit, dammit, dammit!*

—⟡—

Oh Kate. Malcolm watched Kate Barrow, his patient of six months, pound the sand with her fists, whimpering in anguish. The sirens behind him were growing louder. He had only a few seconds to act.

And yet he froze.

Malcolm's mind was blown, his knowledge of the world called into *serious* question.

For years, he had been afraid of monsters.

And now he knew those monsters were real!

Focus on Kate, Malcolm said to himself. *She needs you.*

But did he need her? Did he really want her—and all the craziness she would bring—in his life?

If Malcolm took her in now, he would be responsible for all she did. And would do in the future.

If he just washed his hands of her, he would be free. He could continue with his life, in a world that made sense!

But then Kate would suffer the sting of another figure betraying her. Then what would happen? Would that thing inside her come out again? Commit even more heinous atrocities than Madsen's killer?

Wouldn't Malcolm then be responsible?

—⟡—

It's over, Kate thought, her angry blows against the sand reduced to halfhearted slaps. *I've no place to go.* She slowly hauled herself across the sand. *Should've stayed on the Other Side. At least there I belonged!*

She froze as strong arms encircled her shoulders.

"I have you, Kate," Malcolm declared in a gentle voice. "I have you."

Oh, Malcolm! Kate fell into his arms, a happy sigh escaping her lips.

—⟡—

"So what now?" Malcolm asked as a paramedic treated him for shock.

"We got our killer," McLane answered as her people carted the body of Madsen's killer away. "Case closed. The streets should be safer now, don't you think?"

Glancing at Kate in the adjacent ambulance, Malcolm wasn't so sure. Once she had killed the creature, she reverted to her human form. But that didn't mean the threat was over. Covered in a towel, she looked at her hands and feet, still covered in its blood. "I hope so," Malcolm answered. "May I see her?"

"You still want to?"

"I do."

"By all means," McLane said as she stepped out of his way. "And, Doc?"

"Yes?"

She gave him a proud smile. "You did good work tonight."

A thought entered Malcolm's head. "What about Nina? Is she okay?"

"She got to us, told us where you were."

"And?"

"She's fine," McLane answered. "She's at the station right now, refusing to go home until she knows *you're* okay."

Well, how about that? "Tell her I'm fine." Malcolm looked at Kate. "As I said I would be."

McLane nodded and walked off to the beach.

—◊◊—

Hey, you. Kate felt Malcolm sit next to her in the ambulance. *Right here.* She laid her head on his shoulder. "Thanks for covering for me."

The middle-aged man chuckled and gave her a one-armed hug. "Thanks for saving me."

"Yeah," she chuckled back, rolling her eyes. "*That's* what I did."

"Do you remember any of it?"

"Bits and pieces."

"Maybe that's a good thing."

"I'll second that."

They were silent for a few minutes as officers passed them. Kate noticed a few gave her wary looks. Not as many as before, however.

Maybe things *would* get better.

"You know, Kate," Malcolm said as though he was hearing her thoughts, "I have to tell McLane's people what happened, eventually."

"I know," Kate said, giving his hand a tight squeeze. "But not tonight, okay?"

"Okay, then," Malcolm answered, nodding in agreement. "Not tonight."

Had he looked at Kate's face right then, he would have seen her eyes turn red, then black, then back to normal in the space of a blink.

But Malcolm didn't, and neither did anyone else.

Instead, he and Kate watched the sunrise, the sun's rays promising a new day.

Tonight They Come Back

On a humid night in Gateway City, a police car screeched to a stop in front of an abandoned church on Bridge Row. Two officers, Malory and Johnson, stepped out.

"You ready?" Malory, a fresh-faced officer straight out of the academy, asked. "This is the address Dispatch gave us."

"Okay," Johnson, a slightly potbellied veteran of ten years, answered. "Let's do this."

"We should've waited for backup."

"You a cop, or aren't you?!" Johnson snapped. "We got a call, and we're gonna answer it!"

"But what if"—Malory glanced nervously at the crescent moon hanging just above the building — "*they* come?"

"Jesus." The older cop sighed in exasperation. "They're an urban legend, kid. That's it."

"Right. *That's* why Chief Loeb holds those briefings!"

They shone their flashlights ahead, hoping nothing, or no one, was hiding in the shadows.

"Should've waited for backup," Malory repeated nervously.

"That little girl's not gonna wait, and neither's her kidnapper," Johnson retorted. "We're lucky we got the call at all."

They entered through the front door, their guns trained on all corners. Silently, they checked every room on the main floor, Johnson taking the lead. Malory covered his back, keeping his eyes peeled for any surprises.

"Clear," Johnson announced after checking the last room. "Besides the rats and roaches, there's no one here."

"Then we check the top floors," Malory said, shining a light at a set of stairs. They were about to head up when his ears perked up. "You hear that? Sounds like whistling."

"Yeah," Jonson answered, his eyes wide and alert. "Cellar. Got to be. Let's get down there."

"And what do you know?" Malory shone his light on a set of stairs. "We got ourselves an entrance."

"Stay sharp, kid. Don't get complacent."

"After you, old man."

"Don't call me old," Johnson warned as he crept down the stairs.

"Still think we should call for backup," Malory whispered as he followed. "Just saying."

"Kid, do *not* make me turn around and shoot you."

—⊶⊷—

As they entered the cellar, the whistling turned to high-pitched sighs.

"I knew this tip was good!" Johnson whispered with excitement.

"You really think Dispatch was screwing with us?" Malory asked as his gaze swept over empty wine cases. "C'mon, man!"

That was when they spied the whistler, sitting in the middle of the cellar under a hot light.

An African American girl, couldn't have been more than nine years old. Seeing their uniforms, she raised her hands, dropping the cell phone she had been holding.

"Hold on, kid!" Johnson quickly holstered his gun as he approached her. "We're not gonna hurt you!"

"I hope not." She slowly lowered her hands. "I called you guys."

"That right?"

"A girl like me can't afford to be helpless," she said, looking at Johnson as though he was a rattlesnake. "Especially in *this* town."

"What's your name, kid?"

"Monique."

"You the only hostage here?"

"Yup."

"Okay, let's get you—" That was when he heard shrill screams from upstairs.

"Crap," Monique said, putting her hands to her ears. "Shoulda left like she said!"

"*She* said?" Johnson's face grew white as a sheet. "Oh no."

"I'm on it," Malory shouted as he charged back up the stairs. "Get her out of here!"

"Malory!" Johnson yelled. "Wait for backup, dammit! Malory!"

———※———

With his heart pumping like a piston, Malory raced up the steps, his partner's words mere background noise.

He had heard the stories. Everyone in the department had. They dismissed them as tall tales, but not him. Cops never made up stories like that.

About the couple who lost their son to police bullets.

Then got superpowers, somehow.

And got revenge on the cop that killed their son.

Malory got to the main floor, just as a second scream ringing out from the floor above.

He slowly crept up the stairs, seeing the first room to his left. A cracked door allowed him a slight peek inside.

And a better listening point for more screams, punches, and God knew what else!

Jesus, Malory thought as he crept toward the door. *What the hell's doing that?*

"Stop! Please stop!"

Malory winced as another punch rang out, followed by the sound of crunching bone.

A hellish bark followed.

"I ... I don't know where she is! I don't know!"

Malory gritted his teeth against the sound of a hot laser and the smell of burning flesh. *What's in there with him?!*

"I ... I can't tell you! She ... she doesn't show me her face!"

The door shook, as though a body had been thrown against a nearby wall.

"I … oh God," came a thick, gurgled cough. "I don't … know … where …" It was cut off by gagging sounds, as though something was choking the life out of him.

"Police!" Malory bellowed as he kicked the door in, gun at the ready.

The screamer was on the floor. He had to be about six feet eight, with the body of a gym rat that lost a battle with a meat grinder. A growing pool of blood framed the macabre tableau he had been reduced to.

Good lord! Holstering his gun, Malory knelt by his side while shouting into his communicator. "This is Malory on the abandoned church on Bridge Row! I need paramedics right now! Prep for extensive trauma!"

Then he felt something behind him.

He spun quickly, cursing himself for not checking the corners …

To see a beautiful woman with the most intense set of green eyes, glaring at him. She was wearing a dark suit with a triangular symbol on her chest. Her auburn hair was short, and a long cape ended just above her ankles.

Francine Solomon. Malory swallowed, his throat painfully dry.

"If only your people had showed my child *such* concern," she said in a voice as flat and pitiless as death.

"You're under arrest!"

"Am I?" Her eyes lit up like flares.

What's she— Malory yelped as a lightning bolt shot from her fingers to his gun, making it so hot he had to drop it.

Throwing him a look of disdain, Francine shot through the ceiling and into the sky.

On his knees in shock, Malory barely heard Johnson enter the room with backup.

"Paramedics are on the …" He and the officers behind him stopped dead when they saw the perp. "Kid! What the hell happened?!"

"It was her." Malory got up shakily. "Francine Solomon! I … I never thought I'd see her! But she's real! She's freaking real!"

"Okay, kid." Johnson helped him to his feet. "Be glad you're alive."

"Ch-check on the perp," Malory got out through chattering teeth.

"We will, kid. We will."

"Good lord," another cop—Buchanan—whispered. "You're gonna want to look at this."

"Is he alive?"

"Oh, he's alive. Barely, but he's alive."

"That's all that matters," Johnson said. "Tend to him until the paramedics get here."

"Johnson." Buchanan looked up, his expression grim. "You *need* to see this."

Passing Malory to another officer, Johnson knelt next to the grizzled cop. "What is—" He froze when he saw it.

On the perp's chest—the only part of his body that wasn't pulverized—was the symbol of a bird of prey, with outstretched wings and sharp spines, cut into his flesh.

"Shit! She branded him!"

—⁂—

In another part of Gateway, a towering inferno consumed a factory.

Deep inside, terrified workers huddled against the wall.

"Why hasn't the fire department come yet?!" one worker asked fearfully.

"We're too far inside!" another answered. "They can't get past the fire!"

"How's *that* possible?! It's *their job* to get past the fire!"

"Quiet!" the shift leader snapped. "If we're gonna die, we're *not* dying like pussies!"

"Says the man huddled *behind* us!"

"Hey, look!" someone yelled, pointing at the flames. "I think someone's coming!"

"What are you …" The shift leader, to his surprise, actually saw a man heading toward them! "Well, I'll be damned!"

Astonished, they watched their mysterious rescuer casually stride through blistering flames.

"Who the hell's that?!"

"Where'd he come from?!"

"As long as he's here to save us, does it fucking matter?!"

The workers stood back as the stranger stepped into view. He possessed a muscular physique, clothed in a dark suit with a triangular symbol on his chest. A long cape billowed behind him. Dark eyes gave them a once-over. "Is this everyone?"

"As many as we could find," the leader answered. "We're all that's left, I think!"

"You're not sure?"

"*How* would we be sure?!" The leader doubled over, coughing from the smoke. "It's not like we can check!"

The man's warm look turned to a glare hotter than the flames behind him. "Say again?"

"We don't know," another worker cut in, giving his leader a curt look.

"Right." The man nodded in understanding. "I'll be back. Stay low and stay together."

"I ... what the?" the leader blubbered as the man was suddenly gone. "Where the hell'd he go?!"

"Jesus, Carl!" the other worker snapped. "Do you know who that is?! Are you *trying* to get us killed?!"

"Stay low, he says," another mumbled. "Unbelievable!"

"For cripes' sake! Didn't he check before he got to us?"

"You're right." The stranger had returned. "There's no one else here."

"That's nice," the leader snapped. "GET US OUT OF HERE!"

The stranger's piercing glare returned, his eyes shining like flares. "Please?"

"Better," he said, turning to the flames. "Hold on to something."

An explosive thunderclap jolted the factory, dropping firefighters and nearby onlookers to their knees. It also blew out windows and the fire inside.

As witnesses picked themselves up, four grimy, but grateful, workers stumbled out.

As paramedics rushed to them, they pointed back to the factory as Stan Solomon shot through its roof and into the sky.

—∿—

"So, kid," Randal Solomon said over the phone, "how are things in your neck of the woods?"

"You first," Detective Julie Benz said, sitting up in her bed the next morning. "Has Stan or Francine contacted you?"

"Not since you left here with Kate a few weeks ago." He let out an uneasy chuckle. "Guess I lost my dad appeal."

"I'm really sorry to hear that."

"Me too, honestly."

"If my coming down there had anything to do with—"

"Kid, what happened between Stan and me was a long time coming." Randal let out a weary sigh. "You just happened to see the end of it."

It still happened because of me, Benz thought sadly. *My investigation broke up your family. I'm gonna pay for that, somehow.* "Don't give up yet, Randal. You reached him once. You can do it again."

"No, kid. *You* reached him. By talking to him."

You're going to make me blush. "I didn't do *that* much."

"You did more than anyone else did. That's not saying much, but still."

—∿—

"Hello, Drake," Commissioner Michael Loeb said, standing up from his desk to greet Detective Frank Drake. "How are you?" He was tall and muscular, with dark hair expertly quaffed and a voice that filled the office. He extended his hand, showing a 100-watt grin.

"I've been better," Frank answered, warily shaking Commissioner Loeb's hand. "Enjoying the new job?"

"It's been interesting," Loeb answered, sitting back behind his desk. "How was rehab?"

"Finished," Frank answered bluntly as he took a seat. He took cursory glances around the office, seeing that Loeb had already made

115

himself at home. Any trace of Topher Madsen, his predecessor just months ago, was gone. "So when can I get back to work?"

"I want to ease you in slowly. The department's still smarting from what happened with you and Benz at Kate Barrow's home."

"So am I," Frank said, lightly tapping his knee.

"I looked over your test results."

"Then you know I passed them."

"And the nightmares?"

Dammit. "I have them under control, sir."

Loeb gave him a pointed glance. "Do you?"

"Yes," Frank insisted calmly. "Yes, I do."

—⁓—

"So," Randal said after a lengthy silence, "any blowback on your end?"

"I'm the department it-girl," Benz answered, rubbing her eyes. "Our new police chief gave me a commendation for creative thinking."

"I'm not talking about from your boys at the GCPD. I'm talking about from mine."

Benz stiffened. "I don't know what you mean."

"Come off it, kid," Randal declared in a knowing voice. "I saw the way Stan was handling you. He cares about you."

"Don't make assumptions", Benz thought, suddenly feeling uncomfortable with where their conversation was going. "He's a caring person."

"My ass. The way he held you? Jennifer and me saw it. He's got a thing for you."

Benz hoped to heaven he was wrong. It was bad enough being the "touched one" at the department. She couldn't deal with being "Stan's girl" too. "He's married."

"Doesn't mean he's dead," Randal said. "He has a thing for strength of character. And you've got it in spades. More than anyone else at that damn department."

"He's also a criminal." It was a good thing she was alone because Benz could feel herself bushing. "One I'm investigating."

"Heh, romances have been built on less."

"Randal!" a female voice shouted from his end. "Don't put ideas in her head!"

Wait ... Benz blinked in surprise. *Did I hear right?* "Is that Jennifer with you?"

"Yeah," Randal answered, his voice touched with embarrassment. "She ... moved in a few weeks ago."

Now that's *shocking.* "Wait, isn't she married?"

"*Was* married," Randal clarified, his voice becoming a conspiratorial whisper. "Once you got Kate back, Jennifer returned home with her. Threw it in her ex-husband's face."

And now I broke up a marriage! Benz face-palmed so hard she was sure he heard her smack herself. "You didn't go with her, did you?"

"Hell no, kid. That was *her* battle."

—⁂—

"Tell me what happened that night," Loeb said as he poured himself a cup of coffee.

Do I have to? "Didn't you read our report, sir?"

"I did. I want to hear it from you."

Everyone wants to, Frank thought, his jaw clenching. "I can't add anything."

"Humor me." Loeb gave him an expression that brooked no argument.

Fine, then. "A year ago, Officer Kate Barrow killed the son of Stan and Francine Solomon in the line of duty. Their son's name was Brian Solomon. The shooting went to trial, where a jury of our peers acquitted her. The verdict sparked a firestorm that ripped Gateway City apart."

"I was working in Homicide when it happened."

"I was on vacation when I saw it on television. My wife called me in. She got real broken up about Brian. Even put a rose on his gravestone."

"From what I heard, Kate Barrow did the same thing. When she could get to it without being harassed."

"Didn't stop his parents from taking her," Frank said sourly. "Or from roughing Benz and me up when we tried to stop them."

"I know," Loeb agreed, sympathy on his face. "I'm real sorry about that."

"Thank you, sir."

"Speaking of that night …" He poured a second cup of coffee and handed it to Frank. "Why did Madsen send you and Benz alone to deal with the Solomons?"

———

"So Jennifer just … moved in with you?" Benz needed a moment to get her head around *that* development. "After how you two met?"

"Hey, don't look at us," Randal insisted in a casual tone. "*You* brought us together."

Love how he's trying to use me to rationalize it. "If Stan could see the two of you now …"

"He'd probably kill us."

The statement threw cold water on Benz's mood. "You think he's watching your house?"

"Him? No," Randal answered quickly. "Frannie? Hell, yes."

"How can you tell?"

"There are times in the night, when Jennifer's gone to bed and I'm alone, that I feel eyes on me," Randal answered confidently. "Her eyes."

Francine's still looking after him, Benz thought, remembering how he spoke of her. *Shows a strong bond. If I could get him to agree to it, I could use him as bait to trap her. If we could catch her, we could force Stan to the negotiating table.* "Has she done anything more than staring?"

"No. She won't talk to me. Not without Stan's permission."

"I wasn't under the impression she was under his thumb."

"Just because a woman actually listens to her man, instead of undermining him, doesn't mean she's oppressed," Randal said in a pointed tone. "It just means she trusts him to lead."

"If you say so," Benz said dismissively.

———

The question everyone *asks.* "We were originally sent to deal with a noise complaint," Frank said, giving Loeb an irritated glance. *Can't believe I have to explain this again!* "There was no need for backup."

"But when you saw how powerful Stan and Francine were, why didn't you call for it then? The only reason it arrived at all was because Madsen scrambled everyone after you both failed to report in."

"You really want to know?"

"That's why I asked, Drake."

Okay, then. "I've always been Madsen's go-to guy when it comes to"—Frank sighed, realizing there was no way to finish his sentence without things getting uncomfortable — "cases too dicey for anyone else to handle."

"Dicey, as in ..."

"Off the books."

"Clarify, please."

"Cases that needed to be closed quickly," Frank finished flatly.

"And why would Madsen do that?"

Great, now he's having me explain it. "Look, sir, there are cases in this line of work that are too sensitive for the public. I handle them so no one else has to."

"Uh-huh." Loeb's sympathetic look was starting to curdle. "And what's your success rate with these cases?"

"High," Frank answered, realizing how sketchy that sounded.

"Any of them controversial?"

"A few." *Feel like I'm digging my own grave here.*

"And how long have you and Madsen had this arrangement?"

"A few years."

"Any of these cases make it to the DA's desk?" Loeb asked, his tone measured. "Any that would earn you a few enemies?"

"A few," Frank answered. "But that's the case for any cop."

—⁂—

"So," Randal said for seemingly the fifth time, "how *are* you?"

"I'm fine," Benz lied.

"No strange dreams? No visions?"

119

"Not a one," she got out, bare-knuckling tired eyes.

"Nice try," Randal said knowingly. "But I can hear the fatigue in your voice."

"Can't hide anything from you," Benz said. *I used to have a good poker voice.* She looked out her window, then swallowed quietly to gather her strength.

"When was the last time you got a good night's sleep?" a new voice asked.

"Jennifer?" Benz did a double take. "When'd you get in this conversation?"

"Randal gave me the phone. I asked for it the second he talked about you having strange dreams," she added quietly, "I had them too. When Kate was gone."

"I remember," Benz said, a dull pounding starting in her head. "How is Kate, anyway?"

"Don't know. I hope she's fine."

"You don't know?" Benz didn't like the sound of that. "What do you mean you don't know?!"

"I had her for maybe a week after we got her back home," Jennifer explained, her voice thick with regret. "After she was cleared by your doctors."

"Then what happened?" *Please don't tell me Stan or Francine took her again!* Then Benz steadied herself. *No, if that happened, Mrs. Barrow would've called me earlier. And she would sound angrier.*

"US Marshals showed up at my house."

"Crap."

"I'll say," Jennifer agreed with a touch of sadness. "And they took Kate. Put her in Witness Protection. For her own safety."

"Do you honestly believe that?"

"I have to, Benz," Jennifer answered, her voice breaking. "I have to."

—⚮—

"Well"— Loeb sighed as he sat back in his chair — "that explains it."

"Explains what?" Frank was on the edge of his seat despite his casual expression.

"When I took over for Madsen, a stack of files landed on my desk. They listed detectives to keep an eye on during the department's restructuring."

"And let me guess," Frank said, "I'm in one of those files."

"That you are," Loeb answered, fishing one from a drawer. "It's thick." He placed it on his desk, the sound like a gavel.

"Well," Frank said, pulling at his collar, "there it is."

"Yes, here it is."

"And who collected that?"

"District Attorney McFadden, as a matter of fact," Loeb answered, watching the detective squirm in his chair. "He's really got it out for you."

Damn son of a bitch. Frank snorted derisively. "He's had it out for me since I busted his nephew for drug possession."

"During one of your off-the-book cases, right?" Loeb asked, giving him a pointed look.

"Sir, if word of his nephew's habit had gotten out, the whole city would've suffered. So Madsen and I handled it, privately."

"Well, he told me to watch you," Loeb announced, sliding the file back in his drawer. "You and all the other old-timers that got through IA's purge by the skin of their teeth."

Right, the purge, Frank thought, sinking into his seat. *Let's talk about the freaking purge!*

—⁂—

"But enough about me," Jennifer said, sounding eager to move on to something else. "Let's talk about you."

"I'm fine," Benz answered, feeling an unwelcome sense of déjà vu. "I mean it."

"That's the same thing I said when I started having nightmares, remember?"

How could I forget? Took me days to get the truth out of you. "That was different."

"How, pray tell?"

"You were a mother worried for her daughter. I'm a cop working a case." Benz guided herself back to bed, the covers feeling so inviting under her skin.

"You and I both know this isn't a regular case," Jennifer declared.

"I feel like you're trying to warn me about something." *Or someone.*

"And I can hear the fatigue in your voice, young lady," Jennifer said crossly. "You're having the nightmares now. What are they about?"

Seems I gained a second mother. "I can't tell you," Benz answered, keeping her voice low despite being alone.

"Don't you pull that classified crap on me ..."

"It's not that, Jennifer," Benz said, throwing furtive glances around her room. "For all we know, my phone might be bugged."

"Do you really think the GCPD would do that to one of its own detectives?"

"Normally, no," Benz answered. "In this instance, I wouldn't put it past them."

"The GCPD purge was Mayor Quimby's idea," Loeb insisted. "We had to show we were accountable, given that we cleared Kate Barrow of killing a defenseless child."

The jury cleared her, not us. "I had a feeling," Frank said dutifully.

"You almost got swept up in it."

Don't find that surprising. "What kept me out of the firing line?"

"Madsen."

Madsen? Frank's brow arched in genuine surprise. "Really?"

"You sound surprised, Drake."

"It's just that after what happened, I figured I'd be on his shit list."

"No, he held you high"—Loeb took a casual sip of his coffee—"even as he fell."

"Thanks for the biblical imagery," Frank said, keeping his tone measured.

"Sorry, I keep forgetting this is all new to you," Loeb said, giving Frank a look of guarded sympathy. "For the rest of us, it's ancient history."

Not that ancient, Frank thought, giving the new police chief a suspicious look.

"Yes," Loeb answered, not even bothering to hide his suspicions.

"Well, you can," Frank said, balking at the answer. "But I'll let my record speak for itself."

"You sure that's a good idea?"

"I have nothing to hide."

"Everyone says that," Loeb said in a wary voice, "until the light shines on them."

—⁂—

"Speaking of the GCPD," Jennifer said, trying to sound casual. "What do they got you doing now?"

"Breaking in an old partner," Benz answered quietly as she laid on her bed, her eyes looking to the ceiling.

"Let me guess," came the mirthless chuckle. "Frank Drake."

"Jennifer ..." Benz warned in a strained voice.

"I'm not mad," she said quickly, "but he's not on my list of favorite people."

The nerve of this woman! Benz braced herself, in case their conversation took an uncomfortable turn.

"It's not that," Jennifer said, her voice apologetic. "It's just I heard some bad things about him while I was poking around your department."

"Bad things?" Now it was Benz's turn to chuckle. "What kind of bad things?"

"Things I don't think he's going to tell you," came the wary answer. "How long has it been since you worked together?"

"Since the night Kate was kidnapped," Benz answered cautiously.

"That was a year ago."

"I'm aware," Benz said quickly. "I can count, you know. *Easy, girl, she's trying to help.*

"Has he even been on active duty before now?"

"Not to my knowledge." *Why am I telling her these things?*

"And your bosses decide this case—your case—was the best case to put him on?" The doubt in Jennifer's voice was as obvious as a heart-attack.

"If you're questioning his effectiveness, don't," Benz found herself wagging her finger disapprovingly, despite Jennfier not being in her bedroom with her. "He has a storied career in the force and has more experience than I do. Than anyone in the department."

"And yet, he's still a detective," Jennifer shot back in a resentful voice. "Not a chief, or even a deputy chief. Just a detective."

"You making fun of detectives now?" *How'd we create* this *relationship?*

"Heavens, no. However, the fact that he hasn't advanced at all since making that rank? Says a lot."

She does *think she's my mother!* Benz shook her head at the craziness of it. *I don't need another mother. I already have two.* "As long as that doesn't keep him from being a good partner, I could care less."

"You may have to," Jennifer said, her words dripping with dread. There was a faint rattling sound on her end of the call, as if she'd gripped her phone tighter as she spoke, "if you're going to trust him."

"I already trust him," Benz insisted calmly. "And if I'm going to catch the Solomons, I'm going to need his help."

—⁂—

No wonder the GCPD's a mess. Frank refused to let Loeb see him squirm, despite his accusations making the office seem more stuffy and claustrophobic than ever. Frank, to his disgust, found himself fighting the urge to pull at his collar. "Has everyone *else* gotten this third degree?"

"Anyone who has is now gone."

So I am on the chopping block! "Chief, if Madsen fought for me, why are you—"

"Going through this with you?" Loeb gave Frank a wary look. "Because of the case I'm considering putting you on."

"And what case would that be?" *Think I already know.*

"One investigating the activities of Stan and Francine Solomon."

"Do you think you can catch them?" Jennifer asked, her voice a whisper. "Do you think you can catch Stan and Francine Solomon, after everything they've done?"

"I hope I can," Benz answered, : rising to a sitting position on her bed.

"But they're not common criminals."

"Trust me, Jennifer," Benz said, projecting an easy confidence she didn't feel, "when you've been in this business long enough, you realize there's no such thing as a common criminal."

"You know what I mean," Jennifer insisted in an irritated growl.

Yeah, I do. "I'm formulating a strategy ..."

"Don't quote that department speak to me," Jeniffer said in a voice that wavered between frantic worry and accusation, "we're too close for that."

Jesus, woman! The intensity of the older woman's response took Benz aback, but only for a second. "I'm just saying–"

"Do you think you can catch them?" The question was tense.

"I think I can talk to them," Benz answered carefully. "It worked the night they took Kate. It also worked the night Stan brought her back."

"It's been months since that happened."

Jennifer... Benz felt her shoulders sagging with a sudden fatigue, as if Jennifer's words were sapping her strength. "So?"

"A person can change a lot in a few months."

"I have to hope Stan hasn't."

"It's not ..." Jennifer paused. "It's not Stan I'm worried about. It's his wife."

"Francine," Benz said in a gentle, sympathetic voice. "You can say her name. It's not like she's a boogeyman that'll jump out of the shadows to get you if she hears it."

"I know, but ..." Another pause, as though Jennifer was trying to find the right words. "It's in her eyes, Benz. I saw it the day of Kate's trial."

"When she was acquitted of killing their son."

"Yes!" came the irritated reply. "That day, I saw it. The mania. The rage. She's a spook, Benz! A demon!"

"You're scared of her," Benz whispered, her eyes wide with realization. *And I should've seen this sooner.* She pressed her lips together in thought. I should get her to a therapist.

"I'm terrified of her," Jennifer clarified fervently. "And you should be too!"

"We're choosing *now* to investigate them?" Frank asked, raising a skeptical eyebrow as his hands gripped the armrests of his chair as if they were claws. "What were we doing before?"

"Gathering information, Drake," Loeb answered, a touch of steel in his voice : as he sat behind his desk.

"For what? A history paper?"

"Did you always talk like this around Madsen?"

"More or less," Frank admitted, shrugging.

"Well, do *not* do that around me," Loeb insisted coldly. "It will *not* help your case."

You got *to be kidding me!* "So I'm still under investigation, eh?"

"Yes, you are, Detective Drake."

Frank caught the implication immediately. "I get it."

"I get it ... what?"

Why, you young, underserving…! Frank gripped the armrests as hard as he could to keep from launching out of his seat to strangle the younger man. "I get it, Chief."

At least we got it out in the open. "I can't afford to think like that if I'm going to—"

"Don't bother, Benz," Randal stated in a sad voice. "She's gone."

"How'd you ..." She did another double take. "How'd you get back on the line?"

"Jennifer handed me the phone. She can't talk about Frannie without getting worked up."

"I didn't know that."

"Oh. Well, now you do."

"Where's she now?"

"She went to the bedroom and slammed the door," Randal answered. "Guess I'll be sleeping on the couch tonight."

"Hold on," Benz said, her confusion growing. "She left her husband of many years and moved in with you, on a whim?"

"I'm a little surprised too," Randal admitted. "Guess I still got sex appeal."

Not what I'd call it. Something about Jennifer's behavior wasn't right, but Benz had too much on her plate to put much thought behind it. "Do you have any advice for me? About Stan and Francine?"

"Honestly? Not even a little. You're facing shit I got no context for."

"Still, you raised Stan …"

"His mother and me raised him," he corrected. "Best time of our lives."

"You have to have *some* insight. Some hint as to what he'll do next."

"I don't have a single one," Randal admitted, regret in his voice. "If I'd stayed by his side after Brian's funeral … If I hadn't run away, I could've prevented all this. Kept the both of them on the straight and narrow."

"You are *not* going to wallow in self-pity, Randal. I don't have the time."

"Someone's gotten claws."

"Guess I have," Benz admitted, realizing how harsh her words sounded. *Surviving two near-gods will give you some balls, I guess.* "Sorry about that."

"Don't be sorry," Randal said, pride in his voice. "It shows focus. Drive."

"Francine has that same drive." Benz swallowed back a knot of anxiety. "And look where it's gotten us."

—m—

Now that you've cut my balls off…, Frank thought ruefully. "If you're so iffy about me, why do you want me on this case?"

"Because you're the first person to encounter the Solomons, and walk away unscathed," Loeb answered as he eyed the older detective with barely contained suspicion.

"I spent a year in recovery."

"You're still standing," Loeb insisted. "That's more than anyone else can say."

"Well," Frank said, basking in the minuscule compliment. "I had help."

"Oh, I know," Loeb agreed, his expression brightening as he spoke. "Detective Julie Benz. I had her in here too."

Still not shocked. "She's the reason we survived the Solomons." *Using only her words.* "If not for her, we'd be dead."

"I know that too," Loeb said, flashing that 100-watt grin of his. "That's why we let her keep going after them. And it's paid big dividends for us."

We? Frank felt like he was waiting for the punchline to some unspoken joke. *Is he talking about the GCPD? The mayor? What does he mean by we?* "How?"

"She got Kate Barrow back."

—⁓—

Francine … A solution came to Benz immediately. "Francine's the key!" She was so excited, she almost dropped her phone. "To all of this!"

"What?" Randal asked, sounding absolutely baffled by her words.

"You told me back in North Carolina that all of this was Francine's doing. The powers. All that's come with it. It came from gods …"

"I'm not comfortable with that phrase," Randal replied nervously.

"Fine, 'divine beings,'" Benz corrected, careful to keep the ire out of her voice, "that she called somehow. And they gave her and Stan their powers."

"A bit simplified, but yeah."

"Can she rescind those powers?"

"Honesty?" There was a brief silence on Randal's end, as if he were taking a moment to think about it. "I don't know."

"Best guest, then."

"I'd say yes," Randal answered hesitantly, "long as Stan agrees."

"If I talk to Francine alone," Benz asked with bated breath, realizing that she was playing with fire, just suggesting such a thing, "would she listen to me?"

"You saw her when she kidnapped Kate. Did she listen to you then?"

"Yes," Benz answered, thinking back to that night. Stan had been stoic, but Francine had been furious. Brian's death and Kate's acquittal had made her so manic that Stan had to keep her calm. And yet ... "She said my words were kind."

"That ... was Frannie. She always took the time, you know? To tell you if you were doing good. To compliment you," Randal paused, his normally blunt voice becoming lower pitched, softer, "even if you didn't feel you deserved it."

He's speaking of her in the past tense. "She sounds nice, Randal."

"She was once, Benz. She was once."

—⚬—

"Benz got Kate back?!" Frank almost jumped out of his chair. *Holy shit, I missed a lot!*

"Yeah." Loeb poured himself another cup of coffee. "She did."

Benz got Kate back! Frank's mind reeled. "How'd she even know where to look?"

"She had help."

"From who?!"

"Quite a few people," Loeb answered. "One of whom is ... no longer with us."

"As in ...?"

"Abducted."

Just like Kate. Frank's shoulders sagged. "Anyone we know?"

"Yes. Officer Kevin Jacobson."

Jacobson... It took a few seconds for Frank's brain to connect the dots. *I've seen him before.* "He was Kate's partner."

129

"That he was," Loeb agreed, his lips a firm line on his face.

"And he was there when she shot Brian Solomon."

"Two points to you, Drake."

Another compliment. "And he was present during her trial."

"Three points, good job," Loeb said. "His testimony got the jury on Kate's side."

"Got her off for Brian's death," Frank declared grimly. "How'd he get involved after?"

"Because Kate's mother, Jennifer Barrow, conscripted him."

"She tried to 'conscript' me too," Frank admitted, his heart going out to her.

"She was desperate."

"She cornered me while I was in rehab. Jacobson did too." *Focus on someone else, Frank!* "We got any leads on where he is?"

"No," Loeb answered regretfully. "And we never will. Benz had to trade him for Kate."

"She bartered for Barrow using one of ours?" *Well, shit.*

"I wouldn't bring that up if I were you," Loeb advised calmly. "You'll be working with her."

I have a plan, Benz thought as she moved from her bed to her bathroom, finally, to take a shower. *Or at least the beginnings of one.* "Randal, I gotta go."

"I figure. Me too. You know what you have to do?"

"I have an idea. Just need some help making it happen."

"You need me down there?"

I could use *him.* Benz paused in her steps. *I really could.* But Stan had specifically said that if Randal set foot in Gateway City, he would die.

Either by his hand or another's.

Besides, there was no way Chief Loeb would approve having a civilian on the case. He was already trying to keep the Solomons out of the public eye! If someone as recognizable as Randal was seen assisting detectives on such a high-profile case, it would tank any confidence the people had in the GCPD.

And that was already at a low ebb.

That, and Benz had a feeling anywhere Randal would go, Jennifer would follow. *Going to look into* that *when this is over.* "I already got someone to help me."

"Frank Drake."

"Did Jennifer tell you?"

"I heard her say his name," Randal answered. "Didn't exactly try to keep her voice down."

No kidding. "Don't get on my back about him too."

"Wouldn't dream of it," Randal assured her. "I'm gonna check on Jennifer. You need anything, and I mean anything, don't hesitate to call. I mean that."

"I know," Benz said before ending the call. Tossing the cell phone on the bed, she went to the bathroom to get ready for work.

Now this is starting to make sense, Frank thought as Loeb slid a manilla folder across the desk to him. *We saw the Solomons rise, so he thinks we can bring them down.*

But something was still troubling him. Actually, a lot of somethings.

If Benz had gotten Barrow away from the Solomons, she should've been the department hero. But he had heard no mention of her from anyone, when he arrived at the station.

Also, Barrow's return should've been on blast in the news.

"Why's this the first I'm hearing about Barrow's return?" Frank asked, looking to Loeb for answer. *And why didn't you start our meeting with that, first?*

"Because Witness Protection took her," Loeb answered, making to take a sip of coffee, only to see his cup was empty. "But we had her long enough to do a sexual assault kit on her."

"How'd she look?" Frank asked, dreading the answer.

"Like she'd been through hell," Loeb answered, a grim look on his face. "I spoke to her personally, once she'd been cleared to have visitors. Her mother was close, protective too. If not for Benz, she never would've let me talk to her."

131

Kate's mother, Frank thought, his expressions darkening at the mention of her presence. *As if I haven't had enough of that crazy woman!* He let out a calming breath. *Focus on Kate, Frank. Keep the conversation on Kate.* "What did Kate have to say?"

"That she was lucky to be alive."

"That goes without saying."

"And that the Solomons punished her for what she did."

Uh-oh. Frank's posture stiffened in his seat. "How?"

Loeb's expression soured, a disgusted shudder moving through his body. "By rendering her ... sterile."

Stan Claps Back at Factory Fire!

Damn, Randal, your son's had a busy night. Benz skimmed the newspaper article from the Gateway Gazette as she dried her hair, having just come out of the bathroom. *And everyone's eating it up.*

Her mind latched on to the main details, including quotes from witnesses about what a godsend Stan was for saving their lives. Not just in the article she was currently reading but also in others going back months.

From workers whose place of employment had gone up in flames ...

To a cancer survivor he had convinced *not* to commit suicide ...

Even a battered wife whose husband threatened to kill her ...

The way they made him sound, Stan Solomon might as well have been the Second Coming of Christ!

Huh, Urban Jesus. Benz snorted to cover laughter at her little joke. *Bet that's a movie somewhere.*

Setting the paper on the kitchen counter, she made a breakfast of toast and eggs. Once that was cooking, she toweled off the rest of her body and then went back to the newspaper. *Let's see what Francine's been doing.*

"They," Frank's mouth went dry, "fixed Kate?" He sank a few inches in his seat, a claustrophobic sense of failure permeating his being. *Good lord, the things I missed while I was gone!*

"The term you're looking for is 'neutered,'" Loeb corrected him, a nauseated look on his face. "And yes, they did."

"Like a dog?"

"Yes, Drake," came the sarcastic answer. "Like a dog."

"Jesus," Frank whispered under his breath.

"When I took this job," Loeb said, sitting on the edge of his desk, "I considered working with the Solomons. Like in the superhero movies."

"Really?"

"They're quite effective. Crime's dropped a whopping 60 percent since they got to work. The once-bad parts of the city are safe to walk through now. People are even starting to leave their doors unlocked at night, at least in the low-income areas.

Frank looked at Loeb as if he'd said something crazy, "Aren't they afraid the Solomons will come after them?"

"Only *we* see them as the boogeymen, Drake," Loeb explained. "No one else does."

"So what changed?"

"What they did to Kate Barrow. Loeb shook his head, letting out another shudder of disgust. If they're willing to do that to anyone, for any reason, they can't be tolerated. They have to be stopped."

"Maybe if we told the media what the Solomons did to her," Frank suggested, doing his best to keep his temper under control, "people wouldn't see them as heroes."

"I brought that up," Loeb said, his hands balled into fists at his sides. "With the mayor and the DA, and you know what they told me?"

Don't think I need to, Frank thought, reading the police's chief's expression like a book.

"They told me, 'Such action would put Kate Barrow and her family at considerable risk.'"

"Then what are Benz and me supposed to do?" Frank was still reeling from what he'd learned. "I wanna go after the Solomons too, but we gotta be able to win!"

133

—⟋⟍—

Francine Fries Felon!

Now this *is troubling*, Benz thought as she read about Francine Solomon's torture of Anthony Sikes in the paper while eating her toast. *Very troubling.* Sikes was a low-level thug for the Mala Noche gang, mostly small-time stuff.

The GCPD had been trying to nail him and the Mala Noches for months. A few cops had even managed to haul him into the station a few times. But he had always gotten off, thanks to technicalities.

And surprisingly good lawyers.

Francine, meanwhile, took care of him in one night. There were no pictures, thank God, but the article summed up the grisly details perfectly.

Doesn't make us look good, Benz thought as she finished her toast. *And Gateway City agrees.*

In the past few months, she had seen "Stand with the Solomons" pages on the internet. Teens were taking selfies in front of their symbols, painted on the sides of buildings, and posting them online. There was even a Twitter campaign—#JusticeForBrian—lighting up social media.

Benz's ears perked up, remembering that she was on a clock. She whipped out her phone to check the time. *Crap, I gotta get to work!*

—⟋⟍—

"All I need you two to do is observe," Loeb said after taking a moment to consider Frank's words. "We already know a frontal assault against the Solomons won't work. We tried that months ago."

"How'd *that* go?"

"How do you think?"

Damn, Frank winced as if he'd been slapped. It's just one hit of bad news after another. "So you just want us to tail them?"

"Talk to witnesses," Loeb said, pointing to the file in Frank's hands. "Get a sense of Solomons' attitudes, their motives, how the public sees them."

"Haven't other detectives done this already?"

"Others have tried, but people clam up when we ask about the Solomons. Which means they're either protecting them …"

Or are afraid of them. "What makes you think Benz and me will have better luck?"

"Because you two saw them first."

Already seeing holes in this, Frank thought, biting his lower lip. *Holes the size of a Mack truck.* "Let's say people talk to us, what would we be looking for?"

"Actionable intelligence," Loeb answered in a stern voice.

"Actionable intelligence?" *What are we? The CIA?*

"Yes, indeed," Loeb answered, filling some papers on his desk, before raising his head to look at Frank again. "We do that, we can kick this up the chain."

"To whom?"

"People better equipped to deal with them," Loeb answered, giving Frank a final, appraising look. "So what do you say, Drake? Can I count on you?"

Frank honestly wanted to refuse. To tell Loeb his entire plan was a bad idea. That it was pointless. The Solomons needed to be stopped—especially for what they did to Barrow—but not by him and Benz.

And certainly not by the GCPD.

But if he did, Benz would just go it alone without backup. Like she'd been doing since the Solomons first attacked.

And she would get herself killed. Either by the Solomons or whoever Loeb would assign as her new partner.

And there was no way Frank was going to let that happen. *We started this together. We'll finish this together. One way or the other.* "I'm in."

"Good man," Loeb said, a look of relief on his face. "Benz should already be here. Time to get to work."

—◦◦◦—

Time to get to it, Benz thought as she pulled into the station's parking lot.

She let out an anxious breath after parking the car. It had been so long since she had last worked with Frank. She had changed a lot, physically and mentally.

Could they even work together?

Then she saw him, standing on the station steps.

And she felt green all over again.

"Like riding a bicycle," Benz told herself as she made her way to him. *Or driving the same car with a new paint job.* "Looks like we're back at it again," she announced, forcing a smile as she met Frank on the steps. "Like old times."

"Not quite," he said, walking down to greet her. "Heard you've been earning your spurs."

"I've kept busy," Benz said, shaking his hand.

"Busy, hell. Loeb told me you're the reason we got Kate back." Frank pulled her in for a hug. An uncharacteristically familial gesture. "Good work."

"That's now what I'd call it, Frank." Benz hugged him back, blinking her eyes in surprise. What happened to him during his medical leave? He never hugs anyone!

"You outwitted Stan Solomon, Benz," he said, gently pulling away from her, his face beaming. "That's no small thing."

"By giving up Officer Jacobson," she said, her face full of regret. "Her partner."

"Yeah," Frank admitted, his expression becoming downcast. "Heard about that, too."

"I talked to his girlfriend, after I got back," Benz continued, her mind flashing to an image of Jacobson's girlfriend, breaking into heartrending sobs, before she could stop it, "she was ... inconsolable."

"But you did get Kate back to her family, Benz." Frank held her hands in his, giving her a hopeful look. "Be proud of yourself, okay?"

She looked up, gratitude on her face. "Thanks, Frank."

Frank quickly let her hands drop, as if embarrassed that he'd opened up that much, in front of her, as people moved around the two of them.

"Don't sell yourself short," Benz said as they made their way back to the parking lot. "You were recovering from one hell of a beatdown."

———

She looks leaner, Frank thought, looking at her face. *More angular. As if her baby fat wore away. And her eyes got that haunted look.* "You got it worse, partner. And you were still out there, doing the work."

"You'd be too if our positions were reversed," Benz said as they approached their car. Frank took the passenger seat while she went for the driver's side.

Just like old times.

"So what's in the file?" Benz asked as she started the engine. "Anything interesting?"

Frank shot her an unamused look. "That's a joke, right?"

"Just tell me, Frank."

Before she would've hit me with a witty reply. "This file contains all the information on the Solomons. Looks like Loeb wants us to hit this case running."

"Better than the case running over us."

Not the response I expected. Frank gave her a concerned look. "Seriously, you okay?"

"It's been a crazy couple of weeks."

"I get that. But I'm here now. And I'm gonna work this case with you, okay?" He saw the way her hands trembled before gripping the steering wheel. *What has she seen?* "You need me to drive?"

Now it was her turn to shoot him a look. "With your record?"

"Fair enough." Frank cracked open Loeb's file. "Let's get to it."

———

Benz stood in a crowded park in one of Gateway's low-income neighborhoods an hour later. *Here we go.*

On a bench sat her witness, a nine-year-old girl licking an ice cream cone. A few paces behind her stood her parents, watching Benz with wary eyes.

She stood, waiting for their permission.

Commissioner Loeb had already arranged the interview, but she wanted them to feel in control. She was their kid, after all.

The parents nodded, giving her the go-ahead.

—⁓—

The child's name was Monique Rambeau. She looked remarkably calm, having spent time with a kidnapper and killer.

"Hello, Monique," Benz said, flashing an easy smile. "Mind if I sit down?"

"Who are you?" she asked, giving her a wary once-over.

"My name is Detective Benz ..."

"Whoa! Julie Benz?!"

"Why, yes," she answered, blinking in pleasant surprise. "Have you heard of me?"

"We've *all* heard of you!" Monique's face lit up with excitement. "You met the Solomons first!"

"I hear you met them too," Benz said, sitting on the bench next to her. "I got a few questions about that, if you don't mind?"

"Of course! Ask away!"

"All right then," Benz said, relieved at how easy this was hopefully going to be. "I'm told Francine rescued you. Is that right?"

"That's right!" The little girl answering, puffing out her chest as she spoke.

"Did she try to hurt you?"

"Why would she hurt me?" Monique looked confused. "I'm not the bad guy."

"Oh, I know!" Benz said, backtracking from her statement. "But maybe, by mistake, in the heat of the moment ..."

"You mean, like your police friends do?"

No illusions for this girl. "Yeah," Benz answered, wanting to stay on her good side.

"No," Monique said, shaking her head. "She left me alone when she took the bad man."

"So how did we find you?"

"She gave me a phone. Took it right out of the guy's pocket! Lifted him up by one hand!" Monique demonstrated the move. "He was so scared! You shoulda heard him scream!"

Enthusiastic too. "Weren't you scared?"

"A little, but she told me if anything happened, she'd be close."

So Francine stayed close enough to keep an eye on her, Benz reasoned. *But far away enough to interrogate her kidnapper without being interrupted.* But how'd she learn about Monique's kidnapping in the first place? "Was anyone with her?"

"You mean Stan?"

"Yeah."

"Naw. She was solo."

She was alone. Just like Stan was when he brought Kate Barrow back to me. They trust each other enough to work apart. "Do you know why the bad man was after you?"

"One of the gangs," Monique answered, cocking her head to her parents. "They were trying to strong-arm my dad."

"Strong-arm, how?"

"He used to pay protection money to them," she said, leaning in to whisper into Benz's ear. "It was the only way to keep them off us."

"He used to? What made him stop?"

The little girl pointed to the sky, grinning.

Ask a stupid question … Benz smiled back. "Thank God they're here."

Look at her. Frank beamed as Benz handled the Rambeau kid. *Doing the job despite all she had seen.* He turned to the other witness from that night, Officer Malory. *Time for me to do the same.*

The young officer leaned against the hood of his squad car; arms folded against his chest. His eyes were on Benz and Rambeau too. "Seeing that almost makes getting my hand burned worthwhile." He showed Frank a bandaged right hand. "Almost."

"Thanks for taking the time to talk to me, given what you've been through."

"It's nothing, sir," Malory said, extending his unbandaged hand. "Part of the job."

It shouldn't be. "I read your report," Frank said, shaking his hand. "Says you saw Francine Solomon up close."

"Yup." A sour look passed over Malory's face. "I mean, yes, I did."

"And she was torturing a suspect?"

"Yes, sir. I only caught the tail end of it, but judging from the smell and the screams, she was working him *pretty* hard."

"That sounds like Francine …"

"With a blowtorch."

Frank swallowed back a wave of nausea, remembering how Francine electrocuted Kate the night she and Stan took her. "Any theories on why?"

"He *did* kidnap a little girl," Malory answered, looking annoyed. "Snatched her up in broad daylight."

"When were you and your partner called?"

"Later that night."

Why wait so long to call in their daughter's kidnapping? Frank glanced at the parents, a confused look on his face.

"People like them don't call us about stuff like that," Malory stated, seeing the look on Frank's face. "Or about anything anymore."

"People like them?"

"Folks from the gang-infested neighborhoods. The Rambeaus' shop is dead in the middle of Mala Noche territory."

The Mala Noches. Frank mentally kicked himself for not catching on sooner. "That's right. A new gang. They're supposed to have their hands in all sorts of pies."

"Drugs. Prostitution. Arms dealing. You name it," Malory explained. "And they start young." He reached into his car to grab a steamy cup of coffee. His partner, Officer Johnson, sat in the passenger seat.

Frank was pretty sure he was recording their conversation.

"They're bad guys, sir," Malory continued tensely after taking a sip. "We were trying to bust them, but no one trusted us."

"Any reason why?"

"They were convinced some of us were in their pocket," Malory answered simply.

"And then the Solomons arrived," Frank said, realizing where the conversation was going. Like heaven-sent saviors.

"Like a comet, sir. Attacked organized crime with a vengeance. The Mala Noches are the last gang standing. The rest? They've been run out of town. At least, out of the poorer sections."

Can't say I hate that, Frank thought, impressed. "Damn, a hell of a lot can happen in a year."

"When you don't worry about due process, you can get a lot done," Malory declared casually. Seeing Frank's stern expression, he raised his hands defensively. "I don't agree with them! But obviously, the rest of the neighborhoods do."

"What makes you say that?"

"Because since the Solomons arrived, we barely get any calls. It's like people expect the Solomons to do everything."

We've lost their trust, Frank realized sourly. "Do *you* trust them, Officer Malory?"

"I'm not in their fan club," he answered. "But Francine Solomon did save that little girl. And made sure her kidnapper won't hurt her or anyone else. That has to mean something, right?"

"It sure does," Frank said grimly. *Means they're making us look like incompetent fools.*

—m—

"Monique," Benz continued, giving her a worried look. "Was Francine alone with you at any time? Before she left with the bad man?"

"Yeah," the young kid answered. "After she took the phone from him, she hauled him upstairs. Then she came back to check on me."

"What did she do?" Benz asked with bated breath.

"Asked me a lot of questions," Monique answered quietly.

Not so proud now. "Did she make you uncomfortable?"

"No. But I did feel bad for her."

"Why?"

Monique looked to her parents, then to Benz. "Promise you won't tell them?"

Benz gave Monique's parents a look before turning back to face her. "I promise. As long as Francine didn't hurt you."

"She asked me a lot of questions. About my parents."

Here we go. Benz fought to keep her expression neutral. "Like?"

"How they were treating me. Their relationship with me. Stuff like that."

Benz glanced at the parents, who were starting to look nervous. *Someone's got skeletons in their closet.* "They're good questions. But I get if they made you feel weird."

"It wasn't just that," Monique said, a sympathetic look in her eyes. "She asked about my life."

Didn't expect that. Benz's brow arched in surprise. "Your life?"

"Yeah. What I'm studying, what my plans are for college, stuff like that. You know …"

Dammit, Benz thought, already seeing where the conversation was going. "Mom stuff."

"Yeah. It really made me feel for her," Monique said, her lips curling into a frown. "Then I remembered how she lost her kid. I got a little teary-eyed."

She was trying to relive her time as a mother. Benz's heart went out not just to Monique but to Francine too. In a case like this, it was easy to forget that she was, at heart, a grieving mother.

"She saw me starting to cry, and you know what she did?"

I'm afraid to ask. "What?"

"She told me a joke. It was pretty corny. Made me laugh, though."

Francine wants to be a mother again. Benz was getting close to tears herself, just thinking about Francine, full of regret. *Wants time back with her son.*

"She even gave me some advice. Told me to cherish my time with the ones I love. That I'd never know when they'd be snatched away," Monique finished, wiping her eyes. "Then that look came over her face."

"What look?"

"Like she was gonna kick someone's ass. That was when I remembered the bad man."

From grieving mom to executioner in a split second. "Thank you. I have all I need."

"You sure you don't want to talk some more?" Monique asked, looking desperate for attention.

"Here," Benz said, fishing her card out of her pocket. "If you need to talk to me, for any reason, give the number a call. It's to my personal cell. I'll answer."

"Thanks," Monique said, holding the card like it was more valuable than gold.

"And if you need help with anything"—Benz flashed her parents a wary look — "I'll come running."

—⁂—

"You okay?" Frank asked a few moments later, sitting in the squad car with Benz. "Looks like your session with the Rambeau girl ..."

"Monique."

"Yeah, looked like, it was getting pretty emotional."

"It was," Benz said, looking at him with tired eyes. "It revealed a side of Francine I wasn't ready for."

"That of a torturer?"

"Of a grieving mother wanting to be an active mother."

"Yeah," Frank winced, not expecting the answer. "That'll do it."

"I wasn't ... expecting it," Benz declared, gazing out her driver-side window.

"You need a moment?" Frank asked, eyeing the junior detective curiously.

"No, I'm good," Benz said, shaking her head. "What did Officer Malory tell you?"

"That he and his partner found Monique right after she called them. Matches her claim that Francine handed her Anthony Sikes's phone."

"He'd been leaning on Monique's parents for a while, apparently. For protection money."

"He's not leaning on anyone now. Francine messed him up pretty bad." Frank pulled the file to his lap, flipped through its pages. "There are pictures, but you don't want to see them."

"To go from caring mother to executioner on a dime," Benz said, rubbing her chin as she gazed out of the car window. "Hints at a disturbed mind, partner."

I know a few veterans that did the same in the war, Frank thought grimly. "I agree. But the fact that Francine wants to be a mom might be something we can use."

"You sure?"

"Yeah," Frank answered, rubbing his own chin thoughtfully. "Might have a few ideas on that. But I'm gonna need time to put it together. Let's talk to the next few witnesses."

—⚋—

I'll be ... damned. Benz stood outside an impatient room in Saint Christopher's Hospital, gawking at what was left of Anthony Sikes. *Francine did not spare the rod!*

The infamous gang member lay in a hospital bed, mummified in bandages that covered who knew what type of injuries.

"Hello, Detective Benz," a grey-haired woman, dressed in a white overcoat said, sidling up to her. "Dr. Pettigrew."

"Hello, Doctor," she said, shaking the woman's hand, realizing she was a head shorter than she was. *My goodness, you're a small thing!*

"I take it you have questions about our"— Dr. Pettigrew cocked her head at the comatose gangster, while letting out a resigned sigh— "newest patient?"

"I do," Benz answered, noting the weariness in her voice. "His name's Anthony Sikes. Leg breaker for the Mala Noche gang. He was attacked by Francine Solomon after kidnapping a little girl. I need to know what he saw."

"I assumed, Detective."

Must get visits from us regularly. "This may seem like a dumb question, but is he in any condition to talk?"

"Not now," Pettigrew answered, shaking her head. "Or in the near future."

Now for the other dumb question. "Why not?"

"For one thing, he's in a coma."

Damn. "Why and how?"

"Every time we'd had him stabilized after surgery, he'd start screaming and thrashing." Pettigrew coughed, readjusting a pair of glasses on her head. "That started tearing his stitches and undoing our work. We put him in a medically induced coma so he'd heal properly."

"He's having nightmares." Benz looked to the gang member, surprised at the ambers of sympathy, forming in her gut.

"I'd imagine so, given who he tangled with."

"That a common occurrence with Francine's victims?"

"Yes, indeed." Pettigrew let out a nervous gulp. "They all come here, and they all end up screaming."

She didn't just put the fear of God in Sikes—she's put the fear of God in all of them, Benz realized. "Are any of her victims still here?"

"Once they come here, Detective, they never leave."

"Why?"

"They're all too injured to move. They either end up in a coma, like Sikes here" —Pettigrew tapped the glass — "or they end up dead."

Good lord. The hall seemed to spin for a second as Benz swallowed back a wave of nausea. "Speaking of Sikes, what *are* his injuries?"

"Broken bones. Second- and third-degree burns and a host of internal injuries," Pettigrew rattled off. "He was conscious when your people found him but passed out when they got him here."

"Would you say he was tortured?"

"After what I just told you, is there any doubt?"

Just like Monique heard. A sour look passed over Benz's face. "I saw in the report that he was branded."

"Oh yes." Pettigrew took a picture from her coat pocket. "Just like all the others."

The pictured showed the brand, freshly cut into Sikes's skin. It was of a bird of prey, its wings tipped with spines.

Was it pulsating before Benz's eyes?

Or was it a trick of the light?

—m—

"Okay, fellas." Frank motioned for the workers sitting on benches in Saint Christopher's gazebo to quiet down. "First off, thanks for coming."

"Kinda hard to refuse a police summons," a heavyset man said. "We're not even sure why we're here. We told the police everything."

"But those police weren't me or my partner," Frank declared, seizing up the men who had been saved by Stan from a factory fire the night before. "And worry not, I bring good tidings." He raised his hands, holding a six-pack of beer in one and a box of doughnuts in the other.

"Hell yeah, you did!" a third man declared, practically salivating.

Ah, the working class. Frank put the doughnuts and beers on a table and stood back as the men pounced on them. "Besides, we've a common experience."

"We know," a smaller man chimed in excitedly. "The first person to meet the Solomons! You're like a movie star!"

Actually, Kate was the first. "Which means I have a unique insight."

"I'll say!"

Now that we're all friends. "Let's start with what you saw," Frank started, relieved this was starting out well. "Can you confirm it was Stan Solomon that rescued the bunch of you? Not Francine?"

"We'd know if it was her," another man quipped. "Trust us!"

Right, Frank thought. "How'd he save you?"

"You saw the report," a lanky worker, who looked too small for his clothes, said.

I know, jackass. "Walk me through it."

"We thought we were goners," the oldest one started. "Fire was everywhere. Every exit was blocked."

"How'd Stan enter the factory?"

"He walked in. All heroic-like."

He walked in? Frank scratched at his ear to make sure he heard correctly. "Why didn't he fly in?"

"Maybe he was trying not to disturb any hazardous materials," the oldest one answered. "Anyway, once he found us, he asked if there was anyone else in the factory."

"He didn't check before finding you? He can move pretty fast."

"That's what I said!" another called out from behind the throng. He looked to be the biggest one, with thinning hair and a potbelly.

"And what'd he do?" Frank asked, looking over the rest of them. "Mr. ...?"

146

"That's Carl," another worker, the one closest to him, growled. "Man's mouth almost got us killed."

"Almost got you killed, how?" Frank asked, eyes shining with interest.

"Damn fool decides the fire was the perfect time to pop wise at Stan when he was trying to save us!"

"I simply pointed out the obvious," Carl called out defensively.

"And almost got us killed!" the worker shouted back.

"Easy, boys." Frank impatiently tapped the table. "What did Stan do when Carl decided to pop wise?"

"He glared at me!" Carl answered. "At *me!*"

"Because you were being a jackass," the worker muttered under his breath.

"Yeah, typical Carl," another worker chuckled, making the whole group laugh.

"Okay, okay," Frank said despite letting out a chuckle himself. "Back to my questions. Why would Stan walk in when he can fly in?"

"The factory was a powder keg, Detective," the closest worker explained. "If he moved too fast, he might've triggered a bigger explosion."

He showed caution, Frank thought. *Patience. So did Francine when she tortured Sikes.* "Did he say anything else to you?"

"Just told us to hang on," the older man answered. "Then blew out the flames by clapping his *hands!*" He clapped his own to demonstrate. "Defies physics!"

"With the Solomons around, a *lot* of physical laws are being broken," Frank declared as he turned to leave. "Thanks for the help, guys. Enjoy the doughnuts." Giving the group a wave, he headed back to the squad car to wait for Benz.

—⟨⟩—

That's ... better. Benz looked at her reflection in the bathroom mirror after splashing water on her face. Seeing the Solomons' mark had spooked her. Seeing it move sent her running for the hills.

Or in this case, the bathroom.

Benz inhaled, then exhaled deeply. Her apprehension slid to the back of her mind. *Giving her space but staying close.*

Others. Benz turned from the mirror, leaning against the sink. *What Francine did to Sikes, she did to others.* She felt the sting of betrayal, having just heard earlier from Monique what an angel Francine was. *There are two sides to everyone, Julie.*

She closed her eyes, the painful throbbing of her head returning. *Throbbing, just like the Solomons' mark …*

Maybe I am connected, Benz thought, opening her eyes. *Like Randal said.* She shook her head quickly. *No. I refuse to believe that.*

—m—

Frank was about to get in the car when he felt someone coming up on his six. *Wrong move, buddy.* His hand hovered over his piece, aching to fire it. *No! Not here!* He'd calmed his nerves when someone tapped him politely on the shoulder.

"Detective?"

No threat so far. Frank turned, seeing the worker who started his argument with Carl a little while ago.

Except he was a *she.*

Frank had assumed she was a guy because of her lanky build, boyish haircut, and the fact that she wore coveralls identical to her male coworkers. *Can't believe I fell for that.* "Can I help you, Mrs. …"

"Barlowe."

Interesting name. "Can I help you, Mrs. Barlowe?"

"Just wanted to apologize for what you saw back there."

"Not the first time I've seen coworkers argue." Frank waved away her apology. "Don't worry about it. I'm just glad you guys are alive to argue."

"I knew you'd feel that way," she said, beaming at him. "But the fellas wanted to be sure. Last thing we want to do is get on the bad side of you guys."

"Why?"

"Because that leads to … bad ends."

Excuse me? "We're not the Mafia, Mrs. Barlowe," Frank declared. "Public opinion doesn't influence our desire to do our jobs."

"Oh, doesn't it?" Mrs. Barlowe asked, giving him some serious side-eye. "That's not what I've heard."

This is what Stan and Francine want. For killing their son, this is their revenge. Frank bristled at the admiration in Barlowe's eyes, knew it wasn't for him or his fellow cops. *And they're getting it, ice cold.*

As if confirming his suspicions, Barlowe asked, "You see the Solomons, right?"

Dammit. "I'm not their press agent, if that's what you mean."

"I know, but if you do see them"—she looked around before continuing—"could you tell Stan thank you? For saving our lives?"

"Don't worry." Frank forced a cracked smile. "When I see him, I'll make sure he and his wife get *exactly* what's coming to them."

—⁂—

"Give it to me," Ramona Marconi said, her expression all business. She was wearing a red dress, looking more like a fashionista than the leader of the Mala Noche gang. "And don't spare the details."

"Yes, ma'am." Boris Ryker, her second in command, wore a gray suit. He held a data pad in scarred hands, his fingers flying across its surface, calling up information from the past few weeks. "Do you want the good news or the bad news?"

"Don't play coy."

"All right, then," Boris answered, getting to business. "Francine Solomon got another of our guys."

"Who?"

"Anthony Sikes."

"Huh." Ramona swirled a glass of liquor in her hand. "I don't know him."

"He was a small-time dealer." Boris adjusted his tie. "Worked the shops on First and Fifth."

"Was he a high earner?"

"Yeah," the burly man admitted reluctantly.

"Damn." Ramona's eyes narrowed in disgust. "Where's he now?"

"Saint Christopher's Hospital. Under lock and key."

Ramona gave him a quick side-glance. "He say anything we have to worry about?"

"He's in a coma, ma'am. He's not saying anything."

"We can't take the chance. Send someone to the hospital to deal with him."

"Our guys can't get close," Boris said, pausing before adding. "The guards aren't letting us through."

"Aren't *letting* you?!" Ramona shot him an incredulous look. "We're the Mala Noches! The guards should be terrified of us!"

"With the Solomons doing their thing, everyone's getting bold. Even the guards."

"Damn." Ramona finished her glass in one gulp and then strolled to the stocked bar in the back of her room. After pouring herself another glass and downing it, she looked at him. "What's the GCPD doing?"

"Our informants say they're planning something," Boris answered, checking his watch. "They've assigned two detectives to the Solomon case."

"The Solomon case." Ramona chuckled mirthlessly. "Like it's old times."

"The detectives they've assigned are Julie Benz and Frank Drake."

"The first one to see them face to face?" Ramona gave her second in command a incredulous look. "Do they really think that's a good idea?"

"Actually," Boris corrected in a respectful voice, "Kate Barrow was the first to see them."

"Whatever." Ramona waved off his answer before taking a sip from her drink. "What are the detectives doing now?"

"Interviewing witnesses, including a little girl Sikes kidnapped."

"Are they going to do more than that?"

"I'm assuming," Boris answered calmly. "Either way, the Solomons are picking us off one by one. We wait for the GCPD to do anything, there'll be none of us left."

"Yeah, I know," Ramona agreed, putting her glass on the counter. "It's about survival."

"So what's the plan, boss?"

"Put the word out to whoever's left. It's time for a meet."

—∞—

"Okay, then," Frank started as Benz drove to them to the freeway. "What've we learned?"

"The Solomons are acting benevolent despite their grudge against the city." She got out a deep swallow. "Against us."

"Francine counseling Monica Rambeau. Stan saving the factory workers. It's like they're doing an extreme neighborhood watch."

"And they're targeting the low-income neighborhoods."

"Seriously?" Frank asked, giving Benz a worried look as his nails scraped against the fabric of his seat. *They're pulling on that branch?*

"Yeah. The abandoned church where Francine got Sikes?" Benz answered, keeping her eyes on the road ahead of them. *The factory fire Stan stopped? They're all in poorer neighborhoods."

"Explains why our boys haven't gotten calls from the people living there," Frank said, nodding in understanding. "It's like they're expecting the Solomons to do our jobs."

"And then some," Benz added, cocking her head at his passenger-side window. "Look over there."

What's she showing me? Frank wondered, following her gaze. "Wait, when did *this* happen?!"

"Are you kidding? This has been going on for the past year."

They had arrived on Madison Avenue, but it looked *nothing* like it did from Frank's memory. The streets were too clean, not a single crack in the pavement.

The air smelled too fresh.

Kids played in open fire hydrants that hadn't worked in years.

Even the buildings looked brand new, as though the entire place had been super-gentrified.

Frank turned back to his partner, looking shaken to his core. "The Solomons did all this? All while I was gone?"

"Yup," Benz said as she turned a corner.

"How?" Frank fought back a curse, refusing to lose his cool any more than he already had. "There's only two of them!"

"Yeah, about that ..."

"Benz?"

"There are rumblings," she answered, refusing to look at him, "that there are more."

"More?" Frank felt his stomach flip-flop. "As in more people"—*gulp!*—"like them?"

"Yep." Benz nodded, keeping her eyes on the road. "That's the rumor."

Please tell me that's not true! Frank swallowed nervously, his throat going dry. I'm gone for a few week ... "And why do people think this?"

"Because there are sites like this all over the city."

All over the city?! Frank felt his scars tingle, forcing a strangled breath from his lips. "How many?!"

"Ten, for now. Always in the worst neighborhoods, which are now the best ones," Benz explained, giving her a partner an amused look. "People are flocking to live in them."

It just gets worse! Frank thought, doing his best to calm his beating heart. *The deeper I get in this case, the worse it gets!* "We got proof of this?"

"Back at the station. But why go that far? I can just take you to one of the gardens."

—𝕨—

The look on his face! Benz almost laughed at Frank's incredulous expression.

"I'm sorry," he asked, giving her a freaked out look. "Did you say, the gardens? Like that's somethiing I'm just supposed to know?"

"Yeah," she answered, turning off the main road. "In fact, we're near one now."

"Take me there, partner."

Sighing, she turned the car around a corner, arriving on Madison Avenue. As she parked the car, the Madison Garden spread out before them.

"Jesus," Frank gasped, his eyes wide in shock.

It had once been a desolate park for tired-eyed hookers and depressed homeless. Nothing had grown there but meth and heroin addiction.

But now, before their eyes, stood a dense garden with plants as tall as redwoods. Healthy ferns reflected light from the sun above. Trees flanked the edges of the garden, with happy kids playing hide-and-seek amid the leaves.

"My... god," Frank whispered, looking frozen in his seat. "I can't believe I'm seeing this!"

"Thought the same thing when I saw it the first time," Benz said, amused by his awe. *Weeks ago.* "Takes a bit to get your head around it, eh?"

"You're telling me the Solomons did this?"

"Yup."

"All of this?"

"Like I said, they had help."

"Right, their friends," Frank said, his tone a volatile mixture of desperate, frantic, and angry. "Has anyone *actually* seen these 'friends'?"

"According to the people we've talked to," Benz asked, her amusement turning to worry at Frank's reaction, "no." *Not that we can trust them to be reliable.*

"Why?"

"Because like Stan and Francine, they only come out at night."

—⁂—

"Why does Marconi wanna meet here?" Hiram Diego, of the Diego Crime Family, demanded as he sat at a round table on the top floor of a three-story brick house. "There's a meth lab downstairs!"

Three other figures, dressed in high-end finery, shared the room with him. They were the leaders of the remaining crime families in Gateway City.

The last ones standing.

"She wants to talk about the Solomons," Ashley Mendes, of the Mendes crime family, answered. A red-haired beauty in a green dress, she took birdlike sips from a glass of wine in her hand. Behind her stood her bodyguard, his looming presence promising pain to anyone who upset her.

"Yeah, but why here?" Hiram demanded. His hair was coated with so much grease it looked as though he wore an oil slick on his head. "Why not at the Ice Pick Club? You know, like usual?"

"Because the Solomons burned it down a week ago," Archie Jones, of the Jones crime family, answered. He was wearing a pinstriped suit and was presently checking his watch. "But she'd better get here soon. I don't like being out in the open like this."

"So the club's gone. Okay, then," Hiram conceded. "But why here, dammit?!" An angry bundle of nerves, he got up from his seat. "There aren't even any drinks here, the cheap fuck!"

"Because no one's gonna think we'd meet in a derelict building like this," Jonah Cooper, of the Cooper crime family, chimed in. He was a slim man with a hawklike nose and an entitled sneer on his face. "Not with her product being made downstairs." He shuddered at the sight of a rat scurrying across the room. "But you're right. She needs to hurry the hell up."

—⚒—

It's getting late, Frank thought, checking his watch. "Has anyone gone *inside* any of these gardens?"

"Gone inside?" Benz asked in a gentle voice, "Frank, some people LIVE in them."

"You're kidding me," Frank said as his gaze traveled up the garden's wall of trees, ending at the canopy they'd created, over a hundred feet above the ground. "Who would live in a place like this?"

"The homeless, for starters."

Oh. Those people. "And we haven't cleared them out?"

"Frank," Benz turned to fully face him, one hand on his shoulder, the other resting on the car's steering wheel, "we're too scared to even go INSIDE one of these things."

That's impossible, Frank thought, not even wanting to hear her say such a thing, ever again. *Us? Afraid? Of anything in our city? No freaking way!*

""Did I say scared?" Benz asked, as if realizing she'd said too much, in way too cavalier a tone. "I meant cautious. This is a brand-new era, Frank."

Be it ever so humble. "Well, *this* member of the GCPD isn't." He practically kicked open his passenger door. "What about you?"

"Lead the way."

—⚏—

I got to watch how I talk to him. Benz let out a short breath as they stepped into the garden. *Unintentionally challenged his masculinity, and now he's going in the garden to prove himself.*

"Jesus," Frank exclaimed quietly. "Have you seen anything like this?"

"Not in this city."

The inside looked like something out of a fantasy film. Lush green decorated everything, from the blades of grass to the tall trees that acted like a wall from the outside world.

"Eden," Benz whispered. "It looks like the garden of Eden."

"Didn't think you were a believer," Frank said, giving her an impressed look.

"I'm not, but I read."

The garden had animals. Dogs, cats, and birds. That didn't shock them too much.

But their size? *That* threw them for a loop!

Benz gawked at cats the size of tigers, dogs the size of lions, and pigeons the size of eagles. *What are these animals eating to get so big? And who's feeding it to them?* She expected to see antelope or giraffes next. Maybe even a water buffalo.

"Where'd all these animals come from?" Frank asked, breaking through her thoughts.

"My guess?" Benz suggested, shrugging her shoulders. "They're regular animals that wandered in and never left."

"But to be this big?"

"Has to be something they're eating. Something the garden's producing." *This your handiwork, Stan? Or Francine's?* "They've been altered by the ecosystem."

"They're not the only ones," Frank commented, pointing at a group of approaching people. "We got incoming."

Whoa. Benz took a step back in wary surprise. The shortest of the group looked to be six feet tall. The tallest looked well over seven feet.

155

They were dressed in the remains of clothing they had grown too big for. Most wore no shoes, but they didn't seem to care. As a matter of fact, they didn't even seem to notice.

But they sure as hell noticed them.

"I know some of them," Frank cut in. "Yeah. Some of these cats are homeless."

"Used to be, Frank," Benz corrected quickly. "Used to be."

"Well, they still gotta recognize this," he declared, reaching in his trench coat.

"Hope you're reaching for your badge," Benz declared dryly. "Because a gun would *not* be a good idea."

—⚏—

Frank *had* been reaching for his gun but changed gears after hearing Benz's words. *This is why we're a good team.* But if the threatening looks on the people's faces was any indication, a badge wouldn't be any better. *How'd we get this hated?* He searched the group, hoping to find someone he recognized. "Wait a minute …"

"What?" Benz asked, eyeing the way they came.

Yes! Frank locked eyes with one of the taller men in the group. "I've seen this guy before."

"Frank," Benz said, eyeing the exit a few paces behind them, "we need to get out of here…"

He raised a hand, motioning for silence as he stepped forward. "Gary?"

The taller man stopped, his lips curling into an embarrassed smile. "Frank?"

"Gary Lennox!"

"Frank Drake!" The man's smile went from embarrassed to sure. "Look at you!"

"Hot damn!" Frank held out his hand as Gary approached him. "How are you?!"

"Good to see you," the mammoth of a man declared, lifting the bewildered detective off his feet in a friendly bear hug. "Ain't seen you in a minute!"

———*∞*———

Oh, thank God. Benz let out a breath she didn't know she had been holding as the group peeled off, going back to whatever they had been doing before seeing them. *Still bothered we didn't see them until they were right on us.*

Was that because of the garden?

Or the Solomons' influence?

"Where you been, man?" Gary asked, his voice like thunder. "It's been an age!"

"Screw where I've been," Frank answered, rubbing his ears. "How'd you get this big?!"

"Oh, yeah," Gary answered, glancing at his muscles. "You can thank this place for that."

Frank threw Benz a wary look. "How's that?"

———*∞*———

"So, man," Gary said, taking a seat on a nearby outcropping, "where you been?"

"Rehab," Frank answered, taking a seat across from him. He motioned for Benz to do the same.

"No way!" Gary exclaimed, his eyes wide with surprise. "Really?!"

"Didn't you hear what the Solomons did to me?"

The taller, altered man gave Frank a surprised double-take. "Wait, when?"

"When they kidnapped Kate Barrow! It was in the papers!" *I've got the clippings!*

"Do I look like I read the news?"

"I guess you did have bigger concerns," Frank admitted, gesturing to the garden around them.

"Frank," Benz cut in, an annoyed look on her face. "Care to introduce me to—"

Right, got caught up. "Sorry, Benz," Frank said, pointing a thumb at Gary. "This is Gary Lennox. War veteran, homeless man, and—"

"Citizen of this garden," the large man finished, cutting Frank off.

157

"Nice to meet you," Benz said, before getting down to business. "How long have you lived here, Mr. Lennox?"

"Mr. Lennox!" Gary took a moment to bask in the sound of the name. "Been a long time since I've been called Mr. Lennox!" He gave Benz a warm look. "I've been in this garden, since it popped up a year ago."

"It's been here a year?" Frank asked, his eyes wide with surprise. Benz had told him, but hearing it again still bowled him over. *It's only been a year.*

"Oh, yes," Garry answered, nodding. "And thank God for it, or I'd be dead."

"Oh, come on! You're exaggerating!"

"If you boys ever checked on us," Gary declared, his face taking on a grim expression, "you'd know that."

"Okay, okay," Frank said, raising his hands defensively. "I get it, okay? We screwed up. The Solomons are great. They're freaking messiahs."

———※———

Nice tack, Frank. "How'd you end up here?" Benz asked, wanting to stay on Gary's good side.

"My sister ran a diner. They were robbed one night, and she was killed." Gary paused, biting his lip before continuing. "With her gone, I lost her house. I ended up on the streets. My mental issues got worse, and my body followed."

"That's when I met him," Frank said, letting out a weary sigh. "Covered in rashes."

"Skin cancer," Gary said, his brow furrowed in shame. "I was hard to look at."

"I'm sorry you had to go through that." Benz reached out to give his rock-hard shoulder a supportive squeeze. "Really."

"How'd you end up here?" Frank cut in.

"I heard about it," Gary answered, his chest puffed with pride. "Thought it'd be a good place to rest my bones. The homeless camps aren't safe. Never have been despite the mayor's promises."

"They kept you off the streets."

"And in pens, like freaking cattle."

"Out of sight, out of mind," Benz whispered, more to herself than anyone else. Though she did nothing to cover her voice. "To make Gateway City look good for voters."

"Easy, Benz," Frank said, shooting her a stern glance. "Remember who the good guys are."

"So I came here." Gary stretched his arms out for a second time. "We all did. And after a few days, my aches and pains went away."

"The garden *healed* you?" Benz asked, her eyes wide with surprise. *How is that possible?*

"It healed all of us," Gary clarified, nodding like a grateful dog with a bone. "Not sure how. Maybe it's the air. Or the soil. Or the water. All I know is, after a few nights, my headaches went away. I can think clearly again. Sharp as I ever was."

"And now you're a Solomon fan," Frank declared sarcastically. "Right?"

"What can I say, Frank? They made me feel pride in myself again. Anyone that does that, without wanting anything in return, is aces in my book."

—៕—

"Is everyone in the gardens like that?" Frank asked as he and Benz walked back to their car.

"As in?"

"Drinking the Solomons' Kool-Aid."

"Honestly? Yes, they are," Benz answered as she got behind the wheel. "And if they're anything like your Gary Lennox, they got reason to."

You seem to be lapping it up too. "What about smart people?" Frank clarified, keeping the irritation out of his voice. "Scientists. Scholars. People like that?"

"When the gardens first started popping up, experts from all over the country came here. Even took home samples."

"And?"

"The samples died the second they left the city lines."

"So the country knows how bad we screwed up," Frank mumbled, kicking the street in growing frustration. *How bad I screwed up.* "Perfect."

"The scientific community does," Benz clarified patiently. "The average person? Not so much."

"Hold on." Frank shot her a look of disbelief. "I get the average person is easy to distract, but you're telling me no one, outside of the eggheads, know the Solomons exist?"

"Oh, they know—they just don't care," Benz clarified grimly. "A news program about them came out six months ago, filmed on Bridge Row."

"That's not far from here!"

"No, it's not. It showed footage of Stan and Francine using their powers." Benz leaned closer to Frank, her face taking on a conspiratorial expression. "I heard the journalists even got inside their fortress."

"Wait! The Solomons have a fortress?!" This was becoming too much for Frank. In the time he had been gone, Stan and Francine had gone from an angry couple to an occupying force! Complete with brainwashed supporters!

"Yes, they do, but it only comes out at night."

"And people outside of Gateway still don't believe they exist? How is that possible?!"

"It's like police brutality," Benz answered matter-of-factly. "People have seen countless examples of it in the news but still don't believe it exists."

You had to take it there, didn't you? "C'mon, Benz ..."

"And you know why?"

"I have a feeling you're going to tell me."

"Because people don't want to believe it exists, Frank," Benz answered, a deadpan look in her eyes. "If they can think that way about police brutality, they can think the same about the Solomons."

———

Letting out a tired sigh, Frank checked his watch. "So not only are the Solomons making us look like fools, they're turning Gateway City into their damn playground."

"Only the low-income parts, Frank," Benz clarified, giving him a side glance. *I told you this earlier.*

"Why just *those* parts?"

"They seem to have an affinity for the people who live in those areas." Benz stared at the garden, feeling a subtle tug from its trees. A pain lashed at her head, making her blink.

"So they're allergic to money now?"

"More like privilege," Benz corrected as the pain became a dull ache. "Can't say for sure why."

"Might be because Barrow's 'privileged' parents were integral in getting their daughter cleared of their son's death."

I do NOT like the sound of that, Benz thought, shooting her partner an irritated look. "How?"

"By influencing the jurors." Frank stared at the trees. "Bet Madsen worked 'em, too."

"You've got to be kidding me." Benz shot him a disgusted look. "Seriously?"

"Yeah," Frank answered, a weariness to his tone that seemed to come from his bones.

Good lord, the graft in this town, Benz thought, rolling her eyes in disgust. It's enough to drive a sane person crazy! "How'd you figure that out? Seriously?"

"While I was in rehab, I got Barrow's case file. I put the pieces together."

"And I'm sure Chief Loeb approved that, right?"

"I didn't tell him," Frank answered snidely. "But he's gotta know what Madsen did."

"All this graft," Benz moaned as her dull ache worsened. "I'm starting to think the Solomons have a point. I *don't* like thinking that."

"I don't either," Frank agreed, clapping her on the shoulder. "That's why we gotta catch 'em. To show everyone that the system still works. That *we* work." He gestured to the road. "Now let's get out of here."

—∿—

"Anyone from your crew left?" Hiram asked, taking a seat next to Ashley Mendez.

"Why would I tell you?" she asked, looking at him as though he was a rattlesnake.

"One, to make idle conversation," he answered, gesturing to the other bosses, who had withdrawn to different corners of the room. "And two, because next to me, they're the only ones left to talk to."

"I know." Ashley let out a tired sigh. "God, *what* happened to us?"

"We got outclassed, that's what."

"You're talking like we're already dead."

"We are, Mrs. Mendez," Hiram declared, taking a swig of alcohol from a flask he kept in his breast pocket. "I'm getting the last of my family out tonight."

"That would be your daughter, right?"

His posture straightened. "How'd you know about her?"

"I got spies in your crew," Ashley answered, giving him a superior smile. "Just like you got spies in mine."

"Not bad." Hiram cocked a glance at the other bosses. "Got any in theirs?"

"A few," she answered, leaning closer as her bodyguard hovered over the two of them. "But they got found out. And killed."

"Killed, huh?"

"He," Ashley answered, pointing to Johan Cooper looking out a window, "had one of my spies' head delivered to me. For Christmas."

"Now that's cold," Hiram whistled, sounding impressed. "Efficient, but cold."

"And yet the Solomons dismantled his heroin chain last week."

"Which one? Stan or Francine?"

"Both. Like it was a fricking dinner date. What about you?"

"I got intel on their families," Hiram answered, picking some dust mites off his tailored suit. "Even threatened a few. Not me, of course, my lower-tier flunkies. Told them if they did the job, they'd get a top spot."

"Let me guess," Ashley said, her green eyes twinkling with grim knowledge. "The Solomons headed you off at the pass."

"I'll let you know," he answered, giving her a sad wink, "if I ever find out what happened to them."

—⚏—

"Come on," Frank said as Benz followed him into a convenience store called Hecate's Handiworks a few blocks from the garden.

"What are we doing here?"

"It's a hangout of mine," he answered. "After what we just saw, I need a drink."

"That *can't* be the only reason."

"Frank Drake!" a young Lebanese woman called out from behind the counter. "Good to see you up and around!"

"Ayman!" Frank smiled at her. "How are you?"

"How are *you*?" Dressed in black, she moved from behind the counter to give him a hug. "I assumed the worst!"

"How's business?" Frank asked, taking the short woman in his arms. *How about that?* He thought, smiling to himself. *Someone actually happy to see me!*

"Doing well," Ayman answered, looking over Frank's shoulder at Benz. "And is this the great Detective Julie Benz?"

"I'm great?" she asked, pointing at her chest while looking confused.

"Yes, you are, ma'am."

"Then … yes," Benz said hesitantly.

"Well, then." Ayman walked over to her, taking her hand in hers. "It's an honor to meet you."

"It's an honor to meet you, too," Benz said, looking uncomfortably awkward, shaking her hand.

I thought I was great, Frank thought, shaking off a spark of jealousy. "Now that we all know each other, we can—"

"How'd you and Frank 'meet'? Benz asked, cocking her head in his direction.

"First, let me formally introduce myself." Ayman managed a gracious bow. "I am Ayman Khoury, owner of Hecate's Handiworks. I've lived in Gateway City for ten years after leaving my home country of Lebanon. I am Frank's eyes on the street. I believe you'd call me a CI."

"Criminal informant," Benz rattled off the term. "And I'm guessing not on the books."

"By my request. To keep my family safe."

"But you don't look like a criminal."

Nice one, Benz. Frank shot Ayman an apologetic look. "She's not, and never was."

Benz shot him a confused look. "Then how'd she—"

"Some gangland punks were giving her trouble a few years ago. I took care of them, off the books. In return, she keeps an eye on things for me. Let's me know if something pops off."

"And I'm guessing something's popped off," Ayman declared, flashing a knowing, but also a worried, look at the two detectives.

"Master of the understatement," Frank answered, nodding his head.

———⚉———

"What's the word on the Solomons?" Frank asked, sitting in Ayman's backroom alongside Benz. "Anything?"

"So you *are* investigating them," she said, handing them cans of soda.

"Yes, we are," Benz answered before Frank had a chance. "The both of us." Dammit, Frank, she thought, giving the dusty room a quick once-over, this had better be necessary!

"Interesting. Who approved that?"

"My boss," Frank answered sourly. "Correction, my *new* boss."

"Chief Michael Loeb," Ayman said, lighting a pipe. "He came here once. Part of a community outreach thing."

"Huh," Frank said, grunting in surprise, "I didn't think the man ever left his office."

"He's left it more than his predecessor so far."

"Yeah, about him ..." Frank winced, looking away before taking a gulp of his soda.

"Sorry," Ayman said in a quiet voice. "I'd forgotten."

"Forgot what?" Benz asked, her expression perking up. "What's he talking about?"

"Chief Madsen," Frank answered in a grim voice after giving the backroom a quick once over, "He's dead."

"I ..." Her jaw dropped in surprise. "Really?"

"You didn't know that?"

"All I knew was that he'd been drummed out of the force," Benz answered, gawking at Frank in surprise. "When did he die?"

"A month ago," came the regretful reply. "Surprised you didn't know that."

Please don't tell me Stan killed him, Benz begged mentally. "How'd he die?"

"I'll tell you later." Frank put a finger to his lips. "Let's focus on the case for now."

But ...! Benz wanted to know more but noticed Ayman staring at her. "Fine."

—∞—

"Dammit, when's Maroni getting here?!" Archie Jones blurted out, squashing a roach under his boot. "I got better things to do than this!"

"Like what? Run and hide?" Hiram got up from his seat. "Calm the fuck down."

"You popping wise?!" Archie pulled out twin pistols from his pockets, pointing them at the rival crime boss's chest. "You wanna get capped?!"

"Archie the Bull," Hiram taunted, standing his ground. "That's what the streets call you. Turns out you're just a bitch."

"That's it! You're getting capped!"

"Enough!" Ashley called out, her bodyguard slamming his gigantic fists on the table next to her. "We already got the Solomons killing us! We don't need to be killing each other!"

"Then where the *hell's* Maroni?!" Archie started pacing around the room, nervously eyeing a nearby window. "I'm not waiting here forever! Not with nightfall coming!"

—∞—

"Much as I hate to say it," Ayman declared after taking a puff from her pipe, "the GCPD has had this coming for a while."

"That's what folks have been telling us," Frank said through gritted teeth. "Never mind that we've been doing the best we can."

"If that were true"—Ayman gave him a stern look — "the Solomons wouldn't be here."

A compliment about the Solomons, Benz thought, stifling a chuckle, from a friend, no less! She shot her partner a curious look. *I think I like this one.*

"Yeah, I know," Frank admitted grudgingly as he balanced his body on the fold-out chair.

"But it's not just the GCPD that share blame in this," Ayman continued. "City Hall does too. And honestly, so do we, the people. If we'd held you folks to a higher standard, the Solomons wouldn't have felt the need to be who they are." She cleared his throat. "Or do what they are doing."

"Speaking of that, how *are* the people reacting to what they're doing?"

"They feel pride in their neighborhoods. They haven't felt that in a while."

"Even with the Solomons in the news?" Benz asked, intrigued by Ayman's answers.

"For us, they've made the news something to look forward to, not something to dread."

I didn't think about that. Benz cocked her head in new awareness. *I should have.* "Given what your people have been going through, I'm sure you're long overdue for some good news."

"Acknowledgment from the Solomon Whisperer," Ayman stated, showing off a wicked grin. "A badge of honor."

"The Solomon Whisperer?" Frank looked at her in disbelief. "That's what people are calling her?"

"That's what *we're* calling her."

—◆—

"What in the ..." Hiram approached a window overlooking the parking lot as the other crime bosses talked behind him. "Hey! Guys!"

Everyone fell silent and turned to him.

The hair on the back of Hiram's neck stood on end as fingers of electricity danced across the surface of the window. He jumped as a massive lightning bolt struck the ground outside.

The other bosses leaped to their feet.

Another bolt struck the same spot. Then a third. And a fourth.

Then multiple bolts struck in a circular pattern, closing around the building like a vise.

"It's the Solomons!" Hiram declared, taking a step back from the window. "They found us!"

"Uggh!" Benz put a hand to her head as that familiar throb returned.

"Whoa." Frank was already on his feet. "You okay, partner?"

"I'm fine," she lied, waving him away.

"You sure?"

"Yes, I'm sure," Benz answered, trying to keep the irritation out of her voice. "I'm just having a headache, that's all."

"Interesting time for a headache," Ayman commented, a wary look on her face.

Don't look at me like that! "My headaches aren't important," Benz declared as the room spun around her. "It's just exhaustion. We need to talk about the Solomons and how to stop them." *You are* not *cutting me out of this case!*

"And we will." Frank helped her to her feet. "But why don't you use the bathroom?"

"Frank, I'm—"

"For me," he added, giving her wrist a quick squeeze. To his credit, the puppy-dog eyes he put on showed genuine concern.

If not barely concealed impatience.

I got no say in this, do I? Benz grabbed the edge of her chair to keep from kissing the floor. "Guess I could use a little me time."

"The bathroom's there," Ayman said, gesturing to the back of the room. "Take all the time you need."

Oh, how generous, Benz thought as she stumbled off. "Be right back."

—⚶—

"You see that?" Frank asked once Benz had gone.

"Of course I saw it," Ayman answered, a troubled look on her face. "I'm just glad *you* saw it."

"Why?"

"Because it means that unlike your comrades, you're not ignoring what's in front of you."

—⚶—

Cold. That was all Francine felt.

As she strode through the searing flames of what had once been a meth house, all she felt was cold.

She was deaf to the yammering screams and pleas of fools who hadn't had the good sense to leave when they had the chance. Why else had she done that show with the lightning earlier?

Before Brian's death, the sight of people burning to death would have filled her with horror. That the flames were her own would have filled her with guilt.

Now they only added to the cold.

—⚶—

She enjoys this too much, Stan thought as he hovered over the meth house, seeing people running for their lives. *Way too much.*

He floated just above the building's roof, arms folded across his chest. What passed for a heart thumped so rhythmically he could dance to the beat.

Not that he'd be doing that anymore. Not since Brian had died.

No, not died. Was murdered.

I could be planting another garden, Stan thought, looking up at the moon. *Or saving someone who deserves it.* He let out a weary sigh. *Instead,*

I'm here. Making sure my wife doesn't become a bigger monster than the one who took Brian from us.

Kate. Freaking. Barrow.

—⋘—

How? Ramona Maroni's jaw hung in dumb shock as her motorcade came upon the pyre her meth house had become. *How did they know what we were doing?*

"Mrs. Maroni?" Boris radioed from a truck at the head of the motorcade. "What do you want us to do?"

"Get us out of here," she answered in a frightened whisper, "before the Solomons see us."

"Yes, ma'am."

The motorcade reversed course, quickly and quietly, as crimson flames lit up the night.

—⋘—

Stop. Benz sat on a toilet seat, trying to hold her head together. *Please, stop.* The second the bathroom door closed behind her, her head lit up like a four-alarm fire. She barely got out a groan before falling into the closest stall she could find. *Good thing Frank didn't see that.*

Feeling the contents of her stomach welling up her throat, she turned and vomited into the toilet she had been sitting on. *Or that.*

She flushed the contents of her stomach down, then sat back on the toilet, closing her eyes tightly as the throbbing persisted. *What's causing this?!*

That was when she heard tongues of flames crackling around the stall!

And what is this? Smoke drifted into Benz's nose as she wrenched open the door. *Holy shit!* Her jaw dropped at the destruction around her.

And at the center of it stood Francine Solomon, her eyes wide with surprise!

—⋘—

Getting real tired of people digging on us! "I get it," Frank said hastily. "We got a lot to work on. But I'm worried about my partner."

"She does seem a little high strung." Ayman arched her brow in acknowledgment. "I could feel her ... stress from here."

"She's been through a lot," Frank stated. "And I wasn't there to help her."

"You were hurt."

"So was she. In fact, she got it worse!"

"Did she now?" Ayman leaned back in her chair, giving Frank her full attention. "How?"

"Do you know what happened to me the night Stan and Francine took Kate Barrow?"

"The papers listed you and Benz as among the injured," Ayman answered, taking another puff off her pipe. "They didn't say how badly."

"Stan threw me through Kate's front door," Frank revealed. *Or did he blast me out?* "Anyway, I hit the ground hard, but besides that, nothing else happened."

"You must've had internal injuries."

"That's the thing," Frank continued, the guilt like a bitter taste on his lips. "I really didn't. I suffered some ear damage when Stan and Francine blew up Barrow's house. But that was it. And besides, *everyone* suffered ear damage that night."

"Including your partner?"

"No. She was *in* Barrow's house when it exploded."

—— ᙏ ——

You ... Francine gawked at a detective standing, against all logic, in front of her.

No, she was sitting. Francine couldn't see what she was sitting on— it looked like air—but she was sitting.

You look familiar, Francine thought, racking her brain for where she had seen the dark-haired woman before. *It was recent ... Where ...* Then it hit her. *Benz! Julie Benz!* Her brow arched in surprise. *When we took Kate Barrow!*

The one that got Stan to give her back. To let Brian's killer go free!

You shouldn't be here. Francine's bewilderment turned to rage. *Why are you here?!*

Her lips forming a firm line on her face, Francine pointed a finger at Benz's horrified eyes. Before she could fire off a lightning bolt, Benz's image blipped away, like a character from a glitching video game.

—⚏—

Well now, Stan thought, seeing Detective Benz blip in front of him like a glitchy TV image. *This is unexpected.* "A bit more than professional curiosity, eh, Detective?"

She cocked her head in confusion.

She can't hear me. How is she doing this? Is she doing this? Stan stayed where he was, curious to see what she'd do next. *Or is someone doing this for her?*

He saw glimpses of a stall around her looking like a blurred image. *She's in a bathroom?* "Really hope you weren't in the middle of—"

As she reached for him, Benz's image blipped away.

—⚏—

Jesus! Benz shot up from the toilet seat as though it were made of hot coals, her hand outstretched. *I saw them!*

Stan and Francine, killing people in a meth house not far from where they were! And not only did she see them, they saw her!

Wait … Benz felt something on her arm, saw it was soot and ash. *That's impossible. I was here the whole time!*

Did she … teleport to the Solomons' exact location?!

Focus on what's important, Julie! Benz got to her feet and flew out of the bathroom.

—⚏—

"Benz survived a lightning strike?" Ayman's eyes went wide. "From the Solomons?"

"Yeah, she did," Frank answered, nodding.

"She doesn't even look hurt!"

171

At least not on the outside. "I think the Solomons protected her."

"And that's why people see her as—"

"The Solomon Whisperer," Frank finished, nodding, again. "Speaking of which, how long has *that* been going on?"

"Since the Solomons kicked off their campaign," Ayman answered grimly. "The people need to believe someone can talk to Stan and Francine. To reason with them if they go too far. And they feel Benz is that person since they've seen her consistently chasing them."

"Chasing them? How?"

"Arriving at scenes of their wonders, oftentimes right on their heels."

She's following them. Frank was about to ask more questions when Benz burst out of the bathroom.

"We have to go!" She brushed past them, making a beeline for the exit.

"Benz?!" Frank looked at the bathroom, then at her. "What's happening?!"

"The Solomons are attacking a meth house not far from here! We can catch them!"

Heard nothing over the wire. "How do you know this?!"

"I just do, okay?!" Benz shouted as she left the room. "Come on!"

Dammit... Frank shot Ayman a stricken look as he followed her out.

Hungry flames consumed the meth house from the inside out as Francine watched. Her smile twisted into an annoyed frown at an incessant whimpering. *Where is that coming from?* Tracking the pained sounds to a wrecked table, she threw it aside in one motion.

A scared thug pointing a gun at her.

"Do you really think that's a good idea?"

He lowered the weapon.

Smart boy. Francine cocked her head and regarded the thug. "What's your name?"

"Thomas," he answered. "John Thomas."

Odd name. "How old are you? Really?"

"Seventeen."

So young. Francine's eyes widened, but she recovered quickly. "Do you have family?"

"A mom and dad."

"Do they know"—she gestured at the lab around them—"that you do this?"

"No," he answered, looking into her eyes. "I don't tell them."

"I hope not," Francine said, "because good parents wouldn't let you do this."

"Someone's gotta pay the bills."

"Why can't *they* get jobs?"

"They *have* jobs." The young man pulled himself out of the wreckage and got to his feet. He was a small, wiry boy dressed in black. His innocent face made him look younger than he said he was. "But their jobs don't pay enough."

Reminds me of Brian, Francine thought, momentarily taken aback by the similarity. She blinked back the tear that threatened to run down her cheek. "So you're doing this?"

"It's good money." He took a quick glance around the lab. "Well, *was* good money."

"It's not your job to support your parents."

"But it is my job to do my part."

Touché. Francine cocked her head to the exit. "Get out of here."

"Wait," John practically shouted, "what am I gonna—?"

"Go," she snapped. "Before I change my mind."

—⚏—

Benz drove through Gateway City's streets like a woman possessed, weaving around cars and pedestrians as though they were part of an obstacle course.

Jesus! Frank stifled a yelp of fear as their car took a turn on two wheels. "Keep us in one piece, Benz!"

Her gaze remained laser-focused on the road like a woman possessed. "Benz!"

—⚏—

We're having a talk about this when we get home. Stan coasted to the ground in front of the brick building. *Believe that.*

People ran past him, a horrified look on their faces. He tried to ignore them, but a random kid ran right into him anyway.

"Shit!" The kid cursed, jumping back from Stan as if he were a rattlesnake.

"Whoa, kid," Stan said, keeping him from falling to the ground. *Looks so much like Brian.* "Stay calm."

"You ... you're Stan Solomon!"

"Yes, I am. Are you hurt?"

"Huh? Uh, no!"

"You sure?" Stan pointed at the right side of the kid's face.

"Uh, right." He touched it, came away with blood. "Must've been when the table hit me."

"A table *hit* you?"

"Yeah, that lady inside ..."

"My wife," Stan said calmly.

"Yeah, she brought the lab down!"

Dammit, Francine! "At least no one died."

"A lot of people died!" The kid looked past him with a clear worry on this face. "Crap, I gotta get home!"

"Get home?" Stan made as if to check his watch, then remembered he didn't have one. Or a cell phone, for that matter. "How far is it?"

"What? You gonna fly me home?"

"If I have to."

"But other people! The kid looked around him and Stan with naked desperation. "They need ...!"

"They're not kids," Stan declared in a voice that brooked no argument. "Speaking of kids, how old are you? Fifteen? Sixteen?"

"I ... I ... uh, guess!" The kid took a moment to swallow a lungful of air. Then he started to cough.

"Yeah." Stan took the boy in his arms. "I'm getting you out of here."

—⁓—

Yes. Francine let out a sigh of relief as she felt Stan fly away with John. *Means I can … relish this.* Another drug den wiped off the face of the earth.

As for you lot, she thought, seeing the charred bodies, *I gave you time to leave. You* chose *to stay here. This is your fault.*

And it wasn't like *all* the workers had died!

But the survivors wouldn't work in a place like this again. And she — Francine Solomon — had made sure of that. She beat her chest loudly in celebration, bellowing like King Kong.

—⚉—

At a hospital a mile from the burning meth house, Stan touched down. He eyed various people watching the blaze, the flames illuminating the night. *Guess I'm not the center of attention.* "Excuse me!" he bellowed, revealing the kid in his arms. "This young man needs help!"

Orderlies rushed to him with a stretcher, taking the coughing boy from his arms.

"What happened to him?" a nursed asked without looking at him.

"Smoke inhalation," Stan answered as she checked John for other injuries.

"Where'd he come from?"

"A fire, not far from here." *I'm not exactly lying.*

"You have something to do with that fire?" The nurse finally looked up at Stan, showing an incredible pair of amber-colored eyes. Her gaze was sharp, exacting, and not showing a hint of fear.

"Is that really important?"

"It could be. I need to know how long he's been like this. What was he doing?"

"What his parents should have been doing," Stan answered. "Working to put food on the table."

"A little harsh, but I'll take it," the nurse said, ordering her coworkers to wheel the coughing kid into the emergency room. "Are you staying?"

"I can't."

"He might want to thank you. You did save his life."

"Make sure he's okay, and I'll come back," Stan said before shooting up into the sky.

—⁂—

Benz and Frank arrived at the meth house just in time to see Francine Solomon strolling out of a wall of flames.

We're not ready for this. Frank gave Benz an anxious look. "What now?"

"We talk to her," she answered, putting the car in park. "She controls their powers."

"How the hell do you know that?!"

"Calm down, Frank."

Woman puts me in this situation with no backup or plan and has the gall to tell me *to calm down?!* "No! Seriously!" Frank demanded. "How do you know that?!"

"I have my sources, okay?" Benz kept her eyes on Francine, who miraculously hadn't noticed them yet.

"What sources?!" Frank's hands shook with fear. "And why are you just now telling me about them?!"

Then Stan arrived, landing by his wife's side.

We're so not ready for this! "We need a new plan!" *Hell, I'm not ready for this!* "Benz? Benz!"

She was about to open the car door when the Solomons turned to face them.

Their gaze froze Benz in her tracks and pressed Frank into his seat.

Stan gave them a friendly wink while Francine gave them a withering glare.

"Stay still," Frank whispered once he found his voice. "Stay still …"

"Frank," Benz got in a frantic whisper, "they're right there!"

"I said stay still!"

The Solomons shot up into the sky, leaving the detectives amid fiery devastation, as the squad cars arrived behind them.

—⁂—

"I believe," Loeb said the next day as he, Frank, and Benz met in his office at the GCPD station, "that your job was to gather intel on the Solomons." He took a moment to rub sleep out of his eyes. "Right?"

"It was," Frank said as he and Benz sat in front of his desk.

"Gather intel only," Loeb said, glowering at the two detectives from his side of the desk.

"To be fair, sir," Benz said, raising her hand, "I didn't know that."

"Not the time for snark, Detective," Loeb snapped, shooting her an icy look.

"Right," she said, putting her hand down. "Sorry."

"Your case did not involve you — in any way or fashion — confronting the Solomons," he continued. "Not directly, militarily, or any other way!"

"We know, Chief." It was a struggle for Frank to keep the irritation out of his voice. "But we had a lead. We had no idea the Solomons would be there."

"Really?" Loeb turned to face him, a curious look on his face. "In that case, how'd you end up at the meth house?"

"Sir," Benz started, "it was because—"

"One of my criminal informants," Frank cut in. "She gave us the tip."

"Before it came out over the wire?"

"She's a hell of a CI. Keeps her ear to the ground."

Loeb gave Frank a piercing look, his mouth a tight line on his face. His eyes went from him to Benz. It was clear he knew something was going on between them—he just didn't know what. "Is that what you were going to tell me, Benz?"

"Yes sir," she answered, nodding.

—⚏—

Frank covered for me, Benz realized as Loeb took his eyes off her. *Despite how I acted, he still covered for me.* She tried to catch Frank's gaze.

But the senior detective kept his eyes on Loeb.

"Follow me downstairs," the annoyed police chief said, heading for the exit. "The coroner's got something."

"Downstairs" was code for the morgue. Ironic, given that it was on the same floor as the rest of the station.

Loeb led the way, Frank and Benz moving single-file behind him.

They passed other officers, each refusing to make eye contact with her or Frank.

They're afraid of us, she realized as she followed Loeb and Frank through the morgue's doors. *Like we're marked because we got to the meth house before them.*

"What do you have for us, Alex?" Loeb asked as he approached four slabs, arranged in a row in the middle of the sterile room.

"Quite a bit for you, sir," a dwarf answered, his back to them. He swirled on the stool, facing them while taking off his surgical mask. "I just finished." He nodded to Frank and Benz. "Detectives."

"Hey, Al," Frank said halfheartedly.

"Good to see you," Benz said, giving him a wave.

"Good to see you too," Alex said, relief in his face. "When I heard you faced the Solomons again, I feared the—"

"Can we get on with it?" Loeb cut in, clearly impatient. "We're on the clock."

—m—

"We dug these poor souls out of the rubble last night," Alex said, gesturing to the four slabs. There was a body bag on each, zipped up and ready to go.

Brace yourself. Frank stepped over to one, whipped out a plastic glove, and used it to unzip the bag. The body was burned to a crisp. "And this is ..."

"Hiram Diego," Alex answered.

"Of the Diego crime family," Loeb said. "How'd you ID him?"

"Dental scans. It was the only part of him that wasn't burned all the way through."

"I got another one." Benz unzipped another bag, revealing the burned remains of a young woman. "Who's this?"

"She," Alex said, pointing at the body, "is Ashely Green."

"Of the Green crime family," Frank murmured, glancing over at the other bags. "I'm gonna guess they're other crime bosses."

"The heads of the surviving families in Gateway City."

Frank stood up, realization on his face. "This was a meet."

"Looks like it."

"Only one thing would get bosses from different families to meet," Loeb declared, a knowing look on his face. "The Solomons."

"And they chose to meet at a meth house?" Benz asked in confusion. "With us patrolling the area? Not the smartest move for the top brass of any family."

"It is if they're desperate," Loeb said as he opened another body bag. "Besides, no one would think they'd meet so close to the product. It's so overt it's covert."

Not covert enough. "You think the Solomons knew?"

"Only if Sikes knew. Francine must've gotten the location from him," Benz answered. "Or this meet might've been a spur of the moment and the Solomons just got lucky."

Too lucky. Frank felt as though he was sinking in quicksand, his slight claustrophobia triggered. Intimidation and harassment were bad enough, but this was a culling.

Sure, these crime bosses were scum, but they deserved better than this.

He imagined these captains of the criminal underworld, reduced to hiding from the Solomons like scared children.

Did they hear them coming?

Did they even have a chance to fight back?

—◈—

"So we know what they were meeting about," Loeb said grimly, "but who called it?"

"The one crime boss not in one of these bags," Frank answered. "Though I'll be damned if I know who that is."

"I may have something," Benz said, stepping up to them. "I did some digging before you had us in your office, sir."

"Thank you for that, Benz," Loeb said, looking a little annoyed. "What did you find?"

"The building had been a shoe factory before the owner folded. He was bought out by a generous buyer a few years ago."

"Do we have a name to this buyer?"

"That we do," Benz answered confidently. "Ramona Maroni."

"Well, well," Loeb said, sucking his teeth. "Ramona Maroni, of the Maroni crime family."

Does he know her personally? Benz caught the tender way he said her name. She shot Frank a look, seeing that he didn't bother hiding his suspicions.

"Don't look at one another like that," Loeb snapped as if he'd heard her thoughts. "I met her when I was investigating her father."

"Carter Maroni," Alex chimed in, wanting to be involved.

"Yes, sir. Thing is, Ramona had no interest in the family business, last I checked. Wonder what changed her mind?"

"The Solomons killed Carter a few months ago," Benz answered, "in the early days of their campaign."

"Forcing her to take his place," Loeb said, a thoughtful look on his face. "Mafia life's not the best for women, especially ones newly minted. Makes me wonder if she called the meet to earn some brownie points with the other leaders."

"If she's new, she'd need all the juice she could get," Frank added, giving Benz a proud nod. "Makes me wonder if she had an ace up her sleeve."

"Meaning?"

"Maybe she has a way to stop the Solomons. One that no one else knows about."

One we can use, Benz thought hopefully. "She must've gotten away. That makes her the last boss standing."

"And if we know that, the Solomons do too," Frank reasoned. "We gotta get to her."

"Find her," Loeb commanded, pointing to the exit. "And bring her in."

"Yes, sir." Benz grabbed Frank by the arm and led him out of the morgue.

—⟋⟍—

"So, ma'am," Boris began, standing in one of many safe houses the Mala Noches had in Gateway City. "What do we do now?"

"We stay calm, first off." Ramona stood a few feet from him, looking out a window, stirring a glass of coffee in her hand. "Now you're telling me there's no one left?"

"After what happened last night, no one's stepping up. Congratulations, you're now the undisputed queen of Gateway City's criminal underworld."

Be it on fire or sinking. Ramona's eyes narrowed. "We were right there, Boris."

"I know, ma'am."

"All Stan had to do was turn his head a little to the left, and he would've seen us ..."

"I know, ma'am."

"And we'd be—" Ramona cut off the statement, refusing to look weak. "Makes a girl feel like her luck's running out."

"That has occurred to me," the stocky man agreed as he walked to a nearby table, pulling a map out of his pocket. "So if I may be so bold ..."

"Please be."

"We need to get you out of the city. Someplace warm, until all of this blows over."

Sucking her teeth in disgust, Ramona turned to face him. "You mean until the Solomons go away."

"Or the GCPD deals with them."

"You think either of those scenarios is going to happen?"

"It never hurts to hope," Boris answered, shrugging.

"Hope is for children." Ramona turned back to the window, only to have the ugly brick of an abandoned building to look at. *I miss my penthouse.*

"Do you really think it's safe standing dead in the center of the window like that?"

"Relax, the Solomons only come out at night," Ramona said, taking another sip of coffee. "It's daytime. They gotta recharge or something."

"Do you want to take a chance that's true?"

Ramona looked over her shoulder, about to throw a snide comment. Then she thought better of it and stepped away from the window to join him by the table. "So what are you thinking?"

"The Solomons demolished our regular routes out of town," Boris answered, tapping the map. "That leaves the irregular ones." He put a finger on a spot near the docks. "Here."

What's this? Ramona's eyes widened with indignation. "That's on Wolfenstein Island!"

"And not near any known exit routes. Even the police won't go there. Let's hope that means the Solomons won't go there, either."

"Slim hope there, Boris."

"We get you there. We have a boat to get you out of Gateway City. To Mexico. Maybe even Brazil."

"Europe."

"Fine, Europe," Boris answered in a voice that bordered on exasperation. "Once there, you disappear for a few years."

"What about you?" Ramona asked, looking up at him.

"I stay here, hold the fort until it's safe for you to return."

"I don't like running. It feels like I'm giving ground to these Solomon assholes."

"Hiram Diego felt the same way," Boris stated flatly, a touch of impatience in his voice. "His wife and daughter are at the police station right now, picking up his body."

Jesus, I get it. Ramona swallowed, imagining *that* scene. "All right. Set it up. For tonight."

—⚊—

"Find her, he says," Frank grumbled as he sat at the desk he shared with Benz. "Like we can just pull Maroni's address right out of the phone book!"

"They'd be in directories now, Frank."

"You know what I mean!"

Their office was in the back of the station. Benz had been working there for months before Frank joined the case.

At first, he had thought it an honor. How many people got their own private office in a crowded police station? Now he knew it was because Loeb wanted them out of sight. "Yo, Benz."

"Hmm?" She looked up from her paperwork, her gray eyes as alert as ever.

"Now that we're alone, it's time we had a talk."

"About?" Benz asked, trying to look as innocent and non-assuming as she possibly could.

Franks eyes widened in indignant surprise. "Are you *really* gonna ask me that?"

Benz let out a reluctant sigh. "No, even though I just did, didn't I?"

"What happened at Ayman's store? How you knew what the Solomons were doing and when—how long has *that* been going on?"

—⁂—

Benz had been living in constant dread of this conversation.

That one day someone was going to get curious about her "hunches" about the Solomons. She had assumed it would be Loeb. She knew it would be Frank. He wasn't acclimated to the Solomons like everyone else.

"Do I have to ask again?" Frank inquired as though he had somehow heard her thoughts.

Just tell him. "It's been going on since I got Kate back."

"How?"

"It started out as a dull ache in the back of my head." Benz leaned back in her chair. "I thought it was stress. Or jitters. But as the days wore on, the headaches got worse. There were days I'd be picking myself off the floor—they were so bad."

Frank leaned close, concern on his face. "Anyone here see these pratfalls?"

Yeah, that's what we'll call them. "They always happen when I'm alone."

"When did these headaches become beacons for the Solomons?"

"They weren't beacons, per se," Benz explained, wearing an expression that was a mixture of embarrassment and unease. "It's just ... after the headaches, I ... thought better."

"You *thought* better?" Frank asked, arching his brow in concern.

Sounds strange now that I'm saying it out loud. "My thoughts were clearer," Benz continued, fidgeting in her chair. "My hunches were always on point when it came to the Solomons. I could tell where they were going, what they were going to do. Then I'd just head to where they were."

"Always a few minutes late, right?"

"Yes!" Benz's face brightened. "How'd you know that?"

Frank let out a long breath as if to collect his thoughts. "Ayman mentioned it to me."

"Your criminal informant? How does she know?"

"She told me people always see you at the scenes of the Solomons' crimes. Right after they leave, but always before the rest of us arrive."

Civilians are talking about me? Benz didn't even notice that!

"He also suggested"— Frank paused before continuing —"that Loeb put me on this case to keep an eye on you."

The gamut of expressions that passed over Benz's face pained Frank like nothing else.

Shock.

Disgust.

Disappointment.

And, finally, disbelief.

"Do you think I need to be watched?" she asked in a calm, collected, yet irritated voice.

"No," Frank answered, wishing he had kept his mouth shut. "But with what you've told me, it makes Ayman's theory more plausible."

"Just because I'm having these ..."

"Pratfalls."

"Doesn't mean I'm compromised. I want to catch the Solomons as much as anyone else."

"I know, Benz," Frank said, quick to assure the younger detective. "But I'm not Loeb. I don't have the mayor breathing down my neck." *Way to make excuses for her critics, buddy.*

"So what do we do now?" Benz asked, looking as though she had been kicked in the gut.

Damn you for putting that thought in my head, Ayman. "We work the case." Frank glanced at a clock on the wall, which read 9:00 a.m. "That means finding Ramona Marconi before nightfall."

"How are we supposed to do that?" Benz asked in growing exasperation. "If she knows the Solomons are after her, she's going to be laying low."

"That's why we have to work smart," Frank answered, giving Benz a knowing look. "Now that I know you're our bona fide Solomon detector, I'm hoping you'll have one of your 'pratfalls' and pinpoint where Maroni's hiding. Then we find her and grab her before the Solomons do."

"Frank, by the time these 'pratfalls' hit me, the Solomons are already *at* the scene."

"Then we're gonna have to be on the move." He got up from the table. "C'mon."

—⁂—

Ramona Marconi stood in yet another safe house—Boris's suggestion—as she waited for him to make the necessary arrangements. Unlike the last one, this house was an ugly brick building on Wolfenstein Island just off the coast of Gateway City.

Bootleggers stored liquor in safe houses like this during the Prohibition days. When her father ran the Mal Noches, he had bought most of them.

The Solomons killed him in one of those safe houses a year ago.

Ramona swallowed back a wave of revulsion, remembering the police carrying his remains in a basket.

A very small basket.

She was so sure, the minute she took the reins of the business, that she would be joining him.

In a cramped, dank safe house, just like the one she was standing in.

The sudden ringing of her burner phone almost made her jump out of her skin. "What?!" she demanded.

"We're good to go," Boris answered, sounding a little surprised at her outburst.

"When?"

"This evening."

"What time?"

"Five thirty."

"Cutting it close, Boris." Ramona fought to keep the quivering desperation out of her voice. "Why can't I get out earlier? Like right now? How hard is it to rent a car?"

"Ma'am, the police know you arranged the meet. They're looking for you, going to all your old haunts. Watching all the roads. We move you now, they'll snatch you up."

"And if we wait until nightfall, the Solomons will grab me," Ramona said, feeling as though she was sinking into a tar pit. "What's our window?"

"I'll pick you up at 5:00 p.m.," Boris answered in a reassuring yet urgent voice. "We got a two-hour window to get you to the docks, on a boat, and out of the country. We paid our people in the Coast Guard to look the other way."

"Still wish you were coming with me." Ramona had known Boris since she was sixteen. He'd been her father's second-in-command.

"Me too, but I have to stay here," he answered grimly. "Besides, I'm gonna make sure the GCPD's too distracted to even look for you."

"What are you going to do?"

"The less you know, the better. Just be ready to go when I arrive."

—◊—

An acidic sense of foreboding settled in the pit of Benz's stomach as she and Frank drove around Gateway City. The storefronts they passed were abandoned, the windows and doors boarded up.

Like Florida before a major hurricane.

"It's like they know something we don't," Frank commented dryly.

"The sad thing is, if they do," Benz added, eyeing their surroundings nervously, "they're not going to tell us ..."

"Because they don't trust us. I know."

She could feel nervous anticipation in the eyes of the people they passed. The remaining vendors would give her welcoming nods, but with desperation in their eyes. As if she was the Solomons' emissary. At one point, she had stopped at a 7-Eleven to get coffee.

The owner wouldn't even let her pay.

Coffee, and anything else she wanted, was on the house. With his thanks.

Same thing happened at a gas station she and Frank went to next.

"It's like they think I'll tell the Solomons about their good behavior," Benz noted as they got back in the squad car. "Score them points or something."

"Hence the preferential treatment," Frank said, holding an impressive haul of potato chips. "Gotta admit, I could get used to this."

Spoken like a stereotypical cop. Benz shook her head as she looked through her windshield to see a couple of kids waving at her. Confused, she waved back. *How can people just accept all this craziness? I'm in the middle of it, and I haven't accepted it!*

"Getting a ping on your Solomon alarm yet?"

"I'm not a radio," Benz snapped. "It'll 'ping' when the Solomons do something."

"Just checking," Frank said in between mouthfuls of potato chips.

"How can you be so calm about all of this? The whole city's about to change, and you're just ... eating potato chips!"

"You were pretty casual when you showed me the gardens," he shot back. "And when you mentioned the facelift the Solomons gave the city."

"That was different."

"How?"

"Those are inanimate objects.," Benz answered in irritation. "Not people."

"I know, kid," Frank said, swallowing down the last of the potato chips. "I know."

—⟋⟍—

"All right," he said, throwing his trash away. "Enough prepping. Time to work."

"You call that"—Benz looked over her shoulder at the mess in the back seat—"prepping?"

"In cases like this, you take the time to load up on carbs because you'll be burning them off later. Either by running after or away from something." Frank pulled out his phone and dialed Ayman's number. "Ayman, are you there?"

"I am," the Lebanese woman answered with a touch of annoyance.

Something's happened. Frank's muscles tensed. He put the phone on speaker. *I can hear it in her voice.* "I'm with my partner. You remember her."

"Hello, Ayman," Benz said, trying to keep her words cordial. "Do you remember me?"

"Of course I do," she answered politely. "It was only yesterday."

"We're alone," Frank continued. "You can speak freely."

"*That's* a relief."

A touch of sarcasm. "What happened, Ayman?"

"Your cohorts came by my store."

Dammit. Frank scratched his head, cursing himself for mentioning her to Loeb. "I'm sorry about that. I mentioned I had a CI, but I didn't mention your name."

"He was covering for me," Benz added quickly. "For my …"

"Pratfalls?"

I didn't tell her! Frank shrugged at Benz's incredulous stare. "Did my 'cohorts' treat you right?"

"They put a huge spotlight on my business, Frank."

Okay, then. "Is your bottom line suffering?"

"I've lost customers," Ayman answered, the annoyance in her voice deepening. "People need to feel safe shopping here."

There was a time when we *made people feel safe.* "Given what you just told me, I hate to ask you this," Frank said, wincing at his words, "but is there word on the street about Ramona Maroni?"

"I thought she was killed in the meth-house fire, last night."

"No," Benz said, taking over the conversation from Frank. "But her contemporaries were …"

"Leaving her the last boss standing," Ayman reasoned, her voice going from annoyed to worried. "If she were to take advantage of the chaos, she'd run this town."

"There's no one else to challenge her?"

"From what I've heard?" The Lebanese woman answered. "Not a single one."

—◊◊—

As the sun sank lower in the sky, Ramona bit her nails, something she hadn't done since she was a kid. *C'mon, Boris. Hurry up!*

Feeling a sense of helplessness she wasn't accustomed to, she paced around the room. She eyed her phone, contemplating calling the GCPD to turn herself in. Sure, she would spend time in jail, but at least there she would know what to expect.

With the Solomons, no one knew what to expect.

Boris would be disappointed, but he wasn't her father.

Still, Maroni never surrendered to the police.

No matter how close they came to catching him.

This is your fault, Ramona thought, invoking Officer Kate Barrow. *I'm hiding like a rat! All because you couldn't keep your gun in your pants!*

—◊◊—

"The Solomons won't stop," Benz declared as Frank ended the call with Ayman. "They can't. They're too committed."

"They've practically eradicated organized crime!" Frank practically shouted in frustration. "What else is there?!"

"White-collar crime."

"What?"

"Bankers. Businessmen. Politicians," Benz explained, her voice dripping with a creeping dread. "They're plagued with corruption too. Stan and Francine will focus on them."

"Like City Hall? The mayor?"

"Wouldn't put it past them."

"Given what I've seen those assholes pull," Frank growled, "I'd actually love to see the Solomons roast a few of them."

"Careful, partner," Benz cautioned, shooting him a worried look. "You're starting to sound like me."

"Yeah, well," he said, shrugging, "I never said you were wrong, partner."

—⁂—

Thankfully, Ayman called back a few minutes later. "Getting this wasn't easy, Frank."

"I'll make it up to you." *Somehow.* "Now what do you got for me?"

"Maroni's making her way out of the city. She's on Wolfenstein Island right now."

"The island off the coast?" Benz asked warily. "Why would she head there?"

"Because we got no presence there," Frank answered. *Another mistake coming back to bite us.* "Hasn't been since the riots ten years ago."

"Riots?"

"Tell you later." Frank looked at his cell phone. "You wouldn't happen to have Maroni's exact address, would you?"

"No," Ayman answered in a strained voice. "I had to move mountains to get *this* much."

"And thank you for that. We'll take it from here." Frank ended the call and pocketed his phone. "We gotta get to Wolfenstein Island. Once there, we shake a few trees and get lucky."

—⁂—

Maybe I can appeal to the Solomons, Ramona thought as she took a drink from her flask. *There's always a deal to be made. I just have to find what they want and show them I can get it.* She downed another drink. *God, they're not even in front of me, and I'm shaking!*

Goddammit, this was Kate Barrow's fault!

A noise from behind made her jump.

A quick look revealed it was just a rat scurrying across the floor. She let out a mirthless chuckle. *If Dad saw this, he'd be turning over in his grave.*

So would her mother.

Ramona cast a forlorn look at the door, waiting for Boris to knock.

—⁂—

"And here we are," Benz said when they arrived at Wolfenstein Island. "Where to now?"

The streets were pockmarked with craters and cracks, the buildings looking like bombed-out husks. Benz coasted their car through abandoned streets, eyes on the rooftops. *If anyone wanted to kick off an ambush, this would be the perfect spot.*

"That depends," Frank said, giving her a pointed look. "Are you getting anything?"

"I have a headache, but that could be from being on a sketchy island!"

"Focus. Do these headaches come before your pratfalls?"

"Yes." Benz relaxed her grip on the steering wheel. "What's the time?"

"It's" — Frank checked his watch — "about 5:00 p.m. Why?"

"It's getting close to dark."

"We still got a few hours."

"Is it me? Or are the nights coming faster now?"

"Noticed that too," Frank agreed, looking at the sky from his passenger-side window.

"You think the Solomons are behind that too?" Benz knew the question was stupid the second it came out of her mouth. And yet she had to ask.

"They're not gods, Benz," Frank snapped angrily, "no matter how much people wanna think otherwise!"

"The Solomons are affecting more and more of the city, Frank ..."

"Buildings, Benz! Roads! People! Not the rotation of the earth!"

—⁂—

Ramona pounced on the phone before the second ring. "Hello?!"

"I'm outside," Boris answered in an urgent voice.

"On my way." She grabbed a duffel bag and went for the door. She opened it to see him dressed in his usual black suit. She felt underdressed in her sweatpants, T-shirt, and hoodie. "Say something nice."

"You look nice, ma'am."

Ramona raised a wary finger. "Try. Harder."

"You look beautiful, ma'am."

"Better." She stepped through the door, then stopped dead in her tracks. "What is that?"

"This," Boris answered, gesturing to the black four-door car humming before them, "is a Chevrolet Bolt."

"It's an electric car."

"I'm aware."

"I'd never be caught dead in that."

"That's the point," Boris said, opening the passenger door. "Now get in."

"Goddammit," Ramona muttered, shoving her bag into the backseat before getting in the passenger seat. "Rather be dead than ride in this thing."

"Keep talking," Boris said, pulling away from the safe house. "It might still happen."

—∭—

"Aggh!" Benz gripped the wheel hard as that familiar throbbing chimed in. *Not now!*

"Benz!" Frank shouted, his eyes wide with fear. "What's happening?!"

"It's ... the Solomons! They're ..." She didn't see Frank grab the wheel to keep their car from going off the road. "They're out!"

"That's it!" He coasted their car to a nearby curb. "I'm driving!"

"Wait!" Benz blinked the blurriness from her eyes. "I can—"

"Get out of the driver seat so I can take the wheel, right now!"

"I'm all right," she whispered, opening her door. *Holy ...* She found herself on cold pavement, having spilled out of her seat like clothes from a hamper.

And it was raining. When did it start raining?!

"C'mon," Frank said, pulling her to her feet. "I'm getting you out of here!"

"No!" Benz shouted, fighting to get back in the car. "We're close! We have to—"

"We *have* to get you proper treatment!" he blurted out with desperate insistence. "And yeah, that means telling Loeb! Might take you out of the fight, but better that than—"

A black car screamed past them, its windows spitting gunfire.

On its tail were the Solomons!

"Come on!" Benz slipped back into the driver's seat. "We got them in our sights!"

Before he could think about it, Frank was back in the passenger seat, their car rocketing to catch up. "Our job's to observe! Not to confront!"

"We don't 'confront' now, the Solomons are going to kill Maroni!"

"We can't fight them, Benz!"

"We can't let them kill her, either!"

"So what are we supposed to do?!"

"Call Loeb!" Benz shouted back. "Let him know what we're doing!"

"We don't know what we're doing, *yet*!"

"Just call him, Frank!"

Can't believe she's giving me *orders!* Stuffing down a litany of venomous comments, Frank activated his communicator. "Loeb, this is Drake! You there?!"

"I never left," came the calm, clear response. "What's happening?"

Crap, did he hear us? Frank thought about it for a second, when shook it off. "We found Ramona Maroni!"

"Good job, Drake!"

"Thing is, the Solomons did too!" Frank's stomach flip-flopped as their car jumped the curb to get right next to Moroni's car. *Jesus, Benz!*

"How close are you two?!" Loeb asked, his voice hard to hear over the roar of the cars' engines.

"Close enough to see the whites of their eyes!" Frank answered as Stan and Francine gave him heated looks. *That's right, jackasses, we're on you!*

"Don't lose them, Drake! I'm sending you backup!"

"What kind of backup?!"

"The kind that'll make a difference!"

—⚬—

How did they find us?! Stan wondered when he saw the detectives' car sidle up next to Maroni's. *Benz! This is her doing!*

Francine was on the left side of Maroni's car while he was on top. The detectives were on the right side. Together, they had her boxed in. No chance of escape.

But he and Francine couldn't shake the detectives, either.

"Take care of Maroni!" Stan shouted to Francine. "I'll take care of the detectives!"

"They want to separate us!" she shouted back. "We need to stay together!"

"We can't let them stop us!"

"They can't stop us!" Francine shouted above the roar of the wind as Ramona's car barreled down the street, taking them with it. "No one can!"

"You really want to put that to the test?!" Stan shouted back, cocking his head at the detective's car.

"What are you—" Francine craned her neck to look at the detective car, and saw Benz in the driver seat. "Fine!"

"Don't worry!" Stan shouted back, giving her a reassuring look. "I won't hurt them!"

"I'm not worried about them!"

"But I am," Stan declared, giving her a final look, before leaping off of Maroni's car.

—⚬—

Is he about to…?! Benz wondered as Stan leaped to their car. *Crap!* "Frank!"

He pulled out his gun just as Stan's fist smashed through their windshield almost knocking their car off the road. "Goddammit!"

"Don't worry!" Stan ripped the steering wheel out of the dashboard. "The brakes still work!"

"No way!" Benz put Stan's wrist in a vice grip. "Not this time!"

"Let go!"

"No chance!"

"Stand down!" Frank shouted, pointing his gun at his face. "Right now!"

"Take your shot!" Stan shouted back. "I'll survive it! Will Benz?!"

Wait. Benz saw Ramoni's car getting farther away. *He's the distraction.* She kept the gas pedal to the floor. *Not gonna let that happen!*

"I'll take that chance, jackass," Frank growled, pulling the trigger.

Frank's bullets might as well have been popcorn the way they bounced off Stan's skin. *Dammit, we need better weapons!* He kept firing, hoping one would at least scratch him. *How could Loeb send us after the Solomons without better weapons?!*

"I'm giving you one last chance, Benz," Stan warned, shouting above the wind. "Let! Me! Go!"

"And I'm giving you one last chance to give up," she shot back, refusing to release her grip on his arm. "Turn yourself in!"

"Not! Happening!"

"Would you *stop* talking to him like he's an ex-boyfriend and stop him?!" Frank demanded from his passenger seat.

"You got the gun, Frank!"

"You got us into this, Benz!"

"In that case …" She gunned the engine as far as it would go. "Hang on!"

"Goddamn!" That was the last thing Frank said as their car slammed into Maroni's, sending both vehicles careening off the road.

Ramona's world became a hazy tunnel as her and Boris's car turned over and over. *I knew we needed a better car!* Just when she thought she would die, it came to a lazy stop.

On four wheels, believe it or not.

"Boris …" Ramona saw him slumped over the wheel. "Boris?" She touched his neck. *No pulse. Shit.* She unbuckled her seat belt, closing her eyes tight to will away a wave of nausea. *Have to get out of here!*

She had to get off the island!

Ramona was about to open the door when someone beat her to it. *Shit!* She raised her gun, only to see a middle-aged man and a young woman staring at her. "Can I help you two?"

"Ramona Maroni," the man stated as though it was a punchline to some obscene joke.

"Yeah?"

"Detective Frank Drake." He cocked his head at the woman. "This is Detective Julie Benz. We're here to take you into custody. How about you come peacefully?"

"Always gotta … draw things out," Ramona mumbled before falling back into her seat.

—m—

Benz stared intently at the Solomons, who were picking themselves up across the clearing they had fallen into.

"Benz," Frank warned, slowly shaking his head while giving her his best no-nonsense look, "don't do it."

"Can you get Maroni out of here?"

"Of course, I can, but I won't have to do that," Frank answered, pulling the crime boss out of the car, "because *we're* gonna get her out of here!"

"I can reach them," Benz declared, not taking her eyes off the Solomons. "There'll be no better chance!"

"We're not supposed to confront them, Benz! We have to—"

But she was already gone, sprinting across the rocky terrain.

"Dammit!" Frank gave her a final look before carrying Maroni away from her totaled car.

—◆—

"Are you all right?" Stan asked as he checked Francine for injuries.

"Of course I'm fine! Maroni's getting away!"

"I know," he said, seeing Detective Drake carrying her away. "We'll get to her later."

"I want to get to her now!"

"Cool your jets," Stan said, relieved to see that his wife wasn't hurt. "It's not like they can get far."

"They can if she distracts us!" Francine cocked her head at Detective Benz, sprinting toward them.

"You've got to be kidding me," Stan grumbled under his breath. "What could she possibly have to say to us?"

"Don't ask me, honey," Francine answered, throwing up her hands in growing exasperation. "She's *your* fan!"

—◆—

Here they are, Benz thought as she slowed her approach. *I've been chasing them for months, and here they are!* She took a moment to catch her breath. *What do I say to them?*

"Need a minute?" came the sarcastic quip from Francine.

Always gotta needle someone. "Think I liked you more when I first met you."

"The day we took Kate?"

"The day you *kidnapped* Kate."

"She had it coming," Francine declared, not backing down in the least, "and you know it!"

"She was a person, Mrs. Solomon."

"So was our son," Stan cut in rudely. "And unlike Mrs. Barrow, he's no longer alive."

"I know," Benz said, having caught her breath. "And I'm sorry about that. But you both got your revenge. And you brought Kate back to her parents."

"Doesn't mean we're square. With her, her misbegotten family, or mine."

"Speaking of family, your father asks about you."

"How nice," Stan chuckled. "I've got myself a new sister!"

"And here I thought one was enough," Francine muttered under her breath.

"Hey, hey! My sister's nice!"

—◆—

What are you doing, Benz? Having a fireside chat?! Frank wondered as he dragged Maroni from the scene. *Get away from them!*

Maroni gave off a faint mumble.

Oh, she's got a concussion for sure. "What was your plan to stop the Solomons?"

"Huh?"

"Your plan," Frank repeated, sitting her down by a bunch of trees. "What you called the mob meet. It was a plan to stop the Solomons, right?"

"Wait." Maroni's eyes went wide, either in pain or surprise. "How did you—"

"We're smarter than you think," Frank answered, tapping his badge. "Now what was it?"

—◆—

"Well, now that we have this wonderful talk," Stan said, giving Benz an expectant look, "and got our second wind"—he pointed at Frank and Maroni—"we're gonna take our mob boss and go home."

Dammit, we were doing so well. "I can't let you do that," Benz said, realizing how silly *that* sounded.

Francine threw her head back and laughed. "Believes her own press, this one."

"I don't," Benz insisted. "I just can't let you keep playing judge, jury, and executioner."

"Oh, trust me, we're not playing."

"I can see that. The whole city can see that, especially after last night."

"We don't like to be subtle," Stan said, casually shrugging his shoulders. "Got to make up for the rest of you."

"When we set out to complete a task, we complete it," Francine added with a sinister edge.

"Oh, we all know that. Thing is, you've both eradicated organized crime. That meth-house fire killed every mob boss in the city!"

"Not everyone," Stan corrected, gesturing to Maroni.

Yes, Stan, I know you see her, Benz realized, refusing to follow his gaze. *We all know you see her!* "Let us take her in, Stan. Let us take Maroni back to stand trial."

"No jury in the world would convict her. And more, no one in City Hall would let her get in front of a jury."

"If this is about what happened with Barrow," Benz started, seeing Stan and Francine flinch, "I can guarantee that won't happen with Maroni."

"Give us one reason why."

"Just because the system screwed up with your son's killer doesn't mean it's inherently corrupt. Or that it's beyond saving."

"That's what separates you from us," Francine declared. "You and him," she stabbed a finger at Frank, "are trying to save a system. We're trying to save people."

—❦—

How can she be pointing at me from so far away? Frank wondered in irritated wonder. *Do they just know where I am at all times? Or is it just Francine?* He looked back to Maroni. "I don't know how much time we got here. I need you to tell me everything about your plan."

"Why?" the disheveled mob boss asked. So you can take credit for it?"

"Lady, believe it or not, we're *not* the bad guys here!"

"Of course not." Maroni snorted with laughter. "You're my accomplices!"

—❦—

199

"I've been by the gardens," Benz declared, keeping her eyes fixed on the Solomons standing before her. "Talked to the people living in them."

"Oh, people are doing that?" Stan asked, trying to look nonchalant. "I didn't expect that."

"Oh, please," Francine scoffed. "Why else did you make them so big?"

"I didn't want people to think we're just monsters."

"We're *not* monsters."

"You're acting like monsters," Benz declared, "and people are taking notice. People who have a lot of pull with people like me."

"I don't care what people like you think," Francine shot back. "Since you people obviously…"

"Don't care what you think, I get it," Benz said in exasperation. "But the thing is, you *do* care. You care a lot. I don't need to see Stan's gardens to know that."

"What are you talking about?"

"I'm talking about Monica Rambeau."

"You," Francine blinked, uncertainty creeping into her features, "spoke to her?"

"I did," Benz answered, hoping that would get through to her.

"Is she …?" Francine managed a breathy swallow before continuing, "is she okay?"

"She's fine, thanks to you."

"That's …" She let out a sigh of relief as Stan gave her a one-armed hug. "That's … really good to hear."

—⁂—

"Explain!" Frank yanked Maroni to her feet despite her injuries. "Now!"

"Might as well." A wave of hopelessness passed across her face. "Can't escape it now."

"What do you mean?!" *I am* so *sick of this cloak-and-dagger bullshit!* Then a thought hit Frank like a freight train. "You weren't just trying to get out of town to save your own skin, were you?"

—⟨⟩—

"Monica told me a lot of things," Benz continued. "Things that tell me you're more than killing criminals. That you want more."

"I wouldn't go *that* far," Francine said. "I *like* killing criminals."

"And we'll talk about how bad *that* is later," Stan swore.

"Whatever," Francine said, rolling her eyes in annoyance.

"Mrs. Solomon, you sat down with Monica after saving her from her abductor," Benz said, determined to get her point across. "You made sure she was okay. You even made her laugh."

"She needed to feel safe."

"You then gave her suggestions on how to live her life better."

"Her parents sure as hell weren't going to."

Little harsh. "Actions like that"—Benz raised a finger in emphasis—"show that this random killing? This crusade you're on? It's not you. Either of you. Not the real you."

"Real or not," Stan declared, "it's important."

"And has to be done," Francine added.

"Because it's the only way people will listen."

"But it doesn't have to be," Benz blurted out in frustration. "The people of this city love you two!"

Stan and Francine gave her stern looks.

"Well," she clarified hesitantly, hoping she wasn't losing their interest, "some of them do."

"There it is."

"The point is, a good portion of the people look up to you two. The work you've done, the *positive* work, has improved lives. Given the downtrodden a sense of pride. That's great."

"We know that," Francine said.

C'mon, work with me! "But the killing? The brutalizing? *That's* not you. It's what you've let yourselves become, because you're angry."

"Do *not* demean our struggle," Stan snapped, making the ground shake.

"Demean it? I get it! You think you're the first person to feel stepped on by the law?" Benz demanded, glaring at him. "I'm a woman in the police force! I know exactly how you feel, and I haven't gone through the pain of losing a child!"

"I hope you never do," Stan declared, frowning sadly. "It's the worst pain you'll *ever* experience."

"But you've already given that pain to other people!"

He raised a confused eyebrow. "Excuse me?"

"The people who died in that meth house," Benz explained, "they had parents. People who loved them. How do you think they feel, knowing that you killed their kids?"

"If those parents truly loved their kids, they should've pointed them to another line of work."

"Blaming people for being in the wrong place instead of taking responsibility for causing their pain"—Benz shook her head in amazement—"wasn't that what the court did when it acquitted Kate Barrow of killing your son?"

—🙰—

"I was," Maroni revealed after getting out a swallow that looked way more painful than it should have, "trying to get out before the fighting started.

Oh no. Frank's face went white. "What have you done?"

"Gave us a fighting chance." She spat out a wad of blood. "Since you people weren't doing anything."

Okay, I am done *with people dogging us!* Frank grabbed her collar, wrenching her close. "And how were you going to do that? What's your plan, dammit?!"

—🙰—

"Well, well." Stan chuckled at Benz's comment. "Throwing our words back at us?"

"If the shoe fits, Stan."

"We're nothing like Barrow," Francine insisted, shaking with rage. "Or the spineless fools that acquitted her."

"You're killing people whose lifestyle's different from yours," Benz insisted, "without asking why. You made a snap judgment in the heat of the moment. How is that *any* different from what Kate Barrow did?"

"Because we don't hide behind some freaking badge when we're caught," Stan answered, taking a threatening step toward Benz.

But no one's caught you," Benz blurted out in white-hot frustration. "No one's held you accountable because you don't give anyone a chance!"

"Why would we hold ourselves accountable to a system we no longer believe in?"

"Because you *fought* for that system," Benz shouted, pointing at Stan. "In the military! For ten years, you fought for it! Your son, Brian, believed in that system!"

"Do *not* talk about his service," Francine demanded, taking a menacing step toward Benz while stabbing a finger at her, "or *our* son like you know anything!"

"Besides, look where all that faith got him," Stan added, matching his wife's menacing gaze. "And us."

Dammit, he never gets angry, Benz thought, looking at him all calm and collected, while Francine looked ready to snap. *I know it's his military training, but it's making it harder to get through to him!*

Francine was always ready to snap, but it allowed her to cycle through her emotions faster. Of the two of them, she was the only one who seemed to at least react to her words.

But if she couldn't get Stan on the same page, it wouldn't matter.

The Solomons decided things as a team. How was Benz going to get them on the same page at the same time?!

Look at her, Stan thought. *Trying to divide us when we need to stick together. Maybe she isn't any different than Barrow or her GCPD friends.* He looked past her to Drake and Maroni, who were hiding behind some trees. *Sure as hell isn't any different from him.* He tilted his head in concern. *What* are *they doing over there?*

What were they talking about?

And why was Drake looking from Maroni, to him, Francine, and Benz?

No, he was just looking at him and Francine!

That was when Stan heard the sound of approaching rotor blades.

—⚛—

Oh no. Frank looked up and saw approaching shapes in the nighttime sky.

"And here they are," Maroni said, like some dime-store announcer. "A little late, but still…"

Frank stood up to get a better look. He saw only outlines, but he made out two helicopters, moving like stingrays above him. *Gotta be some kind of cloaking device, but that's only in the movies!*

And yet there they were, moving past him right for the Solomons …

And Benz!

Shit! Frank went to activate his communicator, only to see it was busted. *Dammit!*

—⚛—

Francine tilted her head as the choppers approached them. "Stan, what are those?"

"Helicopters, baby."

"I *know* that. But why can't I see them?"

"Specialized military ordinance," Stan answered, taking a step toward the oncoming aircraft. "I'd heard of them but thought they were only on the drawing board."

"Right, military," Francine grumbled, stepping in front of Benz as if to protect her. She raised her hands at the oncoming choppers. "Well?! Come on, then! Let's get a look at you!"

As if hearing her comment, the choppers dropped their cloak.

"Well, well," Francine whistled. "Looks like your boys got funding." She glanced at Benz over her shoulder. "This some of those reforms I heard about in the papers?"

"As I tried to explain," Stan repeated with a hint of irritation, "this isn't the GCPD."

"I can confirm that," Benz agreed, looking at the choppers with apprehension.

"Why don't you wave your badge at them?" Francine suggested in a haughty voice. "Just to be sure?"

—∿—

They were two helicopters, military-grade, just as Stan suspected.

They looked like the love child of a Black Hawk helicopter and a stealth bomber, dipped in some Flash Gordon aesthetic for good measure. They were silver, blending into the darkness despite being right in front of them.

Who called these things? Benz wondered as the wind whipped around her.

She didn't have time to think of anything else as the choppers opened fire.

—∿—

Holy ...! Stan let out a startled cry as the bullets cut through his body. He hit the ground hard, Francine beside him. *How?!*

"How?!" Francine uttered.

"That's what I'm wondering!" Stan saw Benz duck for cover, but because they were in a clearing, there was nowhere for her to hide.

The bullets hadn't hit her yet, but it was only a matter of time.

Did the pilots not see her? Or did they not care?

—∿—

"Benz!" Frank screamed as she hit the ground. "Hang on!" He dropped Maroni and turned to run to her. "I'm coming!"

He hadn't even taken a step when someone clapped a firm hand on his shoulder, pulling him back.

Get off me! Frank wheeled on his heels to see it was Loeb. "Chief? What are you ... how'd you ... when'd you get here?!"

"We *just* got here," the police chief answered, cocking his head at the officers setting up a perimeter around Frank and Maroni. Medical experts were wheeling the mob boss to an ambulance, hooking her up to drips and such.

Why am I just now seeing them?! Frank wondered incredulously. "Chief, we have to get to Benz!" He gestured in her direction as bullets strafed the ground around her. "We have to help her! She's out there!"

"Sorry, Drake." Loeb gazed at the scene with disdain. "This isn't our play anymore."

"What the hell are you talking about?!" Frank demanded, stabbing a finger in Benz's direction. "That's one of our own out there!"

"One that disobeyed my orders to *not* confront the Solomons!"

"She was doing her job!"

"If she was doing her job, she wouldn't be in this mess now, would she?!"

—⦚—

I'm going to die. Benz knew it in her bones. She had grabbed a tiger by the tail. And now she was paying for it. She was just a simple street detective — if there was such a thing — anot a superhuman wrangler.

But she'd bitten off more than she could chew.

Covering her head while bullets ripped up the ground inches from her face, she chanced a look around.

Stan and Francine were back on their feet, withstanding the hail of bullets. To her shock, the bullets were actually cutting through their skin. *What are they made of?* Taking a chance, she snatched one, which was embedded in the ground closest to her.

It felt warm.

And was vibrating.

—⦚—

They're trying to kill us. Stan leaped to the closest choppers, ignoring the bullets pockmarking his skin. *All we've done, and they're trying to kill us!*

He and Francine were trying to help …

Had delivered the end of crime to Gateway City, gift-wrapped …

And the "authorities" still saw them as the bad guys!

As the monsters!

If they want a monster—Stan ripped the guns out of their mounts and tossed them to the ground—*I'll give them a monster.* His eyes narrowed in cold vengeance. *We both will.*

—⁂—

"Sir, I don't know what's gotten into you," Frank growled, giving Loeb a venomous look, "but you need to let go of me right now." He was already gearing up to slug the undeserving son of a bitch.

Bad as Topher Madsen had been, even by media standards, he had never hung one of their own out to dry.

Michael Loeb was a terrible cop, and a worse commissioner.

He was just a symptom of the cancer the Solomons had infected the GCPD with.

"I'm trying to save your life," Loeb declared, not releasing his grip in the slightest.

The hell with it. Frank hurled his fist right at Loeb's face. *The hell with all of it.*

Loeb caught it quickly, using its momentum to put Frank in a chokehold. "Nice try."

"Let go of me, dammit!" Frank thrashed in his grip. "We have to save Benz, do you get it?! She's right there! We can—!"

"Look up, Drake," Loeb thundered, cutting through his protests.

Dick-sucking son of a bitch! Craning his neck against the pressure, Frank did and saw two more choppers arriving on the scene. *Oh, what now?!*

—⁂—

"Stan! They're automated!" Francine called out from her chopper. The glee in her voice was evident. "We don't have to hold back!"

207

"Good to know," Stan shouted back, raising his fist to smash through his chopper's cockpit. "Rip 'em to shreds. I'm tired of humoring these ungrateful fools."

"Finally!"

Stan was about to let his fist fly when he felt the chopper pulling away. *What is this?*

"Stan," Francine shouted, "they're pulling away!"

"I know that!" He jumped off, and Francine did the same, landing on the ground in front of them. *What are they doing now?* He heaved a wad of blood and spat it out. *God, it hurts.*

"How you holding up?"

"Just peachy." Stan looked to Francine, saw her leaking blood from a score of wounds. The holes in her skin revealed bone, muscle, and then some. "You look marvelous."

"Heh." Francine chuckled wearily, black ichor running down both sides of her mouth. "Liar."

"I'm serious. As good as the day I married you." Stan saw he was a little holey himself, his blood collecting in an ichorous black pool at his feet. "No lie."

"I married *you*, jackass."

"Benz." Stan glanced at the detective, who had finally stopped cowering. "You good back there?"

"Five by five," came the dazed answer.

She's got balls, I'll give her that. "What were you saying about people catching us?"

"Stan." Francine impatiently tapped his shoulder. "We got more company."

—⚏—

The new choppers were like the first two, but bigger.

More robust.

They weren't even trying to hide their arrival, something that stuck Benz as odd.

—⚏—

"Enough of this," Francine declared, electricity dancing across her eyes. "I got this."

"Honey, wait," Stan said in a firm voice. "We're practically falling apart. We need to get out of here and heal."

"What for? They're right there," she said, pointing at the approaching choppers. "I'll just end this right now."

They look bigger, Stan thought darkly. *Bigger than the ones that attacked us before. Why are they bigger?* Then he saw Francine gearing up for an attack. *Wait a minute ...*

—⚡—

Oh no. Thunder drew Benz's gaze to the sky. *I've seen this, before.*

Francine was going to use the sky's lightning to attack the choppers, just like she did on Barrow's home. *She's going to vaporize them!* "Francine, wait! There could be people in those choppers!"

"Those 'people shouldn't have killed my son, but they sure as hell did."

"You can't keep blaming everyone for that!"

"I can when it's true," Francine declared, pointing at the oncoming choppers.

"Francine, think for a minute," Stan declared in a grave voice. "Look at how slow they're moving! It's like they *want* you to shoot them!"

"Then I'd better oblige them.," Francine declared, a look of relish in her eyes.

In the space of a few minutes, Stan moved to stop her.

He should have moved faster.

—⚡—

The sky lit up before Frank's horrified eyes.

"Everyone, take cover!" Loeb bellowed, pulling Frank as far from the horrific scene as he could. "This is gonna be danger-close!"

"Benz!" Frank screamed as he was pulled undercover. "Benz!"

—⚡—

A gigantic bolt of lightning shot out from the sky, striking the choppers …

Only to be absorbed by bulbs sticking out of their sides.

—◊—

"What the …" Francine did a bewildered double take. "What just happened?!"

"Dammit! That's why they approached us so slowly," Stan said in a knowing voice. "They got energy collectors!"

Those energy collectors glowed, arcs of electricity jumping from one chopper to another.

Francine took a step back, fear in her eyes. "Stan?"

"Oh God," Benz whispered after getting down an anxious swallow.

Stan leaped to them, just as the choppers unleashed their payload.

—◊—

"Arrrrgh!" Frank shut his eyes as a searing blue light lit up everything in his sight. *Shit!* He barely had time to react before a massive blast wave washed over the area like a tidal wave.

"Hang on, everyone!" Loeb screamed into his comms. "Hang on tight!"

—◊—

A few turbulent seconds later, the blast wave moved to the rest of the island, giving everyone time to take stock.

Benz! Frank snatched himself away from Loeb and sprinted to where he saw his partner last. "Benz!"

"Frank!" Loeb ran after him, his arm outstretched. "Wait, dammit!"

"Don't touch me!" he shouted back. "Don't *ever* touch me!"

"There could still be aftershocks, you idiot—"

But Loeb might as well have been speaking to the wind, for Frank was already at his destination.

No! Frank's heart sank at what he saw.

In the spot where Benz and the Solomons had stood was a gigantic chasm, drilled deep into the island!

"Benz!" Frank fell to his knees at the rim of the chasm. *She's freaking gone!* "BENZ!"

—◊—

"Drake," Loeb said, gently shaking the older man by the shoulder. "I need you to talk to me here."

"Huh?" Frank looked up, a dazed look on his face.

"It's been thirty minutes," Loeb said, helping Frank to his feet. He gestured to the officers going over the scene.

The crime scene.

With Benz at the bottom of it.

"We left her," Frank croaked, looking for his voice. "We left her to die." *I left her.*

"I'm sorry about Benz," Loeb said, sadness in his eyes. "But that was exactly why I wanted you to get intel on the Solomons, not confront them. We didn't have the resources to defeat them."

"We got some, tonight," Frank said, staring at the crater.

"That ...wasn't from us."

Wait, that's right. "Then where'd those choppers come from?" Frank blinked as if realizing something. "And where the hell are they now?"

"They," a voice answered, "are fueling up back at base. And they came from us."

That's right, lady, Frank thought, head spinning to find the speaker. *Give me a fucking target.*

A short black woman dressed in a black uniform approached him and Loeb. She brandished a warm but efficient grin. Meant to be seen as friendly, but also to show that she was in charge.

Make no mistake.

"Who the hell are you supposed to be?" Frank asked in guttural voice. He was already getting a battle stance, every iota of his body aching to bring pain to the woman in front of him.

"Drake," Loeb warned, shaking his head vigorously as his eyes grew wide with alarm. "Now's not the time—"

211

"Angela Blackfire," the woman answered, stopping a few feet in front of Frank. Maybe she wanted to give him proper space. Or maybe she saw the murderous look in his eyes. Either way, hawkish brown eyes regarded him with wary interest. "Of the Black Wolves."

"The Black Wolves?"

"A private military contracting firm," she explained bluntly. "Sent to deal with trouble spots around the world, quickly and efficiently." She took something from her uniform pocket, flicked at Frank.

Without breaking eye contact, he snatched it out of the air and gave it a quick glance. *A damn business card. Bitch roasts my partner and puts her name on it!* "You killed my partner."

"I apologize for that."

"You. Killed. My. Partner!"

"Drake." Loeb was immediately in front of him, hands on his shoulders. "Calm down."

"What did I tell you about touching me ever again?"

"Do you want her to kill you?" Loeb hissed, getting in Frank's face. "Or worse?!"

Like I give a shit. "She the help you told me about back when you assigned me this case?" *Us. He assigned Benz and me to this case.* Frank swallowed a whimper. *Oh, Benz.*

"Yes," Loeb answered, looking away for a second. "She and her team were called in by City Hall. The mayor clued me in to their involvement from the beginning. Told me to play nice."

"That's what you call offering up one of our own?! Playing nice?!"

—⁂—

"I realize you feel terrible about what happened," Blackfire continued in a sheepish tone. "But we were given explicit instructions to destroy the Solomons. At any cost."

"But not by the mayor, right?"

"What?" Loeb asked, confusion on his face.

You stupid little … Frank laughed as he turned to face his boss. "You really think the mayor would have the stones to call *this* bunch of wreckers in?"

"If you have something to add, Drake," Loeb warned while wearing an expression that exuded authority, "then do it now. Without the sass."

"The mayor didn't call the Black Wolves." Frank gestured to an ambulance carrying Maroni inside. "Ramona Maroni of the Mala Noches did!"

"Hold on." Loeb turned to Blackfire. "Is this true?"

"Yes," Blackfire answered, though she looked uncomfortable doing so.

"*That's* why the mayor got us involved," Frank said. "He didn't want to look bad. Figured if a crime boss can foot the bill for these assholes, he might as well get on board. Makes him look good to the voters." Frank let out a halfhearted, bitter chuckle. "You got played, sir."

"You have to be kidding me," Loeb muttered, shaking his head in disgust.

"And now, Maroni will work out a deal to avoid prison time," Frank continued as his blood boiled, "and be back in business days later! Stronger than before!"

"Well, I'll be …" Loeb paused, looking as though he was still taking it in.

"Either way," Blackfire said, gesturing to the gravel pit, "the Black Wolves will be taking custody of the scene, and this case, until we recover the Solomons' bodies."

"And Benz?" *Say it, you freaking …*

"We'll drop her off, if we find her."

Before anyone could mount a reply, Blackfire turned on her heels and walked off. Her people swooped in like vultures, interrupting the GCPD's CSIs in the middle of their work.

"Blackfire!" Frank shouted after her, wanting to salvage something good from what had happened. "Do you *really* think the Solomons are dead?!"

"If they're not"—she gestured to the chasm her choppers had created—"they will be when we're done."

—∽—

TO BE CONCLUDED